# THE
# WARRIOR'S
# TOUCH

## Angel Lynn

Spicy Historical Romance

New Concepts                    Georgia

Be sure to check out our website for the very best in fiction at fantastic prices!

When you visit our webpage, you can:
* Read excerpts of currently available books
* View cover art of upcoming books and current releases
* Find out more about the talented artists who capture the magic of the writer's imagination on the covers
* Order books from our backlist
* Find out the latest NCP and author news--including any upcoming book signings by your favorite NCP author
* Read author bios and reviews of our books
* Get NCP submission guidelines
* And so much more!

We offer a 20% discount on all new Trade Paperback releases ordered from our website!

Be sure to visit our webpage to find the best deals in e-books and paperbacks! To find out about our new releases as soon as they are available, please be sure to sign up for our newsletter (http://www.newconceptspublishing.com/newsletter.htm) or join our reader group (http://groups.yahoo.com/group/new_concepts_pub/join)!

The newsletter is available by double opt in only and our customer information is *never* shared!

Visit our webpage at:
www.newconceptspublishing.com

New Concepts Publishing, Inc.
5202 Humphreys Rd.
Lake Park, GA 31636

ISBN 1-58608-739-8
2004-2005 © Angel Lynn
Cover art (c) copyright Eliza Black

NCP books are available at special quantity discounts for bulk purchases for sales promotions, premiums, fund raising, or educational use. For details, write, email, or phone New Concepts Publishing, Inc., 5202 Humphreys Rd., Lake Park, GA 31636; Ph. 229-257-0367, Fax 229-219-1097; orders@newconceptspublishing.com.

First NCP Trade Paperback Printing: February 2006

# MASTER MY VIKING

## Prologue

Perched on a the branch, high in the trees, she watched the handsome warrior, who looked to be no more than ten and two, as he crawled through the brush below her. He was magnificent with his long, golden hair--bare-chested, with muscles that her older cousins would swoon at. But she was not interested in that, oh no. It was the way he moved that intrigued her, sleek, like a lynx on the prowl.

Slowly he pulled an arrow from its quiver, his youthfully muscled torso rising as he placed it in his bow, and took aim. Her eyes followed the line to his target and she gasped hard, nearly falling from the branch of the tree. Before she could react further, the arrow was flying and she watched in horror as it pierced her pet rabbit straight through the heart. There was no doubt it was dead. Stunned, she didn't move for a long while. She could only stare in shock as the young warrior skinned her beloved animal and then hung it to dry.

"I will get you for this Zhuwa," she whispered. "I will be a thorn in your side forevermore."

## Chapter One

*A settlement on the coast of Svealand, 867 A.D.*

Sigurd Thorgest stood tall, staring out at the bitter, cold fjord that lay in front of him. Every inch of his naked flesh tingled under the air of the cold early spring. He hoped Nerthus, the sun goddess would shine warmly down upon them soon. The raids of the last several moons had been profitable, giving him and his warriors a large enough plunder to provide for his clan for weeks. And they returned also with five new slave girls to sell. He didn't need more of his own, as he already owned six. Plenty to fulfill his needs.

Sigurd was not a greedy man.

Ah, aye. They celebrated well over their good fortune, which is why Sigurd was now prepared to take this icy plunge. Sigurd snorted and then groaned as the inside of his skull pounded. Having found amusement with two of his wenches and a shits load of the hops, he was suffering a bit of crapulence from indulging perhaps a bit too much. Well, at least his supper stayed put, not like Ivar who spilled the entire content of his guts.

'Twas quite humorous.

A mighty roar bellowed from Sigurd's throat as he took off running into the water. He felt his boys recede into the inner recesses of his groin to escape the frigid blast.

He didn't blame them.

'Twas bone shattering cold.

*Ah.*

Sigurd emerged from the fjord feeling much more refreshed. And as glacial as an iceberg, as well. Walking to the tree where he hung his clothes, Sigurd reached for his garments.

They were gone.

Stupefied he searched the ground and then the surrounding trees thinking he might be mistaken as to where he put them. Nay, his clothes were definitely missing.

A low giggle reached his ears and his head swung in the direction of the sound.

"Wench!" he bellowed. "Bedamned little wench!"

Sigurd gave chase, sprinting toward the figure he spied hiding between the trees. In response her eyes widened and she darted away. "Get yer arse back here, woman!"

He didn't even know her name--didn't care. All Sigurd Thorgest knew was the sorry female was a thorn in his side. For as long as he could remember and for reasons Sigurd could not figure, the wench had set her sights on becoming his greatest irritation.

"Now where did the wench go?" Sigurd halted his running. With a keen ear he listened whilst his eyes scrutinized the forest. And then he heard the crackling of branches followed by a female scream.

His lips curled upward with satisfaction. He had her.

Casually Sigurd strolled along the crudely worn path, feeling quite pleased with his craftiness. At least now he could get his garments and go home to his fire and several refreshing mugs of mead.

He frowned when he came upon her. Though his trap had worked like a wizard's spell, Sigurd Thorgest was sorely disappointed that she had breeches on beneath her skirts. Though he had no desire to bed the annoying wench, like any healthy, red-blooded warrior he hoped that when he caught her in his ropes he would get a nice view of her charms. Perhaps tease her about seeing them and take pleasure in the fury and mortification that would wash over her pretty, little face.

No matter.

He was enjoying watching her struggle as her body twirled round and round. With smug satisfaction Sigurd approached where she dangled upside down from the tree, the cord wrapped nicely around her left ankle. Her right leg was flailing in the empty air as her hands worked frantically to free her skirts, which had fallen heavily over her head.

'Twas quite amusing.

She suddenly stopped struggling, growing very still as though she sensed his presence. Her right leg fell off to one side causing her thighs to spread.

And Sigurd couldn't help but stare at her crotch.

Though 'twas well covered, just the sight of it so close to his face conjured images that made him forget he was freezing his arse off and made him remember he had on not a stitch of clothes. A pleasant tingle nudged at his groin as he pictured what was beneath those boyish breeches she wore.

He pushed the musings away as she began to struggle again.

There was no way in Thor's thunderous skies he wanted to rut on the wench.

He hated her guts.

Sigurd snickered just to confirm to her that he was there.

She stilled once more.

"I will get you for this, Khuwa," she finally said, in and unusually calm voice, considering her predicament.

Why she called him this name, Sigurd knew not. Nor did he know its meaning. Of course he'd never told her his name so he supposed she had to conjure one up. Sigurd liked to think that the word translated to *big strong warrior* or *my, my you are well hung.*

Sigurd scratched the whiskers on his chin. *Hmm.* Wench was all he ever called her. Had she ever told him her name? No, she had not. She probably had a shrewish name and he really did not want to know it anyway. He just wished she would disappear or fall off a cliff or something.

With a devilish gleam in his eyes, Sigurd stepped to within a foot of where she dangled as she finally managed to lift her garments from her face.

"Oh!" she shrieked when she glimpsed what she was face to face with.

*The wench is awestruck*, Sigurd Thorgest grinned proudly.

Despite the cold, his endowments where quite impressive. In a show of agreement, his bequest twitched a bit.

"That is the ugliest thing I have ever seen!" she bellowed. "Get it out of my face."

Sigurd's willy withered immediately at her insult.

"Wench," was all his ego would allow him to say. He harrumphed when she pulled her skirts back over her face and puffed out a breath that sounded more like disgust than delight.

Imagine that. Women adored Sigurd Thorgest. He was said to be good in the bed furs--very good. Maybe even the best.

With a resounding sigh, Sigurd figured he would have to cut her down eventually. But not afore the wench revealed where she'd hidden his clothes. Sigurd Thorgest might be a mightily strong and virile warrior, but at the moment he was starting to freeze his nuts off.

"I will free you, wench when you tell me where you have placed my clothes."

"Nay."

*Nay she says?*

'Twouldn't be an understatement to say that her answer pissed him off. But though he was seething, all Sigurd could do was stand there and watch the wench dangle.

He would like to slap her upside her daft little head, but Sigurd never hit women. What he should do is cut the rope and let her drop. Her skull was surely thick enough to withstand the blow from hitting the ground.

"Khuwa."

The manner in which she said the name made it almost sound like an endearment, but Sigurd was smarter than that. The wench hated him too.

"What?" Sigurd answered.

"I am not feeling very well," she spoke with a muffled voice from beneath her skirts.

"When you tell me where my clothes are, I will cut you down."

There was a pause.

"Khuwa."

"What?"

"I think I am going to vomit."

Not wanting the smelly blessing to land on his feet, Sigurd took a step back from her.

He supposed that in her inverted position it might be true that her belly was getting ill. Again he scratched his chin, pondering how long a body could hang upside down before all the blood went to the skull and the heart labored in beating, causing the person to black out from the pressure of it.

When her arms fell toward the ground and the wench stopped moving and speaking, Sigurd's ponderings turned to concern, and he was now thinking the question had just been answered. With quickness, he lifted her body with one arm and loosened the lash around her ankle with his other hand. Lowering her to the ground whilst pulling the skirts from her face, Sigurd affirmed he liked her much better when she was not awake or moving. But he hoped she was still breathing.

Taunting her was one thing. Killing her was another.

Sigurd knelt down beside her, brushing back the light brown braid that swept across her face. She was as still as an iced-over fjord and he wondered if she was dead. Lowering his head to her chest he laid one ear on her to listen for a heartbeat, ignoring that he was mouth to breast with her, resisting the manly urge to take advantage of the situation and give that mound a good squeeze.

Well, at least her heart was thumping. And from the way his head was raising up and down, he knew she was breathing too.

'Twould serve her right if he took her clothes off and hid them.

And left her there.

Nay.

Though she was bold and galling, Sigurd suspected she was a virgin. Why else would she torment him so? If she were not a virgin she'd be wantin' to tumble with him instead of irritatin' him. What female would not?

'Twould only be a natural thing.

Lifting his head from her chest Sigurd studied her face for a moment. 'Twas a shame she was such an annoyance for the wench had such lovely feminine features. And her body felt rather nice beneath his hold. His eyes moved lower.

*Such plump, round breasts*, Sigurd never noticed them afore.

*Uch.*

One feel could do no harm. She would not even know.

Slowly, Sigurd's hand skimmed along her ribs until the palm of his hand cupped the side of her breast. He ran his thumb along the top of it, feeling the slight push of her nipple through the garment.

His groin tightened and a devious smile came to his lips. Aye. he did like her much better this way, submissive to him--willing.

It mattered not that she was unconscious.

A stinging crack across his face tossed Sigurd from his musings. And before he could sort what happened, the wench was on her feet and darting through the forest.

"You will surely pay, Khuwa," she shrieked as she ran off.

Sigurd pressed his palm to the area on his cheek where she struck him. As he watched her vanish amongst the trees, the only thing he could think of at the moment was that he still did not have his clothes.

## Chapter Two

He could endure the bedamned snickers from the men around him as he casually strolled by them, eyes straight ahead. And he could withstand the appalled gasps of the females who hid theirs and their children's faces as he passed through the village on the way back to his house--stark naked.

The wenches were probably peeking anyway. How could they not? Sigurd was indeed a blessed Viking.

Still, 'twas substantially humiliating. Not the naked part, but the fact that he had lost his clothes at the hands of a feeble female.

But when he reached his house and his stupid brothers Ivar and Ludin and a bevy of his friends caught sight of him, 'twas their roars of laughter and bantering that started Sigurd Thorgest seething.

"Aye!" Ivar roared. "I did not realize you had such a big arse, Sigurd."

"Come 'round to the front." Sigurd narrowed his eyes. "You will be duly impressed with my largeness, arse wipe."

"'Tis good you did not lose yer sword belt, Sigurd." Ludin jested. "Else you would have come home without yer dignity."

Sigurd's nostrils flared with irritation. Ignoring them all, he strolled into his house, groaning that his brothers and supposed loyal men followed him inside.

"We should call him Sigurd the shiny arse!" Ulfrik chortled. "Instead of Sigurd the Brawny."

"Yer beggin' for a shiny eye Ulfrik, if you do not cease this immediately." Sigurd snapped at his closest and dearest friend.

*Closest and dearest friend my arsehole*. Where was the camaraderie, where was the moral support?

"Or perhaps we should call him Sigurd Oddlog!" Ivar chortled as he looked askew at Sigurd's bared crotch.

Runa, his favorite slave girl held a broom that she had apparently just used on the freshly swept, wooden floor. She merely giggled at the horde of Viking warriors as Sigurd brushed by her, moving to the center of the main hall where a fire in the clay-covered hearthstone was ready to warm him.

"Get me a mug of warm mead, Runa." He watched her retreat to the pantries and then he looked around his longhouse, feeling quite proud of his creation and in particular, the second floor loft where he slept. 'Twas reached by stairs not a ladder, a thing he discovered and marveled at, when he traded and raided in Saxon lands a few years past.

Sigurd enjoyed respect as the Chieftain of his village, regarded as a wise and fearless leader to all. And here he sat in his birthday form with all his assets hanging out. If he ever got his hands on that little wench she would dearly pay for his present humbling of him.

*Moo.*

"Did you hear a cow?" Ivar frowned.

"I have thirty cows in the pastures behind the dwelling." Sigurd stated proudly. He surely was a wealthy Viking. His pride however, was short-lived as his head dropped to the area between his thighs and he stared at his shriveling member.

Runa returned baring a pitcher and seven mugs and a fur as well, to warm his flesh. Slipping it over Sigurd's body she smiled lustfully at him, revealing she was in a receptive mood.

Sigurd's lip turned up on one side. He would most definitely have a taste of her in the later evening. She was his favorite and most brazen in the bed furs. He watched as she poured the mead into mugs and passed them all around. His hand slid under her skirts and Runa giggled, squirming at Sigurd's touch.

*Moo.*

"I swear by Odin I hear a cow." Ivar's head turned toward Sigurd's bedchamber loft, and the rest of the lounging brood of

Vikings turned their heads in the same direction.

"'Tis no cow in the pasture, Sigurd," Ludin remarked. He pointed toward the stairs. "The sound comes from up there."

Runa went very still and then slowly backed away. Sigurd's eyes narrowed on her as the color left her usually rosy-cheeked face. The wench knew something.

*Moo.*

'Twas no mistake about it. The sound the beast was making was coming from Sigurd's loft.

"Runa!" Sigurd stood abruptly, his fur covering dropping to the floor. He watched as the slave turned and ran away. Uch! He would find her later to see what she knew about it. For now, his sleeping chamber needed investigatin'.

In six long strides he was across the hall, taking the stairs three at a time as he headed for the room upstairs. Ulfrik, Ivar and Ludin followed just behind him, and the others, never wanting to miss a spectacle were trailing along as well.

When Sigurd reached his sleeping chambers, he halted dead in his pace. Ulfrik slammed into his back, grunting. Ivar, in turn slammed into Ulfrik's back and then Ludin, who did not slam into Ivar's back, dug in his heels and then started laughing. There were two more grunts as Agnar, and Leif fell into one another and then a yelp and several loud thuds as Mord, who was a clumsy oaf, rolled backwards down the stairs.

*Moo.*

"Acquiring new tastes in the bed furs, Sigurd?" Ludin smirked.

"Shut yer yapper." Sigurd glowered at his brother.

Sigurd's face twisted as he glared at the cow that stood in the middle of his bedchamber floor. And she stared back at him like she didn't have a care as long as she had something to chomp on. And she was chomping … on the stuffing from his favorite bench he acquired while trading in the South!

Now when did cows start enjoying feathers? Sigurd scratched his bristly chin. He must have missed the adaptation for he had no idea they did, though this one had a tuft of feathers hanging from her mouth.

*Frp*

"Uch!" Ulfrik fanned his hand under his nose. "The bovine fer sure can pass a potent wind."

Five mighty Vikings sniffed at the air and grimaced. Mord did not grimace because he was still groaning at the bottom of the stairs. Ivar did not grimace either because he was still laughing.

Sigurd closed his eyes and dragged his fingers through his hair. There was only one person he could think of who would have the audacity to do such thing. A very brief and slight smile crept upon his lips. Aye, she's a clever wench.

He wished he had thought of it.

Retribution was now in his field, and Sigurd would surely take his revenge.

"Sigurd!" Thistle, the ten year old boy child who served Sigurd's father came bounding into the room, pushing his way between Ludin and Ulfrik. His brows drew together. "Sigurd, there is a cow in yer bedchamber."

Lifting his eyes to Thor's blessed skies, though the ceiling blocked his view, Sigurd beckoned the gods for patience. He was living among lack wits. 'Twas good he was in charge. Else they might all hurt themselves merely trying to use their brains.

"We are busy child. What do you want?"

"Yer father wishes ta see ya, Sigurd." Thistle's head moved up and down in confusion as he took in the Chieftain's naked state.

Sigurd sighed. Whenever his father summoned him, 'twas usually for an issue he would rather not deal with. Already his head was starting to throb. "Tell my father that I will see him when I get the cow out of my bedchamber."

Nodding, Thistle turned and left the room, taking a hop over Mord who had recovered from his tumble and was now crawling through the door.

"'Tis a cow, Sigurd." Mord said whilst standing and brushing himself off.

*Moo.*

"Yer wisdom has no boundaries, Mord." Sigurd commented acerbically, rubbing a forefinger across one eyebrow.

"You do realize there is a problem here?" Ulfrik said, scratching the back of head.

"Aye a problem!" Ludin agreed.

Sigurd shook his head from side to side, irritation rippling through him. "Aside from the fact there is a cow in my bedchamber, what might that be?"

"How will we get the bovine out?"

"What do you mean?"

Even as Sigurd asked, a sickening feeling twisted in his stomach, for he knew what Ludin's reply would be.

"You know a cow will go up the stairs but cannot go down."

All off the Vikings murmured their agreement and Sigurd

groaned in dismay.

'Twas true.

Why had he built those bedamned steps!

Ivar laughed harder and Sigurd losing his tolerance slapped him upside the back of his head.

"Ouch!" Ivar bellowed, but at least his guffaw simmered to a low snicker.

"Sigurd!" Thistle returned and Sigurd glanced down at the boy, who had obviously run the distance between dwellings because he was panting.

"Yer father tells me to inform you that he does not care how ugly the wench is or how much she desires you. He wants to see ya now."

"Did you tell him it was real cow, Thistle?" Sigurd's eyes widened.

The boy looked at him with chagrin. "I told him you was nekid."

Sigurd's mouth dropped open. 'Twas not turning into a very good day. He had a feeling it was going to get worse.

*Plop.*

"E-e-e-w!" Leif said, looking at the steamy cow dung that oozed on the floor.

Ivar started laughing again.

Sigurd slapped his hand to his forehead, his head dropping into a defeated pose.

"Well then," Mord commented. "Sorry for yer troubles, Sigurd, but I must be going."

"Aye," the rest of the Vikings mumbled as they all began to back towards the door, and then turned ready to make a fast escape.

"Halt!" Sigurd bellowed and they all stopped. He could almost sense the grimaces on each of their sorry faces. Reaching for his spare breeches and tunic, he slipped them on, seething that he no longer had his favorite boots. "Wilst I call on my father you will all come up with a plan to get this beast out of my chamber!"

He swept by them in a heavy stride.

"And get that wench Runa to clean up this mess," he said without looking back. His head was really beginning to throb.

Chapter Three

"What have you done father?"

"You refused to choose a bride when we attended the Thing, two years past Sigurd." Ozur Thorgest said as he casually paced across the room, hands clasped behind his back.

"The women I met at that assembly were all so very dull, father." Sigurd blew out a slow, mournful breath. The only female that caught his eyes at the *Thing* turned out to be another's slave.

A leisurely smile crept across Sigurd's lips as he recalled humping her in the bushes.

"Now you must abide, Sigurd. There is no other choice."

His day musing faded and Sigurd glowered. "But you have betrothed me against my consent."

"I do not need yer consent, son. 'Tis time you marry."

"I told you father, I would choose a wife."

"You have not done so, Sigurd. I beseeched you in yer twenty and fourth year to choose, yet here it is three years later and still you have not done so."

"But father … " Sigurd's voice trailed off and his shoulders sagged. He never argued with his father.

*A wife.*

The idea of it brought a scowl to Sigurd's face.

'Twould be constant naggin' and the shrillin' blah blah blah of a female forever underfoot, making demands, insistin' on her own way.

Did she have to live in his house? Maybe he could put her away with his other wenches.

Nay 'twas a requirement of the marriage she live in his dwelling. Sigurd's peaceful existence was about to escape through the door.

Loki's laughter. He was doomed.

What need did he have for a wife, except to bed her from time to time when he wasn't humpin' one of his slave maidens?

Sigurd plopped onto the bench at the table near the hearth, exhaling harshly.

"Now Sigurd, do not look so forlorn." Ozur picked up a pitcher and poured two mugs full of mead, handing one to Sigurd. "Yer mother wishes for grandbabies, and with yer two brothers still sewing their wiles, there still are none. We are getting old, Sigurd."

Lifting his eyes to his father, Sigurd stared at him for a moment. "I have five sirelings father."

Ozur rubbed a palm along his bristly cheek, pondering that for a moment. "Aye, but they are all bastards, every one of them."

"I have acknowledged them all."

"They were birthed to slaves, son, and the law does not recognize them as legal heirs." Ozur took a gulp of his mead and then set the mug aside. "'Tis yer duty, Sigurd. As Chieftain you must live yer life as a good example for the tribe."

Sigurd's shoulders slumped in defeat. His father, as always, was right. As Chieftain he had to be accountable to his people. He supposed 'twas time to take a bride. Besides, there might be some conveniences to havin' a wife--no more ploddin' through the cold, night air to find himself a wench to bed. He could just roll atop of her and rut on her until his need was satiated.

*Aye.* Now that he mulled this over, it might not be a bad thing a'tall.

Pressing his palms to the table, Ozur leaned toward Sigurd, giving him a stern look. "Aside from yer responsibility there is another benefit to this joinin'."

*Ah,* now comes the true reason for his sire's decision. "And what might that be father?"

Ozur always had motives behind his plots.

"The woman is of the Greylock bloodline, a daughter of the Chieftain's cousin. Comes up from Birka to visit her kin and stays throughout the harvest."

Sigurd's eyebrows rose. "Our clan has been feudin' with the Greylocks over land boundaries for a century."

Many a Viking in both clans had been severely injured or killed, often when taken unawares in the disputed territory.

"Aye, Sigurd." Ozur smiled, his expression revealing utmost satisfaction with his decision. He took another gulp of his drink and sat on a bench across the table from Sigurd. "'Twas a good bargain, costin' a meager bride price of two silver coins in exchange for the titles."

Setting his cup on the table, Ozur leaned back against the wall, folding one arm over the other. He smiled smugly. "We will fight them no more."

Sigurd's eyes widened. His spine stiffened as he bolted upright in his seat, dread boring through every vein. "What is wrong with the wench?!"

Indeed it was a paltry price for such a large gain. There had to be a horrid reason why her clan wanted to be rid of her. Visions of stringy, smelly hair and broken teeth danced through his mind. His breathing accelerated painfully as he imagined putting a sack over her head to tolerate bedding her.

'Twas a good thing he had virile seed. He might only have to bed her once or twice and then be done with her, once he got her with child.

Harrumphing, Ozur scratched his temple. Perhaps he shouldn't have told his son the amount of the bride price. "I have seen her from a distance Sigurd. Outwardly there is nothin' wrong with her."

*Outwardly?*

"'Tis my understandin' she is quite the talented artist," Ozur continued.

*Hmm,* Sigurd contemplated. Artists were known to be daft. He gazed at his father suspiciously. "What picture here are you paintin' over father?"

"She's quite sane, if that is what you are thinkin'."

Sigurd's eyes narrowed. "Is she a virgin?"

He would dissolve the marriage if she'd been bedded by another. Not that he relished the idea of training an untouched female. It would be a tedious task. Sigurd preferred his women to be knowledgeable in the bed furs right from the beginning.

"Her clan promises that she is, most assuredly, a maiden." Ozur nodded his affirmation. "And worry not about her appearance. She seemed well-groomed. At least from the distance I viewed her."

*She probably has warts all over her face.* Closing his eyes, Sigurd winced. He hoped that if she did have warts, her face was the only place she had them.

"Shoot a straight arrow to me father." There had to be something amiss with the woman, and Sigurd's aim was to find out.

"Well .…" Ozur began speaking.

"Well what?" Sigurd glared at Ozur. Rarely did he lose patience with his father, but he was losing it now.

"She's a bit long in the tooth."

"How long?" Sigurd's expression turned worried at the thought of being married off to an old hag.

*Freya!*

*Let her at least be younger than he.*

"She's twenty and three."

Sigurd slumped low on the bench, convinced now that the woman was defective, else she would've been married off long ago. "You are tellin' me no one wanted her?"

"Nay, 'tis not what I'm sayin'."

Lifting his lids, Sigurd gave his father a grim smile. "Stop the bush beatin' father."

"She is a bit too wild for her own good."

"Wild?" Sigurd could enjoy wild. Intrigued, he sat up straighter and leaned on the table. "Give."

"She has a penchant for freedom."

"Meaning?" Sigurd slanted his head, struggling for patience as he awaited his father's answer.

Ozur cleared his throat, brushed off his tunic and smoothed over his gray-blonde hair with his hand.

"Aye … well … she has run from three afore you, straight away from the weddin' ceremony each time, disappearin' into the woods for days and survivin' from the land afore she was found." Pausing, Ozur smiled. "A woman with spirit, Sigurd. She is perfect for you."

"Aye," Sigurd smirked back arrogantly. "I am the warrior to tame her."

He would tame her right into submission and obedience.

"Very well, father. I shall marry."

Like he had a choice.

Standing, Sigurd nodded to his father and left the dwelling, heading through the pastures toward his own home.

"Heave … Ho!"

The sound of Ivar's voice caught his attention and he quickened his stride. What were his warriors up to now?

"Heave … Ho!"

"*Hel* in a hand basket!" Sigurd could not believe his eyes.

"Why do you cry out to Loki's daughter, Hel, Sigurd?" Agnar watched as the Chieftain approached.

But Sigurd was too befuddled to answer. All he could do was shake his head from side to side.

The entire second floor wall outside of his bedchamber was piled in large pieces on the ground near his longhouse, two axes lying along side. The cow was set in a sling, dangling precariously from a rope attached to a pulley that had been hammered to the top beam of his house.

Ulfrik, Ludin and Ivar were in his bedchamber, he could clearly see them through the wide opening. They were holding the end of the rope. Their heels were dug in and their muscles were bulging, all of them leaning at a backward angle, as they slowly eased the bovine downward.

"Heave … ho!" Leif called from below and Sigurd watched as

the cow dropped lower. He walked to where Mord, Agnar and Leif stood and 'twas clear by their bare chests and sweaty brows that they were the ones who had taken his wall down.

"Are you all enjoyin' yerselves?" Sigurd asked.

He didn't want to think of the damage that may have been rendered on his personal effects while his men engaged their task. Forgetting his pending nuptials, his attention returned to the wench in the woods and Sigurd scowled.

"I have found a use for that ice ball we made this winter," he said to his group of men as he watched the cow's hooves come to rest on the snowy ground.

"You mean the one we put behind the barn that is nearly as high as our heads?" Agnar asked.

"'Twould be the one," Sigurd answered.

Was there another?

## Chapter Four

He should be standing proud, not kicking his toe into the dirt like an untried boy or pig being led to slaughter.

Either way this really sucked.

Sigurd was getting married and he was as nervous as a bug in a bird's nest.

He should be focusin' on the days of celebratin' ahead.

There would be friends and feastin' and drinkin' and gamin' and *ah* aye, humpin' 'til his brains fell out.

Sigurd loved the merrymaking, especially the last part. And this eve he would be tasting a new woman. He prayed she was comely.

Groaning, he considered her virginal condition. Sigurd had never taken a virgin. He knew not what to expect or what the proper way was to have her in his bed. Should he take her hard and fast, getting it over with? Or should he be gentle, coaxing and slow? Would it be easier for her on the top or with her on the bottom? Sigurd rubbed his forehead.

'Twould not be pleasant for either of them. She would probably just lay there waitin' for him to tell her what to do.

Perhaps he should kiss her mouth first. It seemed like the proper thing to do.

She might cry. Oh Freya! Please do not let her cry.

Sigurd was at a loss, but didn't dare seek advice from Ulfrik or his brothers. They would mock him until he lost his restraint and was forced to thrash them all. And as for Ozur, his father, the man was old. He couldn't possibly understand the mating habits of the young. His parent's probably did not even rut anymore, maybe even forgotten how. Sigurd grimaced as he considered that they still might be doing the deed.

'Twas not the way a man wanted to picture his parents.

Turning his thoughts and concentrating on the purpose for today's celebrating, Sigurd reminded himself about the alliance that would come from it.

'Twas a good deal.

And there would be legitimate children produced to honor his bloodline, as well, whining, sniveling rush rats that he would be obliged to keep under his roof.

*Uch.*

Maybe he should move to the barn.

But then Sigurd smiled as he affectionately imagined bouncing his youngster on his knee. He was fond of his other children even though they were bastards.

The sound of approaching horses drew his attention and he lifted his head.

"Here comes the ball and chain now, Sigurd." Ulfrik elbowed him and snickered.

"Aye," Sigurd replied, thinking it was time to find a new best friend.

He turned his head from the newly arrived bridal party, wary of laying his eyes upon the woman he was marrying, and instead, looked out over the open field were the witnesses were all gathered.

At least it was a pleasant Frigg's day. The goddess of marriage was blessing them it seemed.

"Uch, she's a pretty one," Ludin said. "If you do not want her, I will have her."

Sigurd's head snapped toward his brother, a low growl emerging from his throat, a feeling of possessiveness threading through him. He cast an expression that clearly warned his brother to keep his hands to himself. This woman would be his wife and she was not to be shared. Sigurd was a bit surprised by his own reaction.

Sighing, he decided to bite the irons and have a look at her.

Slowly he shifted his gaze, but he could not see her. A horde of men had closed around the woman as if they were protecting her.

Or more likely, caging her from escape.

They then parted slightly, giving the woman enough space to step through.

Returning his eyes to the ground, Sigurd caught a glimpse of the delicate slippered feet just peeking out from below the lacing on the bottom of a cream-colored, silk gown, and the edge of the blue, velvet cloak she wore.

*Expensive material.* She was well to do.

He allowed his gaze to wander upward. There was a mild breeze blowing, causing the gown to mold nicely around what appeared to be shapely feminine legs. Feeling more relaxed, Sigurd's eyes drifted further upward. He couldn't retain his smile. She had smooth, rounded hips emphasized by the sash around her waist.

Aye, at least her bottom half was temptin' enough.

He imagined those legs wrapped around him while he grasped her curvaceous hips to rock her beneath him.

Or on top of him.

Or from behind.

His eyes continued their scrutiny and his breath caught when he reached her plump, firm breasts.

*Mmm.* She had big breasts. They were just the way he liked them. Large enough to bury his face between. He would most definitely suckle and fondle those breasts.

Sigurd released a quiet groan with the slight stirring in his groin.

Two lovely hands came up and the woman gathered her cloak around her body.

*Shy too.* Keeping her humble should be an easy task.

Taking a deep breath Sigurd allowed his gaze to wander to her face, noticing that her head was dropped almost despondently, her shiny, light brown hair draping around her head.

He drew his brows together. There was something familiar about her. Tilting his head and hunching slightly he tried to get a better look at her.

Her head came up. Sigurd straightened as his entire body went rigid.

Simultaneously their eyes locked. Two jaws fell open and a gasp came forth from each of their mouths.

"You!" they both yelled in unison.

Sigurd turned to his father with a killing glare, feeling like a sacrificial offering.

"Khuwa!" Hilde said. She recognized who Sigurd Thorgest was

immediately.

Her heart sank. Then it fluttered. Then it sank again.

She turned to run but slammed directly into her father's chest. Her male kin closed around her and she knew there would be no fleeing this time.

"Excuse me a moment while I choke myself to death," she cried to the astonished intakes of air from the nearby witnesses who overheard her.

"Uch. Frigg!" Sigurd beseeched the goddess, pointing in Hilde Greylock's direction. "I cannot marry *her*, father!"

Heads turned at the sound of Sigurd's bellowing, staring in shock.

"You cannot digress from yer decision, son!" Ozur yelled back.

"She is like a tick upon my scalp!" Sigurd's strident voice carried and echoed across the crowd.

The witnesses gasped and started to back away.

"I did not say I had ticks upon my scalp you fools!" Sigurd said even more loudly as he angrily scanned the crowd.

"The arrangement is agreed upon, son. You will marry her." Ozur stated firmly. Ingun, Sigurd's mother, looked as though she were about to cry.

As was his character, Ivar began to guffaw, as did Ludin and his dear, loyal friends who stood nearby. Sigurd scoffed at them and then turned back to Ozur.

"But father! She is like a furuncle upon my arse!"

Again the witnesses gasped, and the circle around Sigurd grew even wider.

"I did not say I had a furuncle upon my arse!"

Bedamned idiots!

Sigurd Thorgest rubbed his jaw. The disapproving look on his father's face told him it was of no use to argue, and he groaned painfully.

"'Twill be a fate worse than death without Vahalla," he mumbled, but his words fell on deaf ears.

Defeatedly he walked to Hilde Greylock's father to secure her hand.

Bram Greylock actually looked relieved when Sigurd approached him, signaling for the lawspeaker to step in.

"Be done with it quickly," Bram urged.

This one was not going to get away.

The terms of the betrothal were immediately declared to all present as Bram Greylock ordered his daughter to take her place at her betrothed's side.

Hilde, who had backed at least ten feet away with her entourage of guards surrounding her, began to begrudgingly move her feet. With her teeth clenched and her lips pursed in a defiant pout, she measured every step she took toward her soon to be husband.

*Of all warriors,* she seethed. *Why did it have to be him?*

Not that she ever wanted to marry at all. When Hilde's father informed her that yet another betrothal had been agreed upon, she argued with her father for days, begging him to reconsider and let her keep her freedom. To her, marriage was as bad as having the status of a thrall. But her father had grown impatient of her refusals, telling her to stop being childish, deciding he'd waited long enough for her to choose a husband. Of course running from three others hadn't helped. And now, she had reached the age where she was almost considered unmarriageable.

Her father promised his choice was a satisfactory one, that the man was a respected Chieftain, assuring her he was handsome and wealthy--a first-born in a powerful clan. The union would ensure an alliance, bring peace to their lands. Additionally, she would produce, for them, an heir.

'Twas her duty.

Out of guilt Hilde finally complied.

But Khuwa?

Imagine him a Chieftain.

'Twas absurd! Hilde bristled as she came to stand at Sigurd Thorgest's side.

With her head bowed she glanced at him askew, the locks of her hair hiding her scrutiny--she hoped.

He was a large man, strong and firm. He would be a good protector.

*Uch!* She needed no protectin'!

Tilting her head back she looked at Sigurd, studying him, as ancestral swords were placed in their hands and, as was the custom, they exchanged them.

His hair hung free along his back, groomed and shimmering blonde in the early autumn sun. His lashes were long and a bit darker than his hair. His skin was smooth. His nose was straight with no apparent damage from his battles. Of their own accord, her eyes dropped to his mouth and she noticed he had full lips--a nicely shaped mouth indeed.

Sigurd Thorgest was very pleasing to look at, even more so than when she first set eyes on him all those years ago. Odd how his handsomeness had eluded her in the years to follow, so focused she was on making him pay for his pitiless deed.

Her heart fluttered again.

*Nay … Khuwa!* Gathering her temper once more, Hilde's body seized. Sigurd Thorgest would be her husband in name only. He was a cruel, merciless murderer of innocent pets. He would never have her body or her heart.

She would rather sleep in pig slop.

Her face reddened with her ire.

Sigurd eyed Hilde as they received the bridal rings, offered from the tips of the traded family swords, and they placed them on their fingers.

*She wants me,* Sigurd smiled inwardly, noticing that her eyes were on his mouth just before she flushed and looked away. He took her hand, only vaguely hearing the lawspeaker offer the blessing, declaring them husband and wife.

Memories of the many times she tormented him came flooding into his brain and his smile turned into a frown.

Sigurd blinked in disbelief.

He had just married the wench!

The crowd around them whooped and they all began to run, but Hilde and Sigurd just stood there, both forgetting what it was they were supposed to do next.

One by one the running witnesses halted when they realized the bridal couple wasn't following. Heads and bodies turning, they all went still and stared.

*Aye.* Hilde remembered, as the befuddlement in her brain began to clear. 'Twas the wedding run to the hall for celebratin'. The clan arriving lastly would be required to serve the other clan their drink.

Suddenly aware of the pleasingly warm feeling of Sigurd's hand surrounding hers, Hilde yanked her hand free. She looked up at Sigurd Thorgest, ignoring the tingling that swept through her body at the thought of him touching her more thoroughly.

"Where is yer house, Sigurd Thorgest?" she asked.

Sigurd glared at her.

The wench damn well knew where his house was located.

He crossed one arm over the other, thinking that if she was too daft to remember, he most certainly was not going to tell her. Perhaps she would lose herself on the way.

Just as he was completing that idea, his father approached him from behind and thwacked him on the back of the head. "Tell her where your house is Sigurd."

Hilde burst out laughing.

*She has a charming laugh*, Sigurd thought, wincing and rubbing the back of his head.

'Twas a shame she was such a pest.

Lifting his right arm he pointed eastward, still unsure of her game.

With a sharp turn on her heels, Hilde dashed away, her clan following closely behind.

"Run, Sigurd!" Ludin yelled. "I do not wanna be servin' the ale!"

"Aye," Sigurd replied as he sprinted to a full run, passing Hilde and several of her family quite easily. When he reached the door to his dwelling he halted and waited until Hilde arrived.

Hilde skidded to a stop just short of his stoop, giving him a baffled look.

As was ritual, Sigurd was supposed to block the doorway with his sword to prevent her from entering unassisted, but he hadn't done so.

"Shall I stumble over yer threshold, Khuwa?"

*And curse the marriage?* He watched her mouth turn up in a devious smile as she started to lift her foot over the stoop.

"Nay!" he started toward her.

Marrying the wench was curses enough.

With that Sigurd dipped low, sweeping Hilde off of her feet in a less than gentle manner. She squeaked as he shifted her, tossing her over his shoulder. Gripping her bottom a bit more firmly than necessary, Sigurd carried her inside, setting her down on a bench at the bridal table. With his arm still around her, he settled at her side. Her cloak fell over his arm, nicely concealing it. Feigning nonchalance, as he scanned the hall to observe the arriving guests, Sigurd's hand began to roam up the front side of Hilde's body. When he reached her breast he gave it a gentle squeeze and then raked his fingertips across the front of it teasing the area of her nipple.

Hilde choked out a subdued protest, trying to be discreet. She attempted to slide away, but Sigurd's palm dropped to her hip pinning her against him. He pursed his lips to keep from smiling. He was making her nervous and he was pleased with that. She tormented him long enough and now 'twas his chance for revenge.

Leaning down he pressed his lips to her ear. Her shoulders

hunched and she began to recoil, but Sigurd held her firmly. Aside from that her father sat on her other side and there was no where for her to flee.

Sigurd blew a gentle, warm stream of air into her ear and then nipped her earlobe, chuckling low when she jumped and then shuddered. She shot him a feral look, her nostrils flaring, her lips pressed tightly together.

He was taking pleasure with her discomfiture and would most enjoy intimidating her with his masculine charms.

'Twas all legal. She was his wife.

"Why did you ask me where my house was, Hilde?" He whispered, bringing his mouth to within inches of hers. She cranked back her head, pulling as far a way from him as she was able.

"Sure as a fly on pig dung, you knew exactly where it was when you were leading that cow," Sigurd added.

"'Twould be unseemly if I revealed I knew that," Hilde answered. She glanced around the hall to see if anyone overheard, but no one paid them any heed.

Sigurd slid his hand up beneath her cloak to cup her breast once more, disappointed when her only reaction was to narrow her eyes in warning and turn her mouth into an irate pucker. He wanted to her to squirm.

Sigurd nodded in reply, letting his hand drop to the bench.

No wife of his would have a tarnished reputation.

He thought back to the time in the woods when she had taken his clothes, his mood souring. He should have despoiled her back then.

Aye he should have.

Then he wouldn't be in this mess right now.

## Chapter Five

Sigurd advanced on Hilde, drawing her into his embrace. How he could despise the wench so and yet desire her so fiercely was beyond his comprehension, but he did.

She stood before him in his bed loft. Prepared by her handmaidens, her long hair was freshly brushed and hung over her breasts, hiding them from his view, but Aye, Sigurd knew they were there--knew what they felt like. The shift she wore was white and of the thinnest material he'd ever seen, revealing every curve along the length of her delicious body.

Hilde too, was quite aware that her garment was transparent for when Sigurd entered the room her hands dropped immediately to hide her womanhood. A discomfited flush spread through her body and her cheeks blushed profusely.

She watched Sigurd apprehensively, pondering what he would do next. The wait was short, for he swept toward her like a starving beast claiming its next meal.

And Hilde was his trapped prey.

Never before had Hilde seen such lust in a man's eyes, and 'twas aimed directly at her. So stunned was she, that all she could do was let him engulf her within his massive arms.

His mouth descended on hers as he smashed her up against his body. She could feel his manhood through his breeches, twitching, growing hard.

Hilde might be a maiden, but she was no halfwit. It was clear he intended to use that thing and she knew exactly how.

But at the moment she had another issue to grapple with.

His mouth.

Not that Hilde was experienced in the kissing all that much, but she had to assume by the way his lips seized hers that Sigurd Thorgest had talents that would make a woman melt.

Surely he possessed talents because she was most certainly melting. And she wasn't even fond of Sigurd Thorgest.

Heat rippled through her from head to toe. Something strange was happening to her knees, as well.

They would not lock.

'Twas good that he held her, else she would doubtlessly be lying on the floor.

And low in her belly, in that place her married cousin, Drifa told her could burst into pleasure with just the right touch--*oh!* Hilde had the oddest urge to take Sigurd's hand and put it there, wanting him to do ... something to it, though she wasn't sure what.

Of its own accord her pelvis shifted against him.

Sigurd groaned when he felt the slight tilt in Hilde's hips. 'Twas a sure indication that she was aroused. Taking advantage he kissed her harder, relishing in the sweet taste of her and the softening of her lips that invited his tongue. He slipped it into her mouth molding his own mouth against hers, arching over her as one of his hands slid down her back to cup her bottom.

Hilde had such a nice arse.

Sigurd began to gather the material of her shift, aching to wrap her legs around him so he could press his manhood to her core.

A scraping sound, one that sounded suspiciously like furniture being dragged across the floor, caught in Sigurd's ears and he went still.

They were not alone in the room.

Lifting his face from Hilde he turned his head, paling when he saw his mother, Ingun, and his mother by law, Grima, sitting side by side in chairs that they pulled alongside the bed. Their hands were folded casually in their laps. Their expressions were passive, as if they were watching musicians play or a rhymester reciting his chants.

"What do you here, mother?" Sigurd asked.

"We come to witness," Ingun answered.

Closing his eyes Sigurd grimaced. His mother and his mother by law?

Nay! He could not stomach Ingun and Grima observing his arse going up and down, up and down whilst he rutted on Hilde.

'Twas his own private affair by Freya!

His willy immediately wilted along with his arousal. Seemed to be doin' that a lot lately.

Hilde snorted and Sigurd released her. Standing to his full height, he faced the elderly women, his expression showing irritation mixed with a heavy quantity of chagrin.

"'Tis the custom, Sigurd." Ingun eyed her son noticing his disapproving façade.

"Aye," Grima added with a nod. "If the consummation is not witnessed there will be no proof and the marriage can be dissolved."

Grima was more than anxious about this entire affair. Her daughter, Hilde was wedded and she was sure to see her bedded.

Sigurd's head snapped around to look at Hilde. Just as he expected, there was a puckish smirk upon her pretty little mouth.

*Humph.* He sensed she was considering exactly what he was considering.

If he refused to bed the wench, Sigurd could be rid of her after a month's time. From the expression on Hilde's face 'twould seem she agreed.

The woman had intelligence after all.

He returned Hilde's smile, suddenly feeling a strange liaison with her. 'Twas a cunning and perfect plot.

"There will be no bedding as long as the two of you sit in this room, mother." Sigurd stated firmly, his head still turned toward Hilde, his eyes skimming along her sensuous body.

He sighed regretfully.

"Sigurd!" Ingun stood hastily pointing at her son's bed furs. "Take Hilde to your linens and lie upon her!"

Astonished at his mother's barefaced words, Sigurd swiveled to face her whilst at the same time Grima began wrenching her hands.

Such emotional nonsense over a mere bedding.

"Woe, oh woe! The alliance will be broken." Grima stood and began pacing the floor. "More arguing, more clashing, more needless deaths!"

Aye, the alliance.

Hilde rubbed her temple and Sigurd raked his fingers through his hair. They both frowned, having forgotten about the wedding terms.

No matter. Their clans had fought for a century. So be it if they fought for a century more.

"As is your wish," Sigurd suddenly said and he turned to Hilde once more, taking her into his arms, hoping she understood that his doings were contrived--well, at least mostly. He pushed aside the sense that he enjoyed touching her.

"Nay, nay nay!" Hilde bellowed, turning her head from side to side as Sigurd chased her mouth, attempting to kiss her.

He released her abruptly, pleased that she played the game.

Or was she truly rejecting him? And why did that thought vex him?

"She will not have me," he said and stomped toward his bed. He plopped down on it, pulled his boots from his feet, and then slid beneath the linens. "And I will not take her by force."

With that, Sigurd turned his back to the women in the room. Shifting a few times, he pretended to fall asleep.

For effect, he snored softly.

"Hilde!" Grima yelled. "Get into the bed furs with your husband."

Hilde blinked at her mother, and then she obeyed, climbing next to Sigurd. Lightly she touched his shoulder, wondering how he would respond. "Sigurd, I am ready for you."

She was grateful her mother and Ingun could not see her face for she was struggling to keep from laughing. Such outlandish dealings, this consummating. Such a fuss!

Sigurd rolled his shoulders and turned around, facing her.

"Nay," he said, lifting his head and propping it with his hand. "'Twill be no bedding tonight. The mood has passed and I cannot perform."

'Twas the truth. As long as Ingun and Grima were in the room his lust would be duly squashed.

Hilde smirked at him.

On a hardy wail, Grima fled the room.

Ingun glared at Sigurd, and then shook her head in bewilderment. Spinning on her heels, she too left his bedchamber in a huff.

They would surely tell the guests below that he was unable to fulfill his duty.

Sure enough, after their mothers had taken their leave of his room, Sigurd heard the roars of laughter from his warriors below, mixed with disapproving female cackles. Sigurd groaned falling to his back and covering his eyes with a forearm. He would suffer much heckling from his brothers and friends in the morn.

For several long moments Hilde stared at Sigurd's unmoving form. He suddenly uncovered his face, turning his head to look at her. Rolling to his side, Sigurd grinned with amusement. He lifted his hand and began to gently trace a finger along Hilde's body.

Unable to determine how to react, Hilde rested her eyes on his face, attempting to dissuade her mind from enjoying the soft caress. Sigurd Thorgest was affecting her in a way that was difficult to interpret. The manner of her emotional response was the last thing she expected. His touch was arousing her senses.

'Twas physical attraction, Hilde decided. It had to be. She hated the Viking warrior.

Didn't she?

Sigurd's manhood blossomed once more as he let his finger roam along Hilde's curves. His hand slid over Hilde's bottom, and he pulled her pelvis tightly to his, deciding the ache assailing his groin was due to insatiate male need and the fact she was alone with him in his bedchamber.

Not because of the women, herself.

Hilde had always been a pain in his arse and nothing more. Still, he had a tempting urge to explore her passion, sensing that the feisty Hilde falling over the edge of arousal would be quite a sight to see.

Dare he take the risk? Aye, his manhood perked up even more, answering for him.

Lowering his head he attempted to kiss her, but afore his lips made contact, Hilde stiffened, bringing her hands up to cover her mouth. His lips landed on the back of her hands and he felt her struggling to get away. Letting go of her, Sigurd sat up straight.

At the same time Hilde sprang from the bed, not wanting to be closer to Sigurd than she needed to be. Her reaction to him was confusing.

"We should seek our pleasure now that our mothers have gone." Sigurd suggested.

"N-a-a-y-y, Khuwa." Hilde backed further away. "If we consummate we will remain married."

"We will not tell anyone." Sigurd shrugged, his eyes feasting on her body once more. Images of Hilde beneath him were taunting his brain, feeding his lust. "No one would be the wiser."

Sigurd would most definitely seal his lips should they do the deed. He wanted to be free of the wench.

Didn't he?

"Oh, Sigurd Thorgest, but I would be the wiser," Hilde placed her hands on her hips and gawked at him. "And 'tis my body that would be changed forever not yours."

"'Tis not like you will save your maiden condition for another," Sigurd commented. "You have fled from three betrothals and you will break from me, as well. 'Tis obvious you will never submit to marry."

Pushing to a sit on the bed, Sigurd flashed his most charming smile, before yanking his shirt from his body and tossing it to the floor. "Why not explore what the pleasure is about whilst 'tis legal a'tween us? Afore you are free."

He opened his arms to Hilde and waggled his eyebrows, mentally praising himself for his smooth-talkin' skills.

Hilde returned a blank expression though her mind was staggered at the sight of his bareness. His shoulders were broad and his arms were sinewy. His chest was strong looking and so well defined. And the ripples of muscle in his belly....

Oh my!

Sigurd Thorgest was truly the most magnificent warrior Hilde had ever seen.

Hilde turned away from him and strolled to the other side of the bedchamber, wanting to conceal her hard swallow and how her breath came out in a quiver. "Tsk, tsk! Such arrogance Khuwa! I will not mate with you."

Sigurd frowned at her rejection. In the past women never refused him. Immediately he shook the disappointed away, forcing himself to remember she was no more than the pesky little wench he wanted to be rid of.

"Then come to the bed furs and sleep," he said indignantly. "I did not want to bed you anyway."

Hilde spun around just as Sigurd yawned and stretched. His arms slid beneath the coverings and he wriggled and shifted finally producing his breeches. With a toss they joined his shirt on the floor.

Her jaw dropped and then she snapped her mouth shut. He was naked in that bed. And he wanted her to join him, just to sleep? How daft did he think she could be?

"If you do not wish to bed me, Khuwa, then why did you ask?"

"I'm horny," Sigurd stated simply. "But I can find another wench."

"On our wedding eve, Sigurd Thorgest?" Hilde bristled that he would do such a thing on the very day they were married. Not that she cared about who he bedded any more than she cared about a squashed flea.

"Hilde. You are here and available." Once again Sigurd pushed to a side sit, the coverings slipping precariously low. "I am a man. I have my needs. Other than that I have no other desire for the wench who stole my clothes, forcing humiliation on me whilst I walked through my village naked."

"You strung me up by my toes!" she answered, trying to refrain from gawking at the hint of blonde male hair peaking above the covers. "And the trap was set afore you knew I had taken your clothes."

"You brought a cow into my bedchamber, the odor left behind was offensive for weeks!" Sigurd bellowed back at her.

"You put an ice ball in my furs. By the time I chopped it small enough, 'twas so wet, I had no place to sleep!"

Sigurd rubbed his forehead wearily, a head throb taunting his skull. He was tired from the day's events, tired from over indulgence in drink, tired of the wench named Hilde.

"In one month's time 'twill be over, Hilde," Sigurd said. "This I guarantee."

On that last comment, Sigurd settled back into the linens, closing his eyes. He was no longer amused or aroused. He just wanted to sleep.

Hilde blinked several times at Sigurd, rigid in her stance and unmoving. Sensing her glare boring into him, Sigurd opened his eyes. He blew out a puff of air and sat up to glare back at her.

When she said nothing, Sigurd finally asked. "Why do you gawk at me like I have a horn growing from each side of my skull?"

Just to be sure Sigurd lifted a hand and touched his head. One never knew when he would be cursed by the gods.

Nay, no horns.

"Where do you expect me to take my slumber?" Hilde asked.

Sigurd shrugged. "On the floor or the bed. I care not."

"I will not sleep on the floor!"

"Then sleep in the bed."

"Not with you in it." Hilde crossed her arms over her chest.

"I am not moving from my own bed furs, Hilde." Sigurd couldn't help but notice the way her folded arms pushed up her breast. Gods bedamned! He wanted to bury his face between them.

"Then I will find another chamber."

"I think not!" Sigurd bolted fully upright, threatening to get out of the bed. "You have disgraced me enough in front of my clan."

"And what will you do if I leave this chamber?" Hilde tipped her head to one side, her pose showing every bit of annoyance she was feeling. "Makes not a bit of sense anyway since we will announce there was no bedding."

"I will follow you." Sigurd wanted her to stay. He wanted to taunt her.

"Uch! Who cares." Hilde waved a hand through the air.

"I will follow you naked as I am, if you attempt to leave this loft, Hilde Grey … Thorgest,"

Sigurd paused briefly thinking about his surname attached to her first. It fell from his lips comfortably and he thought it sounded rather pleasant.

"You would not dare."

"Would I not? Everyone in this village has seen my wares already, thanks much to you." Sigurd threw off the coverings giving Hilde an eye full of the wares in question.

"And here is fare warning, wife." He emphasized the word wife, nearly in a condescending manner, just to remind Hilde that he had a right to her. "When I catch you I will touch you and touch you and touch you."

"Touch me and I will scream." *With pleasure most likely*, Hilde mused but wouldn't think to say it out loud.

"'Twill do you no good. My clan will merely smirk that my

largeness is too much for you to handle."

Of their own accord Hilde's attention dropped to Sigurd's groin. She flustered and blushed, yet she couldn't take her eyes off of his....

*Thingy.*

It seemed to be changing in size. Her eyebrows rose as she studied the swelling flesh.

*Bedamned overconfident bastard!* On that same thread of thought, Hilde was befuddled at how she could move so quickly from desire to anger. The Viking would drive her to madness.

Sigurd groaned. Her eyes upon his manhood was inciting his lust again. Irritated that she affected him so, he mustered his ire, reminding himself that he was forced to marry the bedamned wench who was bent on making his life a misery. He started to rise from his bed furs, hoping to intimidate her.

"Nay!" Hilde held up her hands in surrender. Sigurd chasing her through the village with has arse bared was not what she wanted. 'Twould be embarrassing to both their clans. "I will join you in the bed furs."

She then pointed at his crotch. "But only if you cover that up."

"Happily," Sigurd replied, lowering his arse to the bed and tossing the furs over his body to conceal himself. "And wipe the worry from yer brow. I will stay on my side of the bed furs. 'Twill not be a difficult task. Yer body is unattractive to me."

'Twas such a morbid lie, but he would not let her know that.

The insult ruffled Hilde's pride. Stomping to the bed, she climbed in as Sigurd shifted over, putting as much distance between them as possible.

"I am not attracted to your body either, Khuwa." Hilde reclined to her back, on top of the bed furs. She didn't care if she would freeze this night. There was no way she was putting her body next to his naked flesh, not whilst it trembled with the need for him to touch her, kiss her, give her the pleasure that her cousin, Drifa had described.

Uch! Her emotions were frazzling. In one instance she was furious with Sigurd, in the next she felt passion. Surely she would lose her mind.

One month was such an eternity.

"Accursed wench," Sigurd mumbled reclining to his back. He would not allow feelings for the pest to arise.

"I hate you, Sigurd Thorgest."

"I hate you too woman. Now go to sleep."

Disappointment seized them both, but Hilde and Sigurd were too stubborn to admit that they fiercely desired each other.

## Chapter Six

Sigurd's mind was turning to mush. He could not think beyond bedding Hilde. For ten and two eves, after sharing the wedding mead, they retired together, each lying in their places in the bed furs, a massive space between them.

And Sigurd kept his hands to himself. 'Twas pure agony.

Seeking relief, he attempted to bed Runa, but only one time, 'twas just not the same. Runa was not Hilde and Sigurd desperately wanted his wife.

Such an odd thing.

Miserably he retreated from Runa's pallet, lust unfilled, seeing only Hilde's face in his mind.

Sigurd was a sorry excuse for a virile Viking warrior, his misery only enhanced each morn when he joined the still celebrating wedding guests to partake in the morning meal of stew and bread and mead.

Not a day would pass by when the clans failed to ask him if he and Hilde had done the deed.

His reply was always the same. "My bride refuses me."

This, of course, was contrary to Hilde's tale. For each morn when she joined him to break her fast, her answer was as consistent as Sigurd's. "I am more than willing to have my husband."

And then she would tsk and wear a sad frown. "But his thingy seems not to be working."

"His thingy?" Ulfrik looked at Sigurd wide-eyed the first time he heard Hilde call his man part the ridiculous word. "Ha ha ha ha ha ha ha ha ha ha!"

To Sigurd's grumbling, he suffered a relentless badgering whenever he was around his brood. At every chance they found their amusements using the word *thingy* while conversing.

"Ulfrik!" Leif had said one day whilst they worked in the pastures. "Have you seen my dagger?

And Ulfrik answered, a mocking grin on his face. "Aye Leif, I saw it inside that thingy behind the barn."

"Ha ha ha ha ha ha ha ha ha ha!" Everyone would laugh and the bantering would go on and on.

Runa was of no help. The wench spread rumors that he sought her out one night and 'twas truth Hilde spoke, blabbin' that Sigurd abandoned her pallet unable to satiate his need.

The wench, Runa. He would sell her for sure!

His brothers and brood of friends continued to laugh and heckle. Grima would wail, and Ingun would bluster. Ozur and Bram would glare at him, their expressions showing sore disappointment.

Brawls would erupt between various guests, over which of the couple was lying.

By day ten and three, Sigurd could endure it no longer. He was married to a woman who did not want him, but whom he craved more than the air he breathed.

It was an immense chafing to his Viking pride.

Skipping the morning meal, he walked through the forest beseeching the gods and seeking answers. Thinking a swim might ease his tension he headed for the nearby stream.

Through the tree branches and the brush, Sigurd spied a female form.

"Uch," he grumbled. Loki was surely trailing him. Hilde was already there, but not swimming.

She was mumblin' and grumblin' about somethin'.

Quietly, Sigurd moved closer, ducking behind a bush, so that he could better hear and view what his wife was about, and without being seen.

"Bastard Viking!" Hilde's red paint splattered against the canvas that she strung tightly between two closely planted trees. "I hate you Sigurd Thorgest."

She dipped her bristles into another bowl containing paint and with a jerk of her wrist the green color joined the red. Studying her work, Hilde was satisfied that she sufficiently covered the words she painted earlier.

*Hilde loves Sigurd.*

Her father was correct. She was nothing but a foolish child. Because of her stubbornness, her marriage to Sigurd would be nullified.

*Oh!*

'Twas not what she wanted.

Hilde desired Sigurd, his caresses, his kisses. She wanted to seek his passion, feel him betwixt her thighs. But she could not tell him that. She did not even know how to try.

Hilde was a maiden after all, and she didn't know what to do.

Every eve when they retired to the bed furs, Hilde prayed to the gods that he would touch her, but to no avail. He merely went to sleep. Sigurd Thorgest, her husband was refusing her. He would prefer to rut with his slaves.

Aye, Hilde knew about the night he went to Runa. She followed him, her heart shattering with the understanding of what he was seeking. She returned to the bedchamber with an ache in her chest and tears filling her eyes. When Sigurd returned, Hilde pretended to be asleep.

'Twas normal for a man to seek out other women aside from their wives.

She had no right to protest and so she stoically kept silent, though inside it was ripping her apart.

Anger assailed Hilde as she recalled that night. She slapped yet another splotch of paint on her canvas. "Free of you, Khuwa!"

She watched as streams of paint rolled to the canvas bottom, weeping onto the forest floor. "In ten and seven days more, I will be free."

The idea of it had sadly lost its appeal.

Sigurd's heart sank at Hilde's gnashing words. 'Twas a confirmation that his wife despised him. A decision came to him instantly. Only one more night would he sleep next to her in bed. On the morrow he would be gone.

Backing from his hiding place, Sigurd turned and stomped away.

*Talented artist indeed*, was his next thought. Her painting was nothing but a dribbling, sorry mess.

As was his marriage to the troublesome wench.

Hilde heard the rustling in the brush and glanced over her shoulder, catching a glimpse of Sigurd's retreating backside.

How much of her ranting had he heard?

Nay. She had to resolve this issue with him. Rolling her canvas and placing lids on her paint bowls, she tucked the items in a sack and then headed back to their house.

The first thing she heard when she arrived was the murmuring of male voices.

She moved a bit closer and peeked around the door frame.

"We will go south, here, to Helgeandsholmen, Birka and then Gotland Island," Sigurd pointed at a map flattened atop the table. His brothers, and the rest of Sigurd's warriors stood around listening to their Chieftain's instructions.

"If the thirty days has yet to pass then I may decide to sail on to Jorvik. I hear the trading is profitable."

Hilde gasped. Sigurd was leaving. Did he loath her that much? She dropped her sack of art supplies. It landed with a loud thud, paint seeping through the canvas and onto the floor.

Sigurd's head snapped up at sound.

"What is this you do?" Hilde yelled treading heavily across the room, her angry gaze falling to the map.

Picking it up she examined the diagram and with one whipping motion of her arm she tossed it away. It skimmed the air and then gently floated to the floor.

Not quite the affect she was going for. Her eyes scanned the room seeking something to break.

Preferably over Sigurd's head.

Upon seeing Hilde Thorgest's irate face Ulfrik, Ivar, Ludin, Leif and the rest of Sigurd's men began backing from the room, much in the same manner as the time the cow was in the Chieftain's bed loft.

There was no way in Thor's creation they would get between a furious female and her husband.

"Cowards!" Sigurd bellowed at them, before returning his attention to Hilde.

"I leave in the morn," he said, rubbing the back of his neck in irritation at the acts of his spineless brood.

Hilde gave him a bewildered look. "But why?"

"'Tis for the best," Sigurd's mouth twisted as he contemplated leaving her, but he had no choice.

Absence makes the heart grow distant.

So they say.

And he needed to put as much distance between them as possible, else he would go insane with the lust he felt for her.

"Nay, nay! You must not leave."

Sigurd lifted a finger and placed it against her lips to silence her. Hilde crossed her eyes to look at it.

Thor's thunder! How she wanted to lick that digit, but instead she turned her head away.

"You wish me stay, Hilde?" The thought that she might fancy him had Sigurd's heart leaping in his chest.

Suddenly feeling the fool for the emotions she felt toward Sigurd, Hilde's mind began searching for something to say--to explain her reaction. *Hel's* flaming battles, Aye, she wanted him to stay! But she dared not reveal her true feelings. He would laugh in her face.

Stalling for time she looked around the hall, noticing that it was vacant of all the guests, that is, with the exception of Mord and her Uncle Vog, who were snoring on two separate benches--half into their cups most likely.

She tipped her head looking at the wench draped over Vog's chest, wishing she could be so brazen. "Where has everyone gone?"

"They are in the field, roasting a wild boar they hunted and killed." Sigurd withdrew his finger from her lips, resisting the urge to stroke it inside of her mouth, conjuring images of what he could teach her to do with her tongue.

"Still celebratin' our joining." Hilde's voice was low and despondent. The wedding festivities were a pointless fete. "You would leave me here alone to suffer the consequences of both our scolding clans, Sigurd?"

She took notice that his eyes were focused on her mouth. It caused her lips to tingle.

*Please kiss me.*

*Uch.* Hilde was thinkin' only of herself, Sigurd assumed, but he hadn't much considered the ridicule she would suffer in his absence. Stiffening against his guilt he lifted his gaze to stare into her lovely, green eyes, imagining how they might look in the heat of desire as he brought her body to full blossom, and she cried out his name in passion.

*If only she would let me bed her.* Sigurd groaned inwardly. *I would love her without replete.*

His eyes shut, the stirrings within him becoming clear. *When did I fall in love with her?*

"The mead." Hilde finally said, hoping she'd found a way to keep him from departing. She tipped her head sideways as she looked at his eyelids, wondering what he was thinking.

"What about it?" Sigurd opened his eyes, shifting with discomfort at his swelling member, hurt pride and aching heart.

Uch! 'Twas absurd. No man loved his wife. Perhaps another man's wife, but not his own.

"If we do not share the mead for thirty days, as required of a newly married couple, the gods will frown upon us."

"The gods already frown down upon us, Hilde." Sigurd inhaled deeply attempting to shake the emotions that seized him unaware. He watched as Hilde's brow wrinkled and her eyes lowered.

"'Tis that important to you?" Sigurd lifted her chin with a knuckle. Concern for their beliefs was a thing to consider, but moreover, he cared for Hilde's feelings.

"Aye." Hilde lied, gazing at him with utmost sincerity, her heart lifting, thinking he would now remain. She didn't give two cow dung piles about the mead. She only cared about Sigurd.

Sigurd dropped his hand from her, much to Hilde's disappointment.

Rubbing his temple with a palm, Sigurd pondered the dilemma for a moment.

"Runa!" He called for his slave and when she appeared he ordered. "Bring me sixteen mugs and a decanter of mead."

With much confusion, Hilde eyed Runa scurrying back and forth until she'd gathered all of the requested mugs and placed them on the table, along with the mead. Sigurd picked up the decanter, poured the mead into the containers and then took a gulp from each and every cup.

"I have tasted from all of these and you will do the same each day until thirty days have passed." He leaned back against the wall behind him, folding his arms across his chest, a slight but satisfied grin creasing his mouth. "We will have shared the mead. You are witness Runa."

Runa nodded and Sigurd dismissed her. She left the hall, returning to her chores.

Hilde felt a wretched sinking in her chest as she stared at the mugs on the table.

"What if I accidentally spill one?"

"Then drink from the same cup twofold. 'Twill be the same thing."

'Twas of no use. Hilde sighed. "Yer a clever Viking, my husband."

Hilde tried to smile, but it was a meager response at best. Sigurd was going to leave her. And when he returned their marriage would be no more. "I will have Runa bring the mugs to our bedchamber and will drink from one each morn whilst you are away."

Slowly she rose from the bench and left the dwelling.

Watching Hilde walk away, Sigurd focused on her comments. She called him clever, she referred to him as *her* husband, and she said the bedchamber was *ours*.

If only Hilde understood the impact of those simple statements. If only she was sincere with the words she had to say.

Nay.

Rising from the bench, Sigurd headed for the bay to oversee the preparation of his ship for departure in the morn.

He would suffer only one more torturous night sleeping next to Hilde's sensual body before he set out for the seas. When he returned he would once again be a free man ... alone ... without Hilde.

'Twas an empty and lonely feeling.

## Chapter Seven

Hilde reclined on her side gazing at Sigurd, who was lying next to her, watching his chest rising up and down as he peacefully relaxed in his slumber.

Her mouth watered to plant kisses on his taut and beautiful, but forbidden flesh. She lifted her hand craving to caress him, stopping just short of touching him.

She glanced at the bed furs, a picture of what was beneath forming in her mind. Hilde swallowed, a lusty sensation building inside of her, an ache rising in that area betwixt her thighs.

Hilde wanted to have a peek beneath the coverings, but aye, her innocence was a hinderin' thing. If he awoke and caught her, she would be immeasurably mortified.

She wriggled her hips in a restless manner and then willed them to stop. The sensation seemed to be getting worse.

Her eyes flicked back to his face. She studied his chiseled features for a bit, enjoying the look of his rough, masculine shape. Her attention was then drawn to his hair.

He really did have a nice head of hair. Golden and wavy it spread across his shoulders and chest, nearly to his waist, almost as long as her locks. Unable to resist, she lightly stroked the mane. It felt like a mass of silk.

She sucked in a sob. How was she to bear staying in Sigurd's house without his presence there? 'Twould feel so empty, despite the fact there were at least forty wedding guests still milling about.

But none of them would be Sigurd.

Hilde threaded a finger through his hair, gathering a bit of it in her hand. With her other hand she drew a few strands of her own hair and held it next to his, comparing the differences in the color and thinking how different she and Sigurd were, as well.

A scheme came to her as she unconsciously began weaving a braid--a strand of his hair, over a strand of hers.

She would stow away on Sigurd's ship and he would be none the wiser. He said he would take port in Birka and that was where she lived. 'Twas less than two days away by water vessel.

As Hilde continued to intertwine her hair with Sigurd's she mentally weaved her plot.

Secretly she would depart from his ship when they landed in her home village and then return to her dwelling. The place was empty since all of her kin were presently in Sigurd's house.

*No one would think to search for me there.*

Hilde's hands continued the plait until she reached the ends of the strands. She twisted her handiwork tying it into a knot. Lifting it to her nose, Hilde inhaled the pleasant scent of their combined locks. Sigurd stirred a bit and she held her breath, but he immediately returned to his soft snoring.

She swallowed while blinking away tears threatening to spill onto her cheeks realizing how deeply she would miss the tranquil sound of his breathing.

The idea of going home was much preferred to staying here without Sigurd. There she could wallow in her self-pity, alone and unbothered, without the glares of disapproving eyes. And by the time her family returned, happy to find her safe, she would be fully recovered from her heartbreak, none the worse for the wear. She would go on with her life.

What a miserable thought.

Hilde's hands dropped to the bed furs and she yawned. *Aye 'twas a good plan.*

Slowly her eyes drifted shut.

Sigurd was having a delectable dream. His hands were roaming all over Hilde's body. He could hear her passionate moans, could feel her soft skin beneath his touch. Her breasts were round and supple, the nipples peaking hard as he ran his fingers over them. He groaned, moving his hand lower seeking more of her. Gently he caressed her thigh, skimming his hand upward as he slipped it beneath her shift. He could almost feel the heat as he neared her core. And then he touched her there, and heard Hilde's sigh as he did so. It was a sound of yearning, encouraging him to continue on. She was wet and wanting and he sought to fill her need, stroking his thumb on the female swelling there.

"More," Hilde mumbled. She was having a delicious dream.

"Faster."

*Mmm.*

Her body was aroused, soaring. She was panting, her flesh seeking, climbing and falling like a wave in the sea that sped to the shoreline, only to be pulled back, building to an even larger wave the next time. Low in her belly and even lower still a rush washed over her and Hilde cried out at the bursting sensation that rippled through her feminine flesh, coursed down her legs and marched up her spine.

"Oh Freya!" she yelled out loud.

Sigurd's eyes flew open and the first thing he realized was that his shaft was near bursting. The second thing that took shape in his sleep-fogged mind was that his hand was between Hilde's thighs, a finger gently stroking inside her folds, her female bud throbbing beneath his thumb.

His head snapped to the side. Hilde stared at him with wild, hazy eyes. Her breathing was heavy and her face was flushed like a woman who had just experienced great passion.

Afore he comprehended what was happening, Hilde opened her mouth and released and ear shattering scream, startling Sigurd so acutely that he leapt from the bed.

His head jerked toward Hilde and he pulled back, yanking her head toward him, causing both their heads to crash together.

"Ouch!" Hilde bellowed.

"What the...." Sigurd drew back forcefully not yet understanding what he was caught on. He fell on his rump to the floor. Hilde followed landing squarely on top of him, their bodies mashed together, cheek to cheek, arms and legs entwined.

Hilde gasped when she felt his manhood pressed against her bare thigh. She began to struggle realizing she was bound to the side of Sigurd's head.

"Be still!" Sigurd ordered grabbing her beneath the chin with one hand and Hilde ceased moving. Sigurd's other hand moved to where they seemed to be stuck together. Finding the source of their entanglement, he fingered it, managing to examine it part way by dropping his eyes.

"What is this?" He frowned looking at the knot that combined their locks.

"What?" Hilde frowned back and then grimaced, remembering what she'd done to their hair. Heat flooded her cheeks and she blushed profusely.

"This." Sigurd tugged the plait. Both of their heads shifted slightly.

Hilde attempted to think beyond the pain at the side of her head where she hit it against Sigurd's. She attempted to think beyond the unnerving sensation of his male part resting against her bared thigh, and that her woman part nestled naked against his side. Her arse was likely exposed too.

Never mind the remnants of ecstasy Sigurd bestowed on her that still lingered in her mind. It surpassed anything she ever experienced afore.

"Oh!" Hilde didn't answer but instead began to struggle again.

Sigurd's arms came around her body, his legs locking around the backs of her thighs, firmly trapping her. He groaned, remembering he was a hair's breadth away from mounting her in the bed furs as he started to awaken. "I said, be still!"

And then he chuckled while unconsciously running the tips of his fingers along her bottom.

"'Tis not funny, Khuwa." Hilde tried to lift her head, but to no avail. "And get yer fingers off my arse!"

"'Tis so funny, Hilde." He cupped her bottom instead. "Are you tryin' to tell me somethin',"

"I ... uh...." Hilde stumbled over her words, half from chagrin, half from the intimate touch of their bodies. "Nay, nay! I must have done it in my sleep."

She couldn't admit that she was playing with his hair, though Sigurd was correct, the consequence of her actions was a bit amusing. Hilde firmly refrained from laughing.

"It seems you do quite a bit in yer sleep lovely lady." Sigurd grinned. "Rise to the heat of passion to name one."

But then Sigurd's grin faded. Had Hilde been awake when he touched her so intimately, she likely would have slapped him in the face.

Sigurd sat upright bringing Hilde with him. The movement caused her to slide into his lap and her legs to straddle his thighs. Their sex parts pressed together. His arousal flared, his shaft started twitching. All he had to do was lift her a bit and he could easily slip inside of her.

Instead, he reached for the dagger that sat near the bedside. *Uch*, he couldn't bear it if she denied him. In one quick motion he sliced near the root of his hair and freed his head from Hilde's.

For several moments Hilde didn't move. She could feel the stirrings of his arousal beneath her, which urged her own desires to resurface. But she was afraid--of rejection, of being mocked, of risking her heart on a man who hated her.

Her hesitation gave Sigurd hope, but her expression said otherwise. There was fear in her eyes and something else he was unable to interpret. He would never hurt Hilde, but to say it aloud, well he was about to, when she rose from him and turned away, her actions sealing the death of their marriage.

Springing to his feet, Sigurd slipped into his breeches and left the bedchamber. Hilde swiftly donned her dress and boots, following behind him.

When they reached the hall downstairs, they found Ivar, Ulfrik, Ludin and Agnar sitting at the table with some of the guests, all breaking their fast.

Ivar looked up, and with raised brows he asked Sigurd. "What happened to your hair?"

His eyes snapped from the sheared strands on the side of Sigurd's head to the braided mass of mixed locks dangling from Hilde.

He laughed outrageously.

"I was tangling with my wife." Sigurd snarled, still fighting to tamp his arousal, but his irritation was mostly over his wife's dismissal.

"Aye we heard her scream and could only hope...."

Hilde's eyes went very wide and she blushed, dropping her head to the floor.

"Then yer thingy is workin' again?" Ludin snorted, his eyes falling to Sigurd's crotch.

They all looked at Sigurd's crotch.

"Sigurd's thingy is workin'!" Agnar yelled. "They have done the deed!"

One by one the curtains covering the bed lofts that ran the length of the longhouse walls were pushed aside and heads began peeking out.

"My thingy has always worked properly!" Sigurd bellowed and then grimaced at using the word he loathed.

Sleepy guests sprang from their bed furs and Mord, dragging a wench behind him released a whooping cheer.

"What is this you say?" Bram appeared scratching his arse and yawning. Grima smiled at his side. "They have done the deed?"

"Send word to father!" Ivar ordered to anyone who listened.

"They have done the deed!" Ulfrik laughed, slapping Sigurd proudly on the back of his shoulder. "We knew you could do it my friend."

Voices grew louder as the word was passed and a happy raucous of howling and hollering began rapidly spreading throughout the hall.

Hilde shook her head from side to side and continued looking at the floor. The hubbub gave her an opportunity to slip away unnoticed, since they were all focusing on Sigurd's rediscovered vigor.

She would leave Sigurd to explain their non-joining. Hilde had other things to attend to at the moment.

Namely, boarding his ship.

While everyone shouted their approval, quietly she shuffled to the door, disappearing through it with no one the wiser, not even her mother who was happily celebrating with the others.

## Chapter Eight

Sigurd stood at the bow of his ship, the *Merrymaker,* with his boot propped up on a tied-down chest. His chin was lifted and his shoulders were rolled back--a tall and rigid stance that exemplified every bit of the mighty Viking warrior he was.

The wind blew through his golden hair, catching the plait at his left temple, whipping it in the air. He would have braided the strands on the right side as well, but alas, there was no hair there to weave.

His thoughts drifted to Hilde. Sigurd expected that she would be at the shore to see him and his crew off, but she was nowhere to be found. That saddened him, for he hoped that with all they had endured together, he and Hilde might at least remain friends.

But her absence was a clear declaration of her indifference.

Sigurd scanned the open sea, his scrutiny catching sight of a vessel appearing and disappearing on the water's swells. He squinted, straining to determine if it was friend or foe.

"You see it, Sigurd?" Ulfrik spoke as he stared over Sigurd's shoulder.

"Aye," Sigurd said.

Ulfrik scratched the back of his head. "They seem to be approaching."

"Aye." Sigurd said again, now recognizing the colors on the

ship's sail.

'Twas Harald Guthorm's vessel--Harald the child eater, he was called, because all knew he was a ruthless warrior.

He would sell his own mother if the price were to his liking.

In fact, Sigurd rubbed his chin thinking he remembered hearing that Guthorm had done just that after his father died.

There was no doubt in Sigurd's mind that Guthorm's aim was to plunder the *Merrymaker*. She was riding low on the water, a sign that her hull was full--a bounty for the taking.

"All arms stand ready." Sigurd turned and ordered his men.

The forty Viking warriors that accompanied Sigurd, dropped the ends of their oars in near unison. Standing, they each placed their hands to their swords.

Mord lowered the sail and the *Merrymaker* began to drift.

"We should out run them, Sigurd." Ulfrik suggested.

"Nay, they are too close. 'Tis too late." Sigurd's hand moved to his own sword as he watched the fast moving long ship draw nearer. "Aside from that, running would be a sure indication of cowardice."

Ulfrik nodded his agreement.

'Twould not serve their reputations well to be marked as weak. A rumor such as that might encourage other sea rovers to attack them in the future.

Not that Sigurd and his men hadn't clashed with Guthorm in the past. And though they were vicious Vikings, Sigurd's men defeated them easily, much to Harald's disgruntlement. The Viking would seek revenge, Sigurd was sure, and 'twas most certain he would be better prepared this time.

A bothersome worry creased Sigurd's brow as he scanned his horde of warriors. He had a crew of seventy men back then, but at the moment his ship carried about half that number.

Sigurd watched with a sharp eye as Harald Guthorm's ship came up alongside the *Merrymaker*. Just as suspected Guthorm's ship carried at least seventy, perhaps eighty warriors.

But fierce and as ready as they might be, Sigurd's crew was just as primed. A battle cry rumbled from Sigurd's throat as several of Guthorm's men leapt across the gap separating the two ships, landing on the deck of the *Merrymaker*. They were met by the points of angry swords, their punctured bodies thrown overboard.

'Twas a clean kill.

A sudden rush of Guthorm's men brought the clashing of swords to full hilt as Sigurd's crew fought to maintain their ground. Warriors meshed, fists flew, bodies tumbled over the side. There were wails from the wounded and roars from the victorious, even as blood scourged the *Merrymaker's* deck.

And when the onslaught was done, ten of Sigurd's men lay dead, twenty maimed and lying about, the remaining of his Vikings, captured.

The ship was intact, though Sigurd suspected that Guthorm might set it afire, leaving the survivors of Sigurd's crew to take to the water, unless of course, they were slain first.

The cargo was plundered. Crates and barrels were removed from the hull and sent hand to hand across the deck to be loaded on Guthorm's ship. There was little that Sigurd could do, particularly with two blades to his throat and one to his back. He could only be grateful that most of his crew was alive.

For how long was the question.

"Look what I found, Harald." One of Guthorm's mangy men emerged from below, dragging a special commodity that Sigurd was unaware the Merrymaker carried.

Sigurd's heart seized with horror when he saw what it was.

*Hilde.* He met her eyes in a blatant glare. Her face was as white as a newly fallen snow, her expression just as cold. Sigurd couldn't tell if she was angry or afraid.

"The ship's whore," the man dragged Hilde toward Guthorm, handing her off.

Hilde opened her mouth to speak and Sigurd warned her with a subtle shake of his head, to keep silent. He pressed his lips together, struggling to keep his face unexpressive, lest he reveal to Guthorm that the woman was of import to him.

But his insides were in a rage.

What Hilde was doing on his ship, Sigurd could not even imagine. Was she planning on sinking it? 'Twould be a mightily spiteful task to accomplish, no matter how much she despised him. If that be Hilde's motive, her wish might be attained with the enemy now in power.

A wicked snicker emerged from Guthorm's mouth as his gaze roamed up and down Hilde's body. He placed a hand to her breast, giving a gripping squeeze. Sigurd started forward, but halted abruptly, feeling the sharpness of the blades at his throat sinking in a bit further. He would be of no help to Hilde if he were dead.

Sigurd watched as Hilde bristled slightly, her throat moving as she gulped a harsh swallow. She fixed her gaze beyond

Guthorm's shoulder, staring directly into Sigurd's eyes, as if to gain courage from him.

Pride surged through him at his wife's stoic demeanor. Most women Sigurd knew would be wailing and begging by now.

But not his Hilde.

"Nay," Sigurd stated evenly, fearing that Guthorm would ravage Hilde on the very deck they stood upon and then toss her to his warriors as leavings. His stomach sickened at the idea of it. "Not the ship's whore."

"Not the ship's whore?" Guthorm dropped his hand and turned to scrutinize Sigurd's warriors. "With all of these men on board?"

"I am delivering her to be wed in Birka." Sigurd hoped the lie would encourage Guthorm to hold Hilde for ransom and leave her body alone.

Guthorm snickered. "Do you take me for a fool?"

*Do you wish for me to answer that arse hole?* Sigurd didn't dare articulate his answer aloud.

He kept his silence, tamping his fury, as Guthorm approached Ulfrik from behind, drawing his dagger and threatening Sigurd's friend by pressing the blade to Ulfrik's neck.

"Tell me warrior." Guthorm's voice held a menacing tone that equaled his expression. "Is she as sweet in the bed furs as she appears?"

Ulfrik's face twisted with disgust and Sigurd, knowing his friend as well as he did, could surmise by the way Ulfrik's body quivered that he too was feeling wrath.

Hopefully Harald Guthorm would interpret it as fear.

"The Chieftain is honest, Guthorm." Ulfrik's left eye twitched but he remained composed. "None here have touched the woman."

Dissatisfied, Guthorm sheathed his dagger, signaled two of his men, and then pointed to where Ludin knelt on the deck with his hands tied behind his back. Roughly Ludin was forced to his to his feet, and Guthorm's warriors dragged him to the ship's rail. They tipped him over the side, dangling him above the Baltic waters by his ankles.

Ludin refrained from making a sound.

Guthorm leaned over the rail. "I will spare yer life Viking if you tell me about the whore."

"No whore," Ludin rasped out, struggling for breath in the awkward position.

"Drop him," Guthorm ordered and a splash was heard as Ludin

was released into the sea. Boisterous laughs from Guthorm's brood followed.

Sigurd winced praying to the gods that Ludin managed to stay afloat without his hands free.

"Who here values his life above the woman's?" Guthorm's expression grew even more feral as he turned to glare at Sigurd's men.

His eye's fell to Ivar.

"Nay," Ivar responded, immediately. "Never bedded the wench."

Agnar, who sat tied to the bench next to him, also shook his head. Murmurs rose among Sigurd's crew, each claiming a denial that they had lain with Hilde.

"Not I," Leif said loudly.

"Would not touch her with a ten foot branch," Mord mumbled.

*Sigurd would burn me at the stake,* he thought silently as he glared directly at Harald Guthorm.

Spinning on his heels, Guthorm stalked back toward Sigurd, halting just a foot in front of him.

"It behooves me to think yer men would risk their health for the likes of a whore." He scratched his stained and unruly, yellow beard. Sigurd couldn't help but wonder if it was nesting maggots. Guthorm most certainly was the mother of them all.

Guthorm's hand went still on his chin, as the expression on his face grew pensive. "A maiden woman brings a fortune on the market."

Sigurd's nostrils flared and his lipped snarled with fury, but thankfully Harald Guthorm was too consumed with his thoughts to notice. Through the corner of his eye Sigurd noticed Hilde's tremble.

"Aye," Sigurd agreed.

'Twas not what he expected. Paying a decided sum for ransom would be a much simpler task than buying Hilde back from the slavers, where she would be sold to the highest bidder.

"Her betrothed is quite wealthy, Guthorm." Sigurd offered, hoping the despicable Viking might consider receiving a ransom as more favorable.

"Tell me, Thorgest." Guthorm asked, ignoring Sigurd's last comment. "Is her character biddable?"

"Aye," Sigurd lied, hoping that Hilde's feisty spirit would be her saving grace and not her downfall. He tossed a glance in her direction and she managed a slight smile. His heart warmed to it.

"I think I might get more for her on the markets." With that, Guthorm stomped over to Hilde and grabbed her roughly by the arm. She gasped as he shoved her to one of his men. "Take her the ship and put her below."

Hilde began struggling and Sigurd bellowed to her. "Cease! Do as yer told, woman."

*She never did as she was told.*

Hilde went still as she was handed over to the next ship, her eyes riveted to Sigurd her expression twisted hatefully. It stabbed clear through his heart.

Guthorm inspected the ship and the men he held captive. Just as he was stepping over the rails he turned to his men who remained on the Merrymaker and sneered. "Burn her."

With that, he leapt aboard his own ship, whilst Sigurd's beloved ship was set afire. The blades that held him where suddenly gone as Guthorm's men made their escape.

Sigurd's crew scampered about untying the bound warriors and making every effort to smother the fires, but to no avail.

"We have to jump ship." Uflrik tugged on Sigurd's arm, dismayed by the feral look in his eyes and his frozen stance. He was well aware that his Chieftain was in a fit of rage.

Sigurd watched the gap grow wider as Guthorm's ship made its escape, vaguely aware of the encroaching fire and that he was being picked up bodily and thrown over side.

His focus was on one thing, and one thing only.

Guthorm had his wife--his *virgin* wife.

For that, the bastard would die.


Chapter Nine

"Again!" Sigurd barked.

Mord and Agnar exchanged glances. Shrugging, they dumped Harald Guthorm into the waters below.

"Do you think he has had enough, Sigurd?" Ulfrik stood beside the Chieftain, staring down at the Guthorm as he floundered about, struggling to keep his head above the surface, in order to breath.

A difficult task considering he was bound by ropes that coiled around him from shoulders to ankles, his arms effectively pinned inside.

The free end of the rope was secured to the rail which resulted in Guthorm's body being dragged along, as the ship they were on sailed across the sea.

"Nay," Sigurd growled through gritted teeth. His dealings with Guthorm were nowhere near done. The torturing would proceed. "Bring him up."

Mord and Agnar grumbled. 'Twas the fifth time they'd hauled Harald from the sea. The Viking was far from meager in size, and their arms were growing weary.

But there was no blaming Sigurd for being outraged, however. The warriors who survived the ordeal--twenty in all, were just as infuriated by Guthorm's deeds.

After the *Merrymaker* burned and sank, Sigurd's men were forced to swim the distance to shore and then walk the breadth of the countryside. Two days time, it took, until they finally came upon a clan who shared both their anger and resentment toward Harald Guthorm for his repeated pillaging of their villages. The clan agreed to assist Sigurd and his warriors, providing a long ship, additional men and supplies.

And so, Sigurd, his men and his newly acquired allies set sail to the seas seeking their revenge.

"Is this the best you can do, Sigurd Thorgest?" Guthorm sneered, as Mord and Agnar pulled him up, propping his feet on the narrow planking along the hull and steadying his body against the outside of the ship's rail.

"This is for burnin' my ship." Snarling, Sigurd backhanded Guthorm across his left cheek, the crack loud and so forceful that his head snapped in the opposite direction and his body jerked backwards.

Mord and Agnar tensed, tightening their grips and bracing themselves to keep him from falling overboard.

Guthorm slowly turned his head forward, meeting Sigurd's eyes with a cocky glare. Again, he snickered, as if the blow had no affect on him.

Sigurd raised his arm to strike him again but it was grabbed from behind.

"Allow me," Ludin said stepping closer to their vile captive. "And this is for tossing me over the rails."

Ludin backhanded Guthorm across his right cheek. Again his head snapped to the side. Sigurd placed the sole of his booted foot to Harald Guthorm's chest, and shoved it hard against him.

At the same time, Mord and Agnar released him and Guthorm

splashed into the water once more. They watched with callous regard as the man again fought against drowning.

Several moments passed before Sigurd ordered that he be brought up.

"You hit like a woman," Guthorm mocked through spitting out water and gasps for air, attempting to catch his breath.

"Speakin' of which, you maggot. Where is the she?" Sigurd's own breathing grew heavy, out of irritation, not lack of air. It took every bit of his restraint to keep from breaking the Viking's neck.

Throwing back his head, Guthorm released a menacing laugh. "Nothin' but trouble, that one, I tell you. I did her betrothed a favor."

"Explain," Sigurd glared at him, his blood beginning a slow boil.

Guthorm frowned. "The wench had the audacity to put pepper in our breeches whilst they hung to dry on my deck. My men were jumping overboard to keep their balls from burnin'."

It was Sigurd's turn to laugh and his crew joined him. 'Twould be just like his Hilde to risk such a stunt.

"You did not tie her up?" Not that Sigurd wanted to think that Hilde had been shackled, but the fact that this ruthless Viking would overlook such a thing astonished him.

"The woman picks knots." Guthorm said with a disdainful tone.

Worry suddenly threaded through Sigurd, overshadowing his amusement. His eyes narrowed and his lip turned up into a twitching snarl. "What have you done with her, Harald Guthorm?"

Guthorm met Sigurd's eyes directly, his expression cool--heartless. He said nothing for several moments as he and Sigurd stared one another down.

"Aye, she was a tasty virgin. Fought me even after I pierced her," Guthorm spoke.

The men on the ship grew silent, listening to his bawdy words. Guthorm's mouth curved into a lecherous, gloating grin, when he noticed he had their attention. "She was very, very tight."

Sigurd's nostrils flared and his fury began an upward rise.

"Pity my bedding the wench lowered her value on the market though." Guthorm continued to taunt, his mouth twisting as he sucked air between his teeth and then smacked his lips in an indifferent manner.

Sigurd threw back his head, his voice spewing forth in a rumble that escalated as he roared a thunderous cry.

He pounded a fist against his chest, his senses going berserk. His body convulsed with a bloodthirsty rage, his flesh turning red with fury as the blood rushed to his face, and veins popped from beneath the skin on his neck.

Yanking his dagger from the sheath at his side, he plunged it between the ropes and straight into Guthorm's heart, withdrawing it quickly and throwing it to the deck.

Finding the might of ten warriors, Sigurd continued to bellow his fury. Seizing hold of Guthorm's body, he lifted him high over his head and hurled him into the sea.

"Cut the rope!" Sigurd turned sharply grabbing one of Guthorm's captured men who sat nearby.

Jerking him to his feet, Sigurd roared in his face, seeing nothing but red and an enemy.

With his fists clamped tightly, he cranked back his arm and drove a brutal, right-handed blow to man's jaw. It was followed instantly by one directly to his nose. Blood poured freely from the man's nostrils and he toppled over. Sigurd lunged, landing on top of him and straddling his thighs. The fingers from both his hands curled around the downed man's ears and Sigurd lifted the man's head from the deck and then smashed it back down. There was a sickly crunching sound as he did so. Sigurd lifted him again growling and baring his teeth.

Somewhere in the back of his rational mind, sensibility kept its place, and Sigurd knew he could not kill all of Guthorm's men, else he would never find Hilde. One of them, at least, was privy to her whereabouts.

Those thoughts alone forced him to release the battered warrior who dropped to the deck with a solid thud. He was clearly unconscious or dead.

Whichever it was, Sigurd couldn't care less.

Slowly he rose to his feet, his body rigid, every muscle still taut with anger as his gaze swept the deck. All aboard gawked back at him, some with their mouths agape and in wide-eyed fear, his own warriors included, waiting to see what he might do next.

He felt like killing them all.

"Sigurd." The sound of Ulfrik's voice brought him back to reason, though his heart continued to pound and his breathing remained labored. He clenched and unclenched his fists.

"Question them," was all Sigurd managed to say before stalking to the bow of the ship. He still did not know if Hilde was dead or alive, if she had been ravaged, beaten, or if they let her be. His chest squeezed with an unbearable anguish as he stared out at the open Baltic Sea.

A short time later, Ulfrik approached. Carrying much apprehension he lifted a hand to touch Sigurd's shoulder, but stopped with his hand raised part way. He'd never seen this violent temper in Sigurd afore, and he wondered if it still lingered. Deciding he might find himself on the unwanted side of the Chieftain's fist, Ulfrik lowered his arm.

"Are you back with us, Sigurd?" he asked and hesitantly stepped a bit closer.

Sigurd's head snapped around, his glare boring into his friend's eyes.

The color drained from Ulfrik's face. He gulped and took several steps backward, keenly aware it was foolish to mess with an outraged Viking.

"Yer outburst was all it took to gain information, Sigurd," Ulfrik stated with grave apprehension, waiting for Sigurd's reaction.

"Indeed," Sigurd answered, a strange deadness suddenly washing over him--the after effects of his mind bursting apart, he supposed.

"Aye." Ulfrik stepped in front of him "The remainin' ten captives from Guthorm's crew were more than willing to spill the beans."

Sigurd turned his head back to the water, acknowledging Ulfrik's words with a nod.

"One of them even wet his breeches." Ulfrik chuckled nervously.

*Cowardly bastards,* Sigurd mused. "Is Hilde alive?"

"Aye."

Unable to bring himself to ask more about her, Sigurd turned and fully faced Ulfrik. "Then raise the sail and set the men to the oars. 'Tis past due time I retrieved my wife."


## Chapter Ten

Hilde was having a duck fit.

Three days she'd been holed up in the hull of the ship, trapped inside the tiny room, along with four other women marked as virgins.

*Crying, sniveling, whining virgins.*

And if one more of them started wailing she would surely go insane.

Pacing four steps, Hilde met the wall. She grumbled, spun on her heels and paced four steps to meet the opposite wall.

One of the women began sobbing again.

"Uch! Quit yer yawlin'!"

Hilde rolled her eyes and turned toward the group of females, taking in their ragged clothes and disheveled appearances. From the site of them, they would be better off as slaves--at least as Vikings' slaves, who were well-cared for by their masters.

Wherever these women had come from, they looked malnourished and frail. Hilde should take pity on them, but she did not. She had her own problems to consider at the moment.

For one, she'd been sold.

Koll, the slave seller informed her of this, just a short while ago.

Hilde's lips thinned as she tightly pressed them together. Inhaling through her nostrils, she sucked in the stale air, and started pacing again.

Air.

She needed fresh air. And sunshine and trees.

She needed Sigurd.

Her shoulders slumped and then she stiffened against her longing for her traitorous husband, her fury coming to a full steam.

Khuwa!

He had done nothing to save her as she was dragged to that horrid Harald Guthorm's ship, his crew ogling her as though they were starving and she were fresh kill they would roast for supper.

Uch! Who was she kidding? Hilde knew exactly why their beady, vulture eyes leered.

Lusty bastards! Every last one of them.

'Twas a good thing Harald was a greedy man, else Hilde's maidenhead would've met its defeat.

But it didn't stop their vulgar comments and their lascivious threats. She loathed their appalling behavior and vowed her revenge.

Pepperin' their breeches was too good for them. 'Twould have been the least of their troubles, she first thought, if Hilde had her way. But that misdeed turned a coat on her when Gurthorm became aware of what she'd done.

He was a bit irate.

As his men leapt overboard, one by one, attempting to save their man flesh, Harald Guthorm snatched her by the upper arm and then raised his fist to batter her. 'Twas lucky for Hilde the ship appeared on the horizon just then, setting Harald to mumblin' something about the defrayal he would receive for her.

Releasing her, he signaled the ship.

Koll was the one who traded for her, at what sum Hilde didn't know. But from the grin on Harald Guthorm's mouth, it was apparent he, at least, was satisfied with the bargain.

As she was dragged from Guthorm's ship, Hilde spit at his feet, which only served to widen the detestable Viking's smirk and earn her a smack on the bottom from Koll, who warned her to behave.

'Twas only the beginning of Hilde's degrading, for once she was on the deck of Koll's ship, his men dug through her scalp and pinched her fleshed and inspected the inside of her mouth to determine if she was fit enough to sell.

And all the while Hilde bristled like a duck having its feathers ruffled, glaring at Koll.

Koll laughed heartily at her perturbed reaction, telling Hilde her behavior amused him.

"Feisty women are good for the beddin', maybe even breedin'" he smirked. "And I am sure to find a buyer who will wholeheartedly agree."

He attempted to kiss her then, wrapping her with his arms and smashing her against his body. He crushed his mouth against hers and she bit his lip. He howled, releasing her abruptly. But instead of becoming angry, he laughed again, despite his bleeding lip, telling her if she sought to be struck he would not mar the goods.

"*Gousheng!*" Hilde called him, trying her very best to level her voice and pronounce the expression as if it were a favorable one. She had a sickening sense that the man was twisted in the brain, that he relished in games of rough play.

"And what is this word you call me, wench?" Koll had asked her, swiping his lip with the back of his hand and then drawing it into his mouth to taste his own blood.

*Dog leavings, you shits for brains,* she mocked silently.

"'Tis an ancient Far Eastern name," Hilde told him aloud, biting her lip to keep from smiling at her fabrication. "It means, powerful one."

To that, Koll lifted a brow, but said nothing more. Hilde swore his chest puffed a bit with pride.

Of course in his arrogance he believed her, and Hilde wasn't about to reveal the true interpretation of the epithet. 'Twas enough that it made her feel better just to call him dog crap, as long as she understood its meaning.

"'Tis lucky for you yer a virgin," he said. "Else I would be humping and taming you in the sack."

Hilde started pacing again as she thought about Koll's words. Humpin' her indeed. If anyone was going to bed her, it was going to be Sigurd.

On that last thought, Hilde jerked to a halt and slapped the heel of her palm to her forehead.

Khuwa!

If she ever laid eyes on Sigurd Thorgest again, she was going to chew him a new arsehole ... the arsehole.

Hilde knew Sigurd lived. She saw him jump ship along with most of the crew, and the banks were not far off. Surely he made it safely to shore. Sigurd was a good swimmer, Hilde was aware. She'd watched him many, many times whilst he swam in the fjord. He was firm and strong and able and oh, how she missed him!

A tingling sensation crept between her thighs and simmered. Her mind floated back to their last night together in the bed furs. She recalled his fingers stroking her woman's flesh and how her body responded with a rapturous fall to ecstasy.

Damn, damn, damn! Hilde stomped a foot and squeezed her eyes shut. She crammed her fingers into her hair, bunching it in the palms of her hands, as if yanking her own hair would uproot Sigurd Thorgest from her thoughts.

'Twas hopeless.

Hilde Greylock Thorgest was in love with her own husband.

The woman began sobbing louder, interrupting her musings, her body shuddering as she clung to the others. Hilde opened her mouth to chastise her again, but then noticed all of the women's gazes fell beyond her and to the door. Glancing over her shoulder, she discovered that Koll was there, his massive form nearly filling the entire frame. Spinning on her heels, Hilde flashed a disdainful facade.

She stared at the tall, dark-haired Viking, perhaps a Dane, or a mixed breed.

Aye, he was a mixed breed, a mutt--a mangy filthy mutt, Hilde thought, as she stood in her spot, seething.

"Yer new master is in wanting to claim ya now, Hilde," Koll said and then grasped her by the upper arm, leading her to the above deck.

Hilde's heart beat wildly in her chest, a mix of fear and fury at what was to come.

"Wait here," Koll instructed and left her standing near the ship's rail.

Hilde squinted, her eyelids batting convulsively as her vision strained against the bright sun. She had been kept so long in the dingy hold that now, under the rays of light, she was having trouble seeing. Finally she closed her eyes, her stomach twisting into knots.

*Nay.* A fierce determination seized Hilde suddenly. Never could she be owned as a slave! Opening her eyes and squinting, she attempted to plot her escape.

But where would she find refuge in the middle of the open sea?

Her eyes dropped over the side to the dark waters and a sullen decision befell her. Hiking her skirts to her knees, Hilde lifted first one foot and then the other until she was standing atop the planking on the wrong side of the rail.

"I come to you *Gefjon!*" Hilde started, her voice coming out in a high pitched outcry. "Receive me within your hall!"

The sound of Hilde's voice struck Sigurd, and the first thing that impressed his mind was that if she summoned the goddess of virgins it meant she remained untouched. For a split of a moment he felt relief, but it quickly dispersed as he wondered why she called out to Gefjon.

Sigurd turned about and his mouth fell open at what he saw. In four long strides he leapt across the deck, lunging toward her.

Hilde was falling away from the ship, her arms outstretched in willing surrender. Two strong arms came around her and she was hauled from the brink. Her back slammed against something solid and the air in her lungs expelled.

Whoever had Hilde, held her tightly, neither of them moving for several moments. She could feel his heartbeat pounding against her and realized it matched her own. Hilde was frightened, not only by being grabbed by a stranger, but also because she had just nearly taken her own life. Truth be told, Hilde didn't wish to die, and deep in her gut she was relieved that someone interfered.

Before she could react further however, two lips drew on her earlobe and suckled it a bit and then he moved his mouth to plant a kiss upon her cheek. His breath was hot on the side of her face and she felt his shaft shifting as it pressed into her bottom.

'Twas him, the swine who bought her. She just knew it!

Hilde resisted the urge to reach back and claw his eyes out, not yet familiar with whether or not he was a woman beater. She did however begin an effort to free herself, struggling to slip from his embrace.

"You cost me twenty four ore, woman." His deep voice vibrated in her ear. 'Twas an arousing voice--a welcoming, familiar voice.

"Sigurd?" Hilde went motionless, her eyes scanning back and forth across the water in front of her as she waited for him to speak again.

"'Tis I," returned Sigurd.

Breaking free of his embrace, Hilde spun around, hardly believing her ears, but her eyes did not betray her.

"Sigurd!" she cried and threw herself at him, hugging his neck with her arms and wrapping her legs around his waist. She didn't care that the position hiked her skirts and revealed her legs, clear up to her thighs.

Ludin, who stood nearby whistled a carefree tune as he searched the skies, trying not to stare. Ivar, who was next to him snorted and scanned the deck, the water, the activity around them, looking anywhere but at Sigurd and Hilde. Both of them were trying with all their might not to admire Hilde's lovely bared legs and the brazen position she assumed around Sigurd's body.

Sigurd grasped Hilde's waist to steady her, a bit confused by her reaction, as she planted kisses all around his face. It occurred to him rather quickly that she was probably just grateful he found her. It surely was no more than that.

"Sigurd, oh Sigurd," Hilde gleefully continued. "You have rescued me."

She kissed the tip of his nose.

"Bought you," Sigurd remarked. "And now you belong to me."

"Aye," Hilde replied as she kissed his cheek. "I belong to you, and such a ridiculously high sum you paid."

Hilde went still, the meaning behind his comment dawning. She cranked her head back with a questioning glare. "I belong to you?"

"I bought you and now I own you." Sigurd conjured the idea while bartering with Koll for her. If Hilde was his slave, well, then she couldn't leave him.

"Your slave?"

"Aye, Hilde. You are now my slave."

## Chapter Eleven

"Father!" Hilde barreled through the door of Sigurd's house like she had something to prove.

"Bram, who was sitting at the table with members of his clan and some of Sigurd's, as well, looked up from his cups. "Hilde?"

"Sigurd has made me his slave!" she shrieked.

"Hilde, you are alive!" Grima, her mother rose from her place and approached her daughter.

"Of course I'm alive." Hilde's stiffened shoulders sagged. Her mother was worried about her of course. "I am fine, mother."

She lowered her voice and accepted her mother's hug. 'Twas good to be home and with people she trusted. Hilde turned a sardonic eye toward the door, looking for Sigurd.

*Well some people at least.*

"Now what is this nonsense about being a slave?" Grima held Hilde out at an arm's length to examine her daughter. "Surely you must be...."

"My slave," Sigurd interrupted as he walked into the hall, followed by his warriors. "She stowed herself on my ship. 'Twas overrun by sea rovers. They took her. I had to buy her back."

Sigurd sat on a bench at the table and snapped his finger for Runa to serve the ale.

"At a hefty price," Ludin added, taking a seat next to Sigurd. Ivar, Ulfrik and the others joined them.

"A slave you say?" Ozur said, overhearing the conversation as he came inside the house.

"Aye," returned Ulfrik. "'Twas not an easy bargain either. The slave trader wanted to keep her."

"So you bought her back?" Bram questioned, still unsure of what transpired.

"He did," Ludin answered.

"At what sum?"

"Twenty-four ore!" Ivar exclaimed.

Ozur nearly choked on his next breath. "'Tis a fortune you paid."

"A ridiculous amount for a slave," Bram added.

"Bram!" Grima yelled turning toward her husband.

"Father!" Hilde's entire body shook with irritation.

Ignoring both his wife and daughter, he picked up his ale and took a hardy drink, draining his cup. Bram slammed the cup on the table and then turned to face his wife and daugher. "But twenty-four ore?"

Ozur angled his head looking at his son. "Why would you agree to such an outrageous sum for a mere slave?"

"I am not a slave!" Hilde threw up her hands and then stalked over to the table yanking a mug of ale from Agnar's hand. He stared at the empty space in his palm where his mug used to be and then looked up at Hilde.

In three large gulps she emptied the cup.

"If I refused to retrieve her, 'twould have likely caused another uprisin' between the clans." Sigurd glanced at Ozur. "You and our people would surely have been displeased."

Ozur harrumphed, mumbling his agreement.

"Bram! Sigurd Thorgest cannot make our daughter a slave!" Grima wailed and both she and Hilde faced Bram Greylock squarely, waiting for him to respond.

Bram's gaze darted from Grima to Hilde, and then beyond them to where Sigurd sat at the table.

"'Tis a bit irregular, Chieftain." Bram commented, his brows drawing together into a deep, worried crease. He began wrenching his hands.

Sigurd turned to Bram, regarding his concern with understanding. He winked at his father by the law, and smiled smugly. "'Tis done."

"But what of the marriage agreement?" Bram asked, raising a single brow, eyeing Sigurd speculatively. "The alliance between our clans?"

The Chieftain was wangling something, Bram could tell by the shrewd expression on Sigurd's face.

"The terms of the marriage will be honored." Sigurd slashed a nonchalant hand through the air and then winked once more at Bram.

"Is there a speck in yer eye, Sigurd?" Ivar asked and Sigurd ignored him.

Scratching the back of his neck, Bram studied Sigurd for a moment, pondering what his son by law might be about.

*Aye,* he thought, gaining understanding to the gist of Sigurd's plot. *A clever one he is.*

The warrior was mastering Hilde with her own game.

Bram's face brightened.

"Well then." He clapped his hands together. "There is aught more to say."

"Bram!" Grima started.

"Hush, woman." Bram held up a hand to silence her. "'Tis done. We will gather the clan and leave in the morn."

"Uch!" Hilde threw back her head in disgust and marched toward the stairs.

Sigurd rose from the table and approached her, grasping her by the upper arm. "Hilde." He pulled her to a more secluded part of the hall, away from the

meddlesome ears of the others. Hilde glanced at the hand that held her.

"Where might you be off to?" Sigurd asked with a calm tenor.

"I might be off to the bedchamber," Hilde snapped, annoyance evident in the tone of her voice. "My head throbs with all of this nonsense."

"Nay, Hilde." Sigurd shook his head from side to side, his mouth turning up in a slanted smirk. "A servant does not rest in the Chieftain's bedchamber, unless of course you have somethin' else in mind."

Hilde squawked offensively and jerked her arm free of Sigurd's hold.

Sigurd lowered his head. His lips wisped against her mouth.

"Show me what a biddable slave you are, woman," he said softly--seductively. His shaft stirred at his own words, the feel of her warm lips and the thought of stroking inside of her. Sigurd was immensely pleased to have Hilde back, relieved that there was no choice for her now, except to remain in his household.

Hilde glared at him struggling to ignore that her body was traitorous to her own mind. Even in her ire, heat simmered through her at the nearness of his mouth, tantalizing her seeking senses. She swallowed, going rigid, attempting to suppress the imminent quiver that threatened its way to the surface.

To no avail, Hilde shuddered.

"Come with me to the bed furs, Hilde." Sigurd taunted, keenly aware of her trembling, but unsure of it's meaning--arousal, anger or fear.

Nay. Not fear. Hilde feared nothing. Nor was it arousal. Hilde would freeze a fjord on a hot summer day with the way she was glaring at him.

'Twas anger most likely.

"Over my dead body, Khuwa," Hilde retorted, railing against the onslaught of desire, and narrowed her eyes at him.

Her response confirmed Sigurd's last thought.

Sigurd stepped back from her, disgruntled by her refusal, but expecting nothing other than exactly that from her. He drew in a healthy breath and released it slowly.

"'Tis yer choice, but understand this. I bed all of my slaves," he paused, dwelling on the fact that finding fulfillment with another female other than Hilde would be a blatant fallacy.

"Eventually," Sigurd added.

"I'm sure yer male servants are thrilled." Hilde snorted, casually turning her head aside as if she had just proclaimed a matter of fact.

Sigurd nearly chuckled at her comment--he loved Hilde's spirit and how difficult 'twas to rattle her--but he stifled it, forcing a stern appearance. Crossing one arm over the other he looked down at her with condescension, reminiscent of any slave owner's facade when dealing with a slave.

What he really wished to do was undress her slowly and run his lips along her body.

"You will find, Hilde...." Sigurd shrugged and reconsidered what he wished to say. "You should know, by what you have witnessed, that I am a reasonable master if you comply with my biddings."

"Meaning what, Sigurd?" Hilde tipped her head toward him. What, bed her?

He could have done that afore.

Force her to grovel at his feet? *Never!*

"Master." Sigurd returned.

"Say again," Hilde replied, knowing full well what he was requesting.

"You will start by calling me, master." Sigurd waited for the riled reaction that he was sure would come. Hilde was beautiful when she was angry and he looked forward to it.

*And when had he become so sappy?*

Hilde Greylock Thorgest was most certainly making him soft. 'Twas not such a bad feeling.

Hilde's mouth dropped open. "Sigurd Thorgest! If you have one bit of wit in that pea sized brain that sits like mush within that thick, daft skull of yers, you would know there is no possible day that would dawn in which I would ever call you master!"

Her yelling drew the attention of the others in the hall. Grima started to rise from her bench but she was firmly pulled back down by Bram.

"And furthermore!" Hilde continued to holler. "You can take that useless thingy of yers," she pointed at his crotch. "And stuff it where the sun does not...."

A hand came around from behind Hilde, covering her mouth and muffling her yammering.

"I will show her the servants' house, Sigurd," Runa said nervously, tugging at Hilde, attempting to remove her from the master's presence. Runa had been a slave long enough to know proper behavior in front of a master and Hilde's present manner would earn her a reprimand. Not a beating, as Sigurd Thorgest never beat his slaves, but she might find herself strapped with the most detestable of tasks like cleaning up dung piles or gutting the fish.

"Very good, Runa," Sigurd replied, watching Hilde pry Runa's hand from her mouth. "I'll expect you both in the kitchens to prepare and then serve the supper."

"Uch! And she is permitted to call you Sigurd!" Hilde gritted her teeth and balled her fists as if she were ready to strike.

"Runa behaves herself, Hilde. She is afforded certain privileges."

"Spare me the guess," Hilde answered dryly. Runa tugged on her once more. "Mistress ... er ... Hilde, please," Runa pleaded.

"Fine, Runa. I am shutting my mouth now." Hilde glared at Sigurd with eyes aflame and threatening, her head the last thing on her body to turn as she allowed Runa to lead her away. "Yer enjoying this, Khuwa,"

"Indeed," Sigurd murmured, taking in the sway of Hilde's arse as she followed Runa from the dwelling.


Chapter Twelve


"Would you like more mead, Ivar?" Hilde held the jug, bending way over until her breasts were level to Ivar's head.

Ivar turned to reply, unexpectedly burying his nose into Hilde's cleavage. Jerking his head back he stared at the bounty of bosom dangling in front him.

"Er ... Aye," was all he managed to say after clearing his throat.

The sight of it disturbed Sigurd immensely. But he shifted only slightly in his seat next to Ivar, struggling to keep the sentiment discreet.

'Twas an accident, of course.

Surely Hilde's actions were unintentional. Nevertheless, he

thwacked Ivar upside the back of his head for leering overlong.

Leif burst out laughing from where he sat across the table. Those around the table glanced Sigurd's way to see what was so humorous, but missing the exchange, they immediately returned to their own conversations.

Hilde slowly stood upright, glancing complacently at Sigurd. He appeared to be annoyed with her, but so be it. If he was intent on making her a slave, then she would act the slave--a brazen one.

Who was she to argue?

"Is something wrong, master?" Hilde batted innocent eyes at Sigurd. She wasn't a fool. Hilde knew Sigurd was playing a game--revenge for all of her years of tormenting him. She supposed it was deserved, yet it was in her nature to strike back, and that was exactly what Hilde intended to do.

Hmm, Sigurd took a sip of his drink. Her behavior was irregular, much too compliant. "Nay, Hilde, nothing is wrong."

Docile was a word that was absent from Hilde's lexis. He would keep an eye on her.

Sigurd watched her disappear into the kitchen and return a short while later, carrying a large platter filled with more food. She set it down next to Mord.

"May I serve you m'lord?" Hilde whispered sweetly, her lips a hairsbreadth from Mord's ear as she pressed the length of her body against his back. Reaching around him, she sank his eating dagger into a chunk of meat and held it to his lips.

Mord tipped his head to look at her and Hilde smiled seductively. At least she hoped it was seductively not ever having acted the shameless part prior to this.

Sigurd slammed his mug to the table, catching Mord's attention, riveting his gaze upon his warrior, his expression a murderous warning to refrain from responding to Hilde's lusty behavior. Mord shrugged, giving Sigurd an *I did not do nothin'*, look in return. He took the dagger from Hilde and slid it into his mouth, careful to refrain from looking at her.

"Come here, Hilde," Sigurd ordered.

"Aye, master." Hilde casually strolled in his direction.

"Sit," Sigurd patted his thigh.

Hilde's eyes dropped to his legs and then snapped back up to his face. "But master, I have much work to do."

Sigurd rolled his eyes. As he requested, she'd been calling him master ever since returning to the house and yet he despised the word falling from her lips. 'Twas unbefitting of her--his wife.

Aside from that the manner in which she spoke it, held a sound of contempt instead of compliancy.

"Part of yer duty is to please me," Sigurd grasped her hips and pulled her into his lap. "And it pleases me much to have you sit with me."

*It does?* Hilde thought briefly. But Nay, Khuwa's intent was to intimidate her. 'Twas not going to work.

Hilde wriggled in Sigurd's lap and then froze as the heat of his desire became evident beneath his breeches. She heard him release a low groan as he shifted his pelvis, pressing his hardness against her bottom. Her feminine flesh quivered and tightened, and Hilde felt moisture build in that sensitive area between her thighs. One of his hands slipped from her hip coming to rest on her belly, and his fingers circled gently, moving dangerously lower and lower.

*Oh Freya! Touch me!* Hilde's mind screamed, an ache to feel his finger stroking her building like a fire raging through a forest.

"Come to my bed furs," Sigurd murmured in her ear.

*Aye, aye, aye!* her libido shrieked. Hilde was lusty! She was aroused!

She was pretty damn horny.

"Nay!" Hilde shouted. Not whilst she was Sigurd's slave. Never, whilst she was his slave!

Forty and some at the table turned to stare as she jumped to her feet.

"Khuwa!" her voice came out in a hoarse cry. Her gaze swept across the room as she aimed in on a target.

Poor Ulfrik.

Poor, unsuspecting Ulfrik.

He was half in his cups when Hilde threw herself into his lap, whilst maintaining a glower on Sigurd. Ulfrik nearly toppled from his seat as he lifted his drunken head, struggling to focus on what felt like a female on his thighs.

Loki was surely laughing.

"Pretty slave," he slurred, his eyeballs crossing. Hilde's demeanor relaxed as her head turned to Ulfik, her lagging eyes the last to break from Sigurd's returned glare.

"Aye pretty slave," she responded and Ulfrik, poor drunken Ulfrik, slobbered a kiss at the corner of her mouth, and then nuzzled his lips at her neck.

Several chuckles emerged from the Vikings at the table, as all became aware of the outlandish travesty ensuing between Sigurd and Hilde. A few of the women gasped at Hilde's less than dignified deeds. Bram and Ozur both closed their eyes, shaking their heads with disbelief, while Grima dropped her head to message her temple with her fingers.

Ingun watched her son intently observing the continuous tick in his jaw, knowing he was becoming enraged. She was about to offer him soothing words when both of Sigurd's fists came crashing to the table top, causing plates to bounce and mead to spill.

The hall fell silent as Sigurd flew to his feet, toppling the bench and the three Vikings that sat upon it.

Ulfrik startled and fell backwards carrying Hilde with him and they both laughed aloud when they hit the floor.

'Twas a disgraceful scene.

Two hands lifted Hilde, setting her upon her feet. Squaring her shoulders, she spun around, stifling her amusement at seeing the outrage apparent in every line of Sigurd's face.

She stepped back apprehensively, her head dropping to brush off her skirts. Choosing to ignore him, she then held out her hand to help Ulfrik rise, but the Viking was unconscious from his indulgence and snored from where he was sprawled on the floor.

Sigurd was rattled with frustration. Never had a woman affected him as such. He wanted to squeeze his fingers 'round Hilde's neck. He wanted to seize her mouth with his own. Sigurd clenched and unclenched his fists pondering which he should do.

"Runa!" he hollered, and the slave quickly scampered to his side.

"Aye, Sigurd?"

"This eve you will share my bedchamber," he told her, his eyes never straying from his wife. "And Hilde, scrub the kitchen floor."

With that he slipped his arm around Runa's waist and guided her to the stairs.

Heat flooded Hilde's cheeks, part humiliation and part anger. She swallowed the lump in her throat. And then another sensation crept in--a heaviness in her chest like it was being crushed by stone. Hilde lifted her hand and pressed it firmly against her bosom trying to stay the pain assailing her and ease her cracking heart.

Chapter Thirteen

"Die, die, die, you bastard!" Hilde looked down at the blood on her hands as she continued her brutal attack.

She hadn't even noticed she'd rubbed her knuckles raw as she scoured the kitchen floors.

Hilde sat on her haunches, leaned back on barrel of mead and tossed her scrub rag in the bucket. Her eyes welled with moisture and she tightly squeezed her lids shut.

'Twas more than her knuckles that were stinging at the moment. Her dignity was as raw as her open wounds. Scrubbing the floorboards at least five times did little to ease her anguish, the whole time of it her mind imagining what Sigurd and Runa were doing.

*Was he kissin' her?* Hilde whimpered. *Touchin' her body?*

She shook the picture from her head, sniffling down her sob.

Grima kept her company in the kitchen for a spell, but her mother's words gave Hilde little comfort.

"'Tis the way of men," Grima told her.

"'Tis why I wished not to marry, mother," Hilde responded.

"You are woman now Hilde, and 'tis time you take yer place." Grima returned, wrapping an arm around Hilde's shoulder and kissing her brow. "And yer place is at Sigurd's side."

"You forget I am now his slave, mother."

"That my dearest daughter is a bed you made for yerself to lie in." Grima hugged Hilde tighter. "I am grateful to Sigurd for bringin' you back unharmed, Hilde. He could have left you with the traders."

Grima then admitted that it was she who suggested Sigurd as a husband for Hilde.

"You, mother?"

"Aye. 'Twas a perfect match, and Sigurd is an honorable man."

"But I detested him."

"Nay, daughter. 'Twas passion not hate I witnessed in yer eyes each time you returned from yer frolics. You loved him even then."

"You knew of my tricks?"

Grima took Hilde's hand between her own, and gave her a gentle pat. She chuckled softly. "I am wiser than you realize."

Hilde mused over her mother's words and they talked quietly for a while. Eventually, Grima dismissed herself to retire for the eve, whilst Hilde returned to attacking the floor, her aggravation and anger re-igniting.

Shifting, Hilde rose to her feet. Carrying a tallow, she went into the main hall, hoping to find someone awake to talk with and perhaps share some mead. She was exhausted, but loath to sleep next to Runa's empty pallet in the servants' house, unable to bear contemplating what was occurring in Sigurd's furs.

'Twas dark in the hall, except for a few embers still sparking in the hearth. Hilde resisted the urge to glance at the stairs leading to Sigurd's bedchamber. Instead she looked around the room.

The curtains were drawn on the bed lofts, and she could barely see the shadowy forms of those slumbering on the benches. Soft snores filled the air.

It appeared that all were asleep.

Her clan would all depart in the morn, leaving her to fend for herself and settle into her mess of a new life as a slave.

Hilde blew out a slow breath of air through gritted teeth. Her pride then reared its ugly, misled head. Through the darkness of the night her vision sought out Ulfrik, and she found he remained on the floor where he had fallen.

*I will show you Sigurd Thorgest, that I too can play yer game.*

In a huff, she spun around, snatching the covering from Vog who slept on the bench closest to the kitchen. Rolling to his other side, Vog drew up his knees and grunted at the sudden coolness brushing his body, but he didn't awaken.

Inside of the kitchen, Hilde blew out her taper and then stripped off her clothes until she was wearing nothing but ... well nothing. Wrapping the cover tightly around her and tucking in the top seam to keep it in place, she returned to the hall, and sidled up next to Ulfrik, grimacing at his wretched breath. She picked up one of his arms, slung it over her hip and then settled her head on his shoulder.

Ulfrik stirred and sat up causing Hilde's head to thump on the floor.

"Hilde?" Ulfrik rasped out, sleepily. "What ... er."

'Twas obvious by his glazed-over eyes and the way he swayed that Ulfrik was still half drunk.

"Go back to sleep," she told him, pushing hard against forehead with the heel of her hand. "You are dreaming."

"Aye," he responded weakly, slumping back to the floor and shutting his eyes. They popped open again and Ulfrik attempted to focus. "If I am dreamin' then

I am already asleep."

"Shut up, Ulfrik," Hilde whispered. "Jest close yer eyes."

Ulfrik nodded and his eyes drifted closed again. Hilde watched him for a bit, until she was sure he was back to sleep. She nuzzled up to him once more. Ulfrik didn't stir after that and Hilde was grateful, unsure of what she would do if he awoke and tried to mount her--probably resort to hitting him over his head with a mug. When he awoke in the morn with a head throb and lump, she would tell him it was the result of too much drink and falling from his seat. He would believe her. She had witnesses to verify it.

Hilde settled against Ulfrik, her lids becoming heavy. Yawning she allowed her drowsiness to take her into slumber, craving the man call Sigurd Thorgest, the man who deemed her a thorn in his side.

*We will see what you think of my sordid liason, Khuwa,* was her last thought, along with the hope that Sigurd would awaken before Ulfrik did and catch them together.

Why Hilde did this, she wasn't sure. Perchance Sigurd might not care, but she had a strong feeling that he would.

Sigurd's bed was a lonely place without Hilde in it and he held little if any interest in Runa. Once he was sure the household was asleep, he sent Runa back to the servants' dwelling without even touching her--not a single stroke of her body or a kiss. Hilde was the woman who held his heart and his head. He had no desire to bed another.

The restlessness was overwhelming so he decided to leave his chamber, to walk outside or perhaps find someone awake to converse with. He made it as far as the bedchamber door when he spied Hilde emerging from the kitchen carrying a candle. Sigurd went no further. Instead, he perched himself on the top step, unseen in the shadowy darkness of the stairwell, observing the whole of Hilde's antics.

If he was a different sort of man he would have swept her from Ulfrik's side and taken her in his bed furs. If he were a different sort of man he would have let his presence be known to her. Ah, but Sigurd was Sigurd, so he did nothing except watched her sleep until the wee hours of the morning dawned, his temper slowly boiling.

When the first signs of light trickled into the room he decided that enough time had past, and he made his move. Standing, Sigurd bound down the steps with heavy treading feet, intent on waking the household.

"What goes here!" he boomed in his fiercest, deepest voice. 'Twas loud enough to bring the roof down.

Several curtains on the bed lofts drew open, and those on the benches began to stir.

"My closet friend, my trusted warrior, with my wife!" Sigurd continued to rant as he approached Hilde and Ulfrik. Grasping the edge of the massive supper table he roared out a yell as he toppled it to its side, the tableware that remained upon it crashing to the floor. Nearly the entire household was on their feet by then.

Hilde and Ulfrik both bolted upright, Ulfrik scratching his head in confusion.

"Slave, Sigurd!" Hilde returned, coming fully alert. "Not wife."

Sigurd yanked his dagger from its sheath and Hilde's eyes went wide. She put her body in front of Ulfrik's to shield him.

"I bedded you?" Uflrik peered over her shoulder, blinking in an attempt to shake his grogginess. "Did I enjoy it?"

He then scratched his head, trying to remember what Hilde felt like.

"Oh Hilde! Did you do such a thing?" Grima yowled from behind Sigurd, an appalled expression on her face.

"Hush mother," Hilde replied.

"Move aside, Hilde!" Sigurd yelled. "I am going to slit his throat."

"For what reason, Sigurd?" Hilde stood gathering the covers and tightening them around her. She stalked toward Sigurd at a heavy pace, unconcerned with the blade he wielded. She shot him a venomous look. "I am a slave. Or did you forget? Available for any and all to take."

Hilde was delighted Sigurd showed such a reaction, but at the moment 'twas imperative she save Ulfrik's neck.

"'Tis true, Sigurd." Agnar remarked. "You have always been generous with yer females."

"She is my wife!" Sigurd argued.

He called her wife--not slave--wife. Hilde dropped her head to hide her smile, her unbound hair shielding her face.

"Nay Sigurd," Ludin argued back. "You have declared her yer slave. That makes her status different. Even Runa carries the keys to yer buildings. That in and of itself puts Runa's standing even higher than Hilde's."

Sigurd swung around to face his brother, his eyes wild with his fury. Still, he couldn't argue with that small but significant detail. He had purposely given the keys to Runa because he wanted to annoy Hilde.

His attention swung across the hall, his glare moving from one kinfolk to the next. But how dare they defend Hilde's sordid behavior. "Is the entire house of the same accord, that Hilde is a slave for the taking?"

A few tentative *ayes* fell through the mouths of his Viking warriors.

Sigurd went still. He hadn't considered the implications of making Hilde a slave. Such a grave error in judgment on his part. Never would he allow another to have her as a bed mate. 'Twas unthinkable.

Sheathing his dagger, Sigurd drew in a lengthy breath of air, filling his lungs to capacity. He held it briefly and then slowly released it, thinking on how to resolve this predicament.

"I hereby on this morn, declare that Hilde will no longer be called slave."

Hilde's head snapped up and her eyes brightened. Sigurd was freeing her.

"She will hence be known," he continued, feeling quite cunning at his impromptu resolution. "As slavewife."

"What in Frigg's name is that?" Hilde frowned.

"'Tis a new word," Sigurd turned to her, his chin lifting to an arrogant pose. "I made it up."

"Can he do that?" Ludin asked, looking around the hall.

"I think he just did." Leif replied shrugging.

"Is it lawful to create a new word?" Mord chimed in. "Send for the lawspeak."

"What does it mean?" Ivar asked.

"A slavewife," Sigurd began, raising his arm and pointing a finger into the air, as he began his recitation. "Is a slave who cannot be bedded by anyone but her slave owner. That would be me."

He tipped his head toward Hilde, his expression baring every bit of the smugness he felt.

"Uch!" Hilde threw back her head. She thought to thrown her hands up as well, but if she'd done that, her covering would've dropped, exposing her. "Yer just miffed that you might not be the first."

Hilde didn't wait for Sigurd's response to her rebuttal. She stalked across the hall and left the dwelling, absent of both her boots and her clothes, save the bawdy covering that wrapped around her body.

Sigurd caught her sly little innuendo that he might not be her first. Smirking at her cleverness, he followed her outside.

Forty and some of their kinfolk followed him outside.

Hilde stopped in the grass momentarily to swipe the mud she'd stepped in, from her feet.

Sigurd stopped just a few paces behind.

Forty and some of their clans stopped just a few paces behind him.

Hilde continued walking into the field for several more steps, and then she halted, turning around.

Sigurd began to pace.

Forty and some of their kinfolk halted their forward progress also, and began to pace with him.

Sigurd snapped his head toward the crowd and snarled, before returning his attention to Hilde.

"There are rules is my house you will follow, woman!" Sigurd pointed at her as he treaded back and forth like a restless lynx.

In like their kin followed him en bloc.

Hilde's eyes tracked Sigurd's movements as he trudge in front her.

"Pft." Hilde slashed a single hand through the air. "Rules to benefit who?"

Sigurd halted, facing her, cringing when he heard the shuffling of their kin ceasing behind him as well. He could almost feel their eyes boring into his back. "Rules to benefit me of course. I rule my household. I am the Chieftain."

He pounded of fist against his chest.

Once again, Sigurd began his crosswise course in front of Hilde, and aye, forty and some tagged along. "You will bed no other but me. Is that understood?"

Hilde ignored him, her eyes twinkled with mirth as she watched the horde pace along with Sigurd like buzzing flies drawn to a pile of excrement.

She snorted, realizing she'd just compared Sigurd to smelly gut contents.

"You find being a disloyal wife amusing, Hilde?"

"Slave." Hilde stated simply whilst she chuckled at the comical scene.

"Slave wife," Sigurd retorted. He was going to wallop each and every one of those behind him if they didn't cease tracking him. His pique was rising higher.

"Aye, Sigurd," Hilde stood with her arms akimbo and frowned at him--taunted him. "A declaration made after I lain with Ulfrik."

Silently, Hilde praised herself at the double implication. 'Twas not a deceitful statement. After all, she hadn't bedded Ulfrik, she merely lain beside him.

Sigurd drew up to Hilde, his expression ceding to what appeared to be a look of angst. Hilde's brows tightened further. She could nearly feel his pain. What was this all about?

"Why Hilde? Why would you feign taking Ulfrik as a bed mate when such an act would break my heart?" Sigurd winced at his own admission, never intending to reveal the inner sentiment, not alone the fact he was aware that Hilde's affair was fraudulent.

Hilde's brows lifted. *Break his heart ... wait, feign?*

She lifted her hand, fisting it fist tightly around the covering as though she were trying to capture her beating heart, confusion setting in. Unable to believe that Sigurd had affections for her, she concentrated on his first comment.

"What do mean by saying the word feigned?"

Finding no way around it, Sigurd confessed. "I observed you the entire eve from my bedchamber doorway, Hilde."

"All of it?"

"Aye," Sigurd crossed his arms over his chest. "From the first time you came from the kitchen fully clothed and then the next."

"Then you saw I did nothing with Ulfrik but sleep?"

Sigurd nodded.

From behind him, Ulfrik blew out an audible gust of air whilst rubbing a palm at his neck.

His throat was safe.

"What behooves me is why you sidled aside Ulfrik with nary a stitch on, putting yerself in a position of scandal."

Hilde's eyes lowered.

"Aye," she agreed, shamefully. "'Tis quite disgraceful for a wife to betray her husband."

"Then why?" Sigurd asked, his voice conveying a recognizable sadness.

Hilde's mouth twisted. Sigurd was clearly disconcerted. 'Twas not as satisfying as she thought it would be. She decided 'twas time to be truthful.

Inhaling nervously, Hilde tipped back her head, meeting Sigurd's searching eyes.

"Hel's fury can never equal a woman's scorn," Hilde attempted to keep her voice even, but it cracked despite her effort.

"Explain," Sigurd replied.

"I...." Hilde closed her eyes and winced, preparing for Sigurd's mocking that was sure to follow.

"I was resentful of Runa in yer bed furs." Hilde's swallow caught in her throat, and she kept her gaze averted, humiliation from her feelings for Sigurd preventing her from facing him.

"Resentful?" Sigurd's arms dropped to his side, his head tilting in perplexed surprise.

"Aye."

"But why?"

"I longed for it to be me." Lifting her head, Hilde forced herself to face him, so that Sigurd could see the truth in her expression. Her arms crossed snugly over her chest and she hugged herself, seeking to self-comfort. "I love you Sigurd Thorgest."

## Chapter Fourteen

Sigurd's stern expression fell. He stared at Hilde letting her words thread through his mind. Neither of them blinked, neither of them spoke through several heartbeats. Only vaguely did Sigurd hear the mutterings of their clans who stood behind him, but what he did hear from Hilde ...

Nay, he heard wrong. Or 'twas one of her tricks.

"'Tis cruel to tamper with a man's heart, Hilde," Sigurd finally said.

Could he even hope to have heard her words correctly?

Hild's bottom lip quivered. "'Tis no game, Sigurd. I speak the truth."

Turning from him, Hilde started to walk away. To where, she knew not, but her pride incited her need to hide her tears.

Suddenly, Hilde's feet left the ground and she sucked in a startled breath of air, her hands grasping at her covering to prevent it from falling open.

Sigurd's arms wrapped around her body, and he held her close to his chest. His lips came down to Hilde's, taking possession of her mouth.

Resounding cheers rose from the horde of witnessing Vikings.

Hilde closed her eyes tasting his tongue as it slid into her mouth, listening to the sound of Sigurd's soft groans as he kissed her. Her brain was muddled, a mix of emotions--pleasure, confusion and fear.

Sigurd withdrew, skimming his lips along her cheek, nuzzling at her neck, and then he buried his head in her hair, inhaling deeply, sighing at her longed-for scent and the feel of her curves molded to him. His lips returned to her mouth, his shaft perking to life with need for Hilde--his wife.

He had to have her. Now.

Carrying Hilde in his arms, he headed back toward their dwelling, reluctantly breaking the kiss. After all, he had to see where he was walking, and 'twould be Loki's greatest laugh should he fall with Hilde and they suffered cracked bones.

Aware of what Sigurd was about, Hilde pressed her palms to his chest and pushed her body away, attempting to loosen his grip on her.

"Nay, Sigurd. Not with Runa's mark so fresh upon your flesh." Surely the wits had fallen from her brain. Sigurd desired her and yet, the tear in her heart was still raw from the thought of Sigurd's intimacy with the slave.

"I did not bed Runa," he told her without faltering his pace.

"Truly?" Hilde looked at him with disbelief.

"Truly. I have bedded no female since the day we wed."

Hilde could hardly believe her ears. "Not a one?"

Nearly thirty days was a long time for a man to be without a woman, but she trusted that Sigurd wouldn't lie.

"'Twas an impossibility when my mind was tangled with aching thoughts of you every waking moment," Sigurd added.

Hilde's heart thumped an unruly beat and her mood brightened. A mischievous smile crept across her lips as she recalled their night of fondling. "And whilst you slept too."

Sigurd harrumphed. "Forgive me for that."

He wasn't really sorry. Sigurd savored the memory of her passion from that eve, though he decided it was better not to say it.

"Nay, Sigurd. 'Twas a tease," Hilde responded. "Show me more."

His clasp tightened around her, his pace increased, his arousal seizing every coherent thought except sinking into Hilde.

Hilde wrapped her arms around Sigurd's shoulders, resting her chin atop his collarbone. Her attention went to the forty and some of their clans that lagged behind them, all with nitwitted grins smeared on their faces.

Sigurd halted abruptly, as he reached the door of his house. He heard the shuffling and grunts of forty and some of their clan tumbling into each other--except for Mord, who jumped neatly out of the way.

"They follow us." Sigurd stated.

"Aye," Hilde answered.

Sigurd rolled his eyes, finally realizing why his parents insisted on keeping their own home, claiming they required privacy. He shuddered at the thought as he caught sight of Ozur and Ingun slipping away from the crowd, in the direction of their dwelling.

*For the love of Freya, they were too old. One of them would surely break something.*

His attention returned to the issue at hand--forty and some of their clans wishing to bear witness. "Ulfrik, Ludin, Ivar, stand watch at the door. No one enters. The rest of you find another place to stay."

"Might we go in now, Sigurd?" Hilde asked.

Sigurd smiled at Hilde. "Anxious, wife?"

"Er ... Aye. But mostly I am freezing my arse off."

Chuckling, Sigurd stepped through the doorway, leaving forty and some of their kin grumbling outside. He wasted no time, his urgency to feel Hilde, taste her, breathe her in, overwhelming his senses. Heading directly for the stairs, he passed the table, thinking he would enjoy taking her on the top of it, if he hadn't toppled the piece of furniture earlier.

*Another time ... many times.*

Sigurd set Hilde on her feet inside his bedchamber and then he stepped back, admiring her from head to toe.

Hilde inhaled nervously, apprehension of what was to come edging into her thoughts. Her breath quickened, and her heart beat rapidly at Sigurd's devouring gaze, but she waited for him to show her what to do next, for she was truly at a loss with the lovemaking game.

"Beautiful," Sigurd whispered removing the sheath holding his dagger at his side.

He dropped it to the floor and then reached up, tugging at Hilde's cover and allowing it to bundle at her feet. Air snagged in his lungs as his eye's roamed her naked form. He blew out the trapped air and sucked in another quick breath holding it briefing and then releasing it slowly.

"Beautiful," he whispered once more, his body jerking with his growing arousal.

Hilde blushed, but despite her shyness, his gaze heated every area of her flesh, her craving for Sigurd to touch her abounding. She watched in awe of him, of his desire for her, as he untied his breeches and they fell to the floor.

His chest was already bare from the eve before, when he sat vigilant on the stairs.

Feeling slightly abashed, but wanting to see all of her husband, Hilde let her eyes travel his body, from his strong, broad shoulders, to his well-formed chest and straight down that line of golden hair that led to ... *there.* She studied the stiffened appendage with amazement, somewhat afraid, but also with a craving that ached to be filled. Her nipples hardened and her female muscles clenched. She felt a warm, slick moisture building between her thighs.

"Magnificent," Hilde said softly, almost timidly. But Sigurd heard her and he smiled.

Lifting a hand, Sigurd gently molded his palm beneath one of Hilde's breasts, his thumb lightly skimming over her nipple. Hilde's body swayed at his tender touch and she thought she might faint from the whelm of rousing sensations surging through her

She wanted to touch him but didn't know how and she looked at Sigurd to help her.

His eyes gleamed with understanding and his smile widened, his heart leaping at her innocence. Taking her hand into his own, he guided it, wrapping her palm around his manhood, showing her how to stroke him. Hilde closed her eyes on a slow exhale, relishing in the silky heat of the flesh there, as she ran her hand along its length.

It jumped in her hand.

Startled Hilde jerked her hand back as if it might bite and Sigurd laughed, not mockingly, but with adoring amusement.

Hilde's lips turned up into a slight smile as she realized it was supposed to do that. It meant Sigurd liked what she was doing.

Sigurd's arm slipped around Hilde's waist and he pulled her to his body. His other hand skimmed the flesh of her neck and he sighed.

"From the first time I saw you in the forest so long ago, Hilde, all I wanted to do was squeeze yer little neck." Dipping his head, Sigurd skimmed his lips along her earlobe and whispered, his voice low and sensual, "But now I merely want to kiss you until you are mindless."

He pressed his mouth to her jaw line and Hilde's head tilted to one side, savoring his sensual nuzzling. "I have been a naughty girl, Sigurd."

If Sigurd wanted to kiss her mindless, he didn't have far to go.

"Mmm," he replied moving lower to suckle the flesh at her throat. "Aye."

He captured her lips whilst both of his hands moved around her to caress her bottom, his fingers dipping between her thighs from behind, tantalizing, brushing along the crease of her female flesh.

Hilde whimpered, her body begging for more, and she went limp in his arms. Sigurd gathered her in his embrace, carrying her to his furs, his head moving downward to lick her breast before molding his lips around the pale-colored peak and drawing it inside of his mouth. Slowly he lowered her to the bed without breaking contact.

He nipped at her already stilted bud. Hilde gasped, her back arching, her hands raking his wonderful hair, her mind reeling with the excitement of Sigurd Thorgest's passionate touch, heightened when he moved to her other breast offering it the same attention, whilst his hand skimmed down the side of her body seeking the utmost source of her pleasure.

His fingers delved, deftly parting her, his finger flicking and rotating on the swelling nestled there, and Sigurd groaned. She was wet and nearly ready, but there was more that Sigurd yearned to give her. He rose from her, stopping to admire her green, passion-hazed eyes as they opened to greet him. Moving to her legs, he knelt between them, drawing up her knees and then gently parting them.

And all the while Hilde watched, wondering what Sigurd was going to do. Her eyes widened when his head fell between her thighs and she felt the first touch of his mouth and tongue.

"Sigurd," she gasped breathlessly before her mind went numb, her body bending willfully to his ministrations. She moaned out, her hips shifting against him in a natural rhythm, and innate drive, her fingers desperately clenching fistfuls of his hair to anchor herself, to hold him there as the most incredible sensation surged through her loins and stretched through her body in a potent rush. "Freya! Oh."

Sigurd held his head still until she ceased her trembling, tasting her sweetness, relishing in all that was his, all that she shared with him.

'Twas an ultimate game of passion and they were both the victors.

And now he would claim his prize--*Nay*, 'twas a gift she offered--her love. And Sigurd would wrap it like the finest gem, and hold her close to his heart.

Moving over Hilde, he reclined atop of her body, careful not to crush her with his full weight, his hips moving slowly, stroking her folds with his burgeoning manhood. Worry touched him at the discomfort he would cause her, his concern battling against his arousal.

Arousal won.

Sigurd shifted restlessly. He could wait no longer. Cradling her head he looked deeply into her eyes and she stared back at him unblinking.

"I love you, Hilde," he softly said and slipped his shaft inside, groaning at her heat and the tightness of her female core. On an intake of breath, Sigurd plunged. Hilde shuddered and whimpered her pain, a single tear falling from the corner of her eye. Sigurd kissed it away and smiled down on her lovely face, stilling himself at her suddenly rigid body, but aching to push harder inside.

And then Hilde snorted.

Sigurd frowned at her ill-timed humor. "What amuses you, woman?"

"Such and odd thing to say before spearing a person ... I love you." Hilde willed her body to relax. "Perhaps if we attempted it on our enemies they would go willingly to the grave."

Sigurd smirked, withdrawing from her part way. Her sense of wit was odd at times, but he found it quite charming. His expression grew serious as his attention turned to the reason for her comment.

He'd hurt her.

"I'm sorry, Hilde."

"Nay, you are not." She cupped his cheek and lifted her head, planting a kiss on his mouth. "And neither am I."

Sigurd exhaled a growl of pleasure and plunged again, his shaft swelling, growing rigid, near to spilling inside her. All sensibility retreated from him as Hilde's arms wrapped his waist, her hands drifting to grasp his bottom, urging him on.

She pushed aside her discomfort, concentrating fully on Sigurd's body and the slide of his shaft inside of her, his slow steady rhythm in and then out, how he filled her and how wonderful it felt to be this close, this intimate with him. Her muscles clamped around him as he pressed deeper. Though she was raw within, her legs fell wider and her bud swelled once more and tingled. A mutter of approval escaped her lips and Sigurd lifted his head to look at her, catching the stirrings of renewed passion in her sparkling, green eyes.

It made him wild for her.

Sigurd stroked inside of Hilde, his heart beating faster, his breathing coming in short, hastened pants as his hips moved in accord to his escalating excitement. Bending down he kissed her hungrily, his tongue sliding between her lips, murmuring his pleasure when Hilde's tongue did the same in return.

A quake ripped through his loins, every muscle growing rigid as he hunched, squeezing shut his eyes, pressing his pelvis tightly against Hilde's mound, his eruption coming hard and strong.

He listened to the sound of Hilde's subtle crooning grow louder, felt her shuddering beneath him, and he opened his eyes, watching the peak of passion wash over her once more. Never had he witnessed a more glorious thing.

They collapsed into each others arms.

And then they slept, finally content in their satiated yearning.

## Chapter Fifteen

'Twas near the supper hour as they rested in the bed furs. Sigurd admired Hilde whilst she dozed in the crook of his arm, his expression soft and adoring as he listened and felt her peaceful breathing from where she lain by his side. His free hand played with her hair, rolling it between his fingers. The hand on the arm that cradled her body rested on her hip, occasionally moving to caress her flesh. Hilde reclined on her side, facing him, her body molded firmly against him. He could feel her naked breasts nestled on his ribs, her arm thrown over his chest, and the hair of her mound against his thigh as she casually entwined her leg around his. If she failed to wake soon he would bring her to life slowly.

The thought alone stirred his manhood.

Sometime past midday, Runa brought them a platter of food and a pitcher of mead. She dutifully left the keys to Sigurd's buildings for Hilde who accepted them with dignified regard.

As they shared the meal, Sigurd thought about the mead that he and Hilde were to share. Surely the gods would not curse them for breaking the ritual, not after suffering the calamity of events before he and Hilde finally found their peace with each other. He touched the sides of his head assuring himself there were still no horns there. He then picked up the covers and checked his groin thinking perhaps the gods issued a worse punishment.

But *nay,* Sigurd was whole, so his groin reminded him as it perked up yet again.

Hilde stirred, murmuring in a soft voice as she stretched the length of her body along his flesh. Groaning, Sigurd shifted and slipped his begging shaft inside of her. Hilde tittered at his rude prodding of her before she came fully awake. Nevertheless, she adjusted to accommodate him. Rolling to his back, Sigurd pulled Hilde atop of him, her legs astride his hips. He laced his fingers through her hair, pulling her face close to his and tenderly kissing her brow.

"I pondered much while you slept, wife."

"Aye?" Hilde cranked back her head to get an easier look at him.

"Explain to me why all of these years past you have made it your aim to torment me." Sigurd's hands leisurely skimmed along her sides until they reached her breasts. He cupped them with the palms of his hands, smiling at their fullness and rounded shape.

A devilish smile played along Hilde's lips. "'Twas my revenge for yer slaughtering of my pet rabbit."

Sigurd's brows drew together and he let his hands drop. "I killed yer pet?"

"Aye, with an arrow straight through his tiny, beating heart."

Sigurd rubbed his fingers across his brow. He'd hunted many rabbits over the course of his lifetime, mostly in his younger years, until he was prepared well enough to pursue bigger game. "I fear I do not remember, Hilde."

All of her games over a small, fury creature that was meant to be stewed?

"You were very young and I was just in my eighth year."

"Remind me never to rile you woman. You hold a grudge for quite a lengthy time."

"Nay, Sigurd. I ceased caring for that rabbit long, long ago."

Sigurd stared at her curiously. "Then why the pranks that drew me to retaliate?"

"A girlish fancy." Hilde shrugged, her expression growing sheepish. "I knew no other way to lure your attentions."

To this, Sigurd smiled. Hilde tormented him because she secretly admired him from afar. "Then why such fury on the day we married?"

"In case you failed to notice Sigurd Thorgest, I am a stubborn woman." She slapped Sigurd playfully on the shoulder when he snorted in response. "I was not willing to admit those feelings.

Perhaps I was even unaware of them. But 'twas something my mother said to me last eve, and I realized the truth."

Hilde paused, gazing down at Sigurd, her fingers played with the hair on his chest and her mouth turned up into a mischievous smile. She wriggled atop of him.

Sigurd's shaft twitched inside of her, and Hilde clenched in reaction.

Sigurd growled, eyeing her with a predator's gaze, thrusting upward, as he grasped her hips to steady her.

"This name," he rasped out, his voice laden with lust. "Khuwa ... what is its meaning?

Hilde grimaced, and she squeezed her lids shut. Sigurd stilled his rotating hips and looked at her.

One of his eyebrows rose.

"Hilde," he said sternly.

Hilde opened a single eye to briefly glance at him. She closed it again and blew out a relenting breath. Sigurd cupped the back of her head and pulled her body against his chest. He cupped her under the chin with his other hand and kissed her mouth.

"Tell me, woman," her urged sucking in her bottom lip. "Or you'll get no more of this. He flexed inside of her.

Hilde chuckled, pulling herself free from his embrace. She sat upright and bit her lip before speaking. "'Tis a Far Eastern word."

Hilde pursed her lips, eyeing Sigurd's questioning look as he patiently awaited her answer. Would he be miffed at her?

"Khuwa...." her shoulders slumped in defeat. "It means pig baby."

Sigurd expression dropped and he stared at her wide-eyed. 'Twas not what he expected a'tall.

Their eyes remained locked, Hilde waiting anxiously, assuming he would toss her to the floor.

Sigurd's nostrils flared and then, his face alit with amusement.

He roared mightily, a bellowing laugh that sent a wave of delight through Hilde's body and she smiled broadly. He rolled her beneath him, his mouth claiming hers and he kissed his wife soundly, passionately, his tongue mingling with hers, his hips beginning the mating strokes. "I may be your Khuwa wench." Sigurd nipped her chin, her earlobe and then the top of her breast, forcing a squeak to burst from Hilde's mouth.

"Ah, my beautiful wife, but 'tis you who squeals."

## The End

# PASSIONS OF THE FLAME

It's May! It's May!
The lusty month of May!
Those dreary vows that ev'ryone takes,
Ev'ryone breaks.
Ev'ryone makes divine mistakes!
The lusty month of May!

~Lerner and Lowe~

## Prologue

Enter the lands of Scottish Dalriada before the settlement of Scotland's Argyll, an ancient era of mystic beliefs. It is the season called *no time* when the shrouds between the world of the others and the human world, grows very thin.

One might spy the faerie seeking mischief or amusements.

Magic abounds!

They are upon the threshold of summer. And the fertility celebration begins. What has lain dormant beneath the Earth's frigid soils rears their precious heads. The weary are coming to life, emerging from the *dark time* season casting off the mundane which has tamped their spirits and taunted their souls. The lands will now grow vibrant and warm. Seeds will come to bloom. Hungry bellies deprived because of diminished food stores, will soon be filled.

Be merry and cheer!

'Tis the eve of Bealtuinn, a time that all souls long for, the mark of winter's lackluster end. The sacred fires will be lit. Union with the nature spirits will begin.

All will feast and dance and sing around the flames. Their voices will rise up beseeching the spirits to bring down the nourishing rains and the sunlight to spur growth. And they will cry out for blessings, for a harvest aplenty, fertility to all beasts and human creatures alike, and give hallows of good health for all.

Good fortune, good friendships, good marriages. All will be asked for.

All will honor life, as they come to celebrate!

All will be fire struck, for no being, whether he be mortal or descendent of the otherworld, is immune to enchantments brought forth by the Bealtuinn flames.

Lust seeks love, and passion burns the heart.

Garments are optional.

## Chapter One

Scottish Dalriada 495 A.D.
Pre-Christian era
The eve of Bealtuinn

It was early in the morn, and the activity in the Gaelic village was already full of merriment as the clans prepared to herald the growing season. The sacred woods were being gathered to pile the pyres high. And children weaved among the market stalls frolicking in their youthful playfulness and taking advantage of their youthful delights. Others gathered flowers with which to bedeck themselves, their families, and their hearths. The sounds of mallets performing their seasonal mendings could be heard throughout the village. The clashing of metal by men in swordplay and the clinking of sticks as many play precision games resonated through the market square. But best of all, the mouth-watering smells of simmering foods wafted through the air.

"Nevin!" Perched atop his mighty destrier, the warhorse at a lazy walk, the stranger who had just entered the village shouted to his friend.

Pausing with his wood-cutting task, Nevin Selby turned toward the caller and smiled broadly. He would recognize that strong, mighty form, that sturdy, leather chest shield he wore--scratched and battle worn--even if he were a blind man. "Why look who it be!"

Two seasons had passed since he had laid eyes on his friend. It was the warrior who saved his life during Nevin's last battle, when his leg was nearly torn off by the sword of the *painted ones*--the Picts. "Kane Siosal, I see yer sorry arse still be movin'"

Using a long stick for support, Nevin limped closer.

The warrior dismounted from his beast and straightened the *brat* he wore draped thrice around his chest. Pushing the hood of his *leine* from his head, a deep chuckle emerged from his throat, causing passing females to turn their heads to the rich sound and the handsome stranger that had just entered their village.

"Me arse is a sturdy thin', but a bit of luck helps."

Giggles emerged from three nearby women who overheard Kane and he tipped his head toward them in greeting. Again they giggled, their bodies closing, their heads tipping tightly together to whisper secrets, occasionally glancing Kane's way.

"Who might this handsome warrior be?" Another woman approached and slid into Nevin's arms, her gaze grazing along Kane's shoulders before snapping up to his face.

"'Tis Kane Siosal, wife." Nevin gave her a squeeze.

"Ah, so ye be the man who saved me husband's life." Moving toward Kane the woman grasped his shoulders to keep her balance as she rose on her tiptoes to give him a thankful kiss on each cheek. "*Cead Mile Failte*." A hundred thousand welcomes.

Kane dipped his head to accommodate her or else she would not have reached, for he stood more than a head above her tiny frame. "And this be the woman whose name Nevin called from his restless sleep ev'ry eve."

"I be Glenna Selby." She smiled broadly. "Where did ye learn such a talent, mendin' a torn leg?"

"Kane has talents aplenty, wife."

The eavesdropping ladies nearby, murmured and giggled once more.

"Hmm." Glenna scanned the village, observing the women who beamed a lustful eye at Kane Siosal. Her expression became amused. "Ye will be joinin' us for the celebrations I gather? It seems there will be females in abundance who will wish to make yer acquaintance if ye know my meanin'."

"Aye, of course he will," Nevin answered in Kane's place. He leaned in closer to Glenna. "But perhaps he will catch yer fancy this eve, woman."

Nevin grinned at his wife.

"Oh ye old fool," Glenna gave Nevin a gentle slap on his shoulder with the back of her hand. "Ye know I only have eyes fer ye, husband."

Unseen by Glenna, Nevin's gaze rolled upward, and Kane crooked a brow, understanding exactly what his friend meant. It was the eve of Bealtuinn, when the marriage vow could be ignored and a man could bed another's wench. He and Nevin had talked about this deed. Though Nevin loved his wife dearly, he lusted after a neighbor's woman, but he would only bed her if Glenna too desired to taste another's passions.

It was only proper in Nevin's mind.

Kane's sight meandered up and down Glenna's body. With skin so fair and brownish-red hair she was a pretty lass, but bedding his dear friend's woman seemed like an awkward thing.

He would find another willing woman this eve.

"Ye must stay in our dwellin', Kane Siosal," Glenna offered. "We have room aplenty."

Nodding vigorously, Nevin agreed. His eyes alighted with another kind of invitation.

"Room aplenty," he said waggling his eyebrows.

"Come, Nevin. We have preparations to make for the festivities." Glenna grabbed her husband's hand and began leading him away. "Our house is beyond the knoll, Kane Siosal. Look fer the blue shutters. And despite me husband's keenness, I will tell ye now that seekin' me body is forbidden by me."

With that, Glenna grinned as she and Nevin walked off.

"I will be snatched by a faerie!" a man yelled.

Kane turned, his lips curling into a deep smirk. Cullen Agar called his name, another acquaintance in arms. They fought side by side in many a battle and he was gladdened to see yet another of his friends had survived.

"Ah Cullen!" Kane chuckled.

The man approached and dropped the sack of oats he carried. He embraced Kane with a hearty hug.

"I see ye have come ta take us up on our proffered hospitality, Kane Siosal."

"Well, I had none the place better to go." Returning the hug, Kane slapped Cullen twice on the back before the two men released each other, laughing as they did so.

Cullen hooked an arm around Kane's shoulder and waved his hand through the air. "Alanna, ale for me friend!"

A woman, who was just across the village market, lifted her head from the water well she peered into as she pulled up her now filled bucket. Setting her pail on a nearby horse cart, she swiped the sweat from her brow with the back of her hand.

"Aye!" She waved to them, her gaze lingering overlong on the man who stood by her papa's side.

Smiling in return Kane tipped his head toward Cullen. "Yer daughter?"

"'Tis me eldest, Alanna, and still unwed." Cullen sighed. But then his expression brightened. "Perhaps ye might leap the flames with her?"

Casting a glance toward Alanna, Kane studied her briefly. She was certainly desirable enough, but he had no wish to remain for a season, or least of all be bound to the lass.

As was the rite on the eve of the fertility celebrations, couples could consummate in trial marriages lasting a year and a day. Though they were not legally binding, it allowed a man and woman time to *taste the waters*, one might say, before deciding to take a further step into a permanent situation.

"Nay, Cullen. I be a man of a warrin' nature, and a wife is no' what I seek."

After all he served under Fergus Mor mac Eirc--who most claimed would become the king--and Kane was needed on the battlefield. Though he would not mind slaking his lust on the lass, it would not be a fitting thing, for Kane would turn her aside when it was time for him to leave. He also doubted he could be faithful to her, as he was a man who enjoyed assortment in his female company.

Shaking is head in the negative, Kane looked at his friend. "She might find herself with a babe in her belly and me far off in another land."

"Ye might grow to love her, Kane, and return with haste. She be a bonnie and biddable lass. Aside from that, there are few men I would trust with me daughter save ye."

"Ye have much faith in a man who teems with lusty need at the moment." Kane gave Cullen a cordial pat on his shoulder.

To prove his point, he turned a libidinous eye on Alanna as she approached them.

Noting the expression on Kane's face, Cullen tossed his head back and laughed uproariously. "Aye, ye see. I be correct in me assumption. Ye be an honest man, Kane Siosal, to admit to yer manly need. But in that regard, I will tell ye then to keep yer hands from me daughter."

Kane responded with a snort.

Indeed.

He had much respect for the man who taught him many of the battle skills he now possessed and would not put their friendship at risk for one night of pleasure.

"A good morn to ye." Alanna dropped the reins of the horse and cart she led. She placed her hands akimbo, glancing at Kane before casting a suspicious gaze at her father. "What plot might ye be up ta papa?"

"Do no' interfere in the dealings of men, child." Cullen tipped his head in warning. "Now fetch us our drink."

To that comment, Alanna squared her shoulders. "I be hardly a child."

Her eyes flicked to Kane as if her words were meant for his ears and not her father's. She then put her back to the two men. Reaching into her cart, Alanna retrieved two mugs and a decanter, and poured the ale. With the mugs in her hands, she turned back toward the two men, offering one each to Kane and her father.

"And who might ye be, warrior?" she asked Kane.

"'Tis Kane Siosal in the flesh," Cullen answered. "Come to celebrate with us."

Taking the cup from Alanna, Kane tipped his head toward her and smiled. He drained the ale with three large swallows.

"I have heard much of yer bravery." Alanna inspected Kane's *brat*, noting it was thrice wrapped. He was man of high standing. It, in like, had a trio of colors--lavender and blue, most likely his clan colors and the third was green. He must be an honored man to have the liberty of wearing the sign of the would-be king. "Ye are famed warrior."

A smirked touched Kane's lips at her words. Famed was not a word he would use to describe himself, but if it would gain him favor with the other lasses in the village so be it.

"I give no more of me service to Mor mac Eirc than any other honorable man," Kane returned, hoping he appeared humble, though he was mighty proud of his close alignment to the respected warrior royal.

Alanna smiled brightly, and Kane noticed she had all of her teeth. It was a desirable quality in a woman. Pity she was forbidden, least of all by him.

"Well then," Alanna took Kane's empty mug and refilled it. "Ye deserve another cup of ale."

Nodding his thanks, Kane smiled. "'Tis much appreciated, lass."

His hand closed around the mug, unintentionally around her fingers and he noticed she was slow to remove them. Looking up he saw the interested sparkle in her eyes as she fixed an overlong gaze upon him. There was no mistaking the amorous intent in her expression. He would need to find a wench quickly to avoid the pretty lass this eve, lest he find himself witless with drink and between her thighs.

"Tell me, Kane Siosal." Alanna's eyes roamed downward along Kane's body. "'Tis true the Picts stain their naked flesh blue with the woad flower to make themselves look fierce in battle?"

"Enough, Alanna," Cullen interceded, watching with dismay at his daughter's wanton behavior. "There be no talk of war with ye!"

But Alanna protested. "Papa!"

"Yer mother needs ye to prepare the supper," Cullen persisted, slashing a hand through the air. "Now off with ye!"

Huffing, Alanna reached for her horse's reins, grasping them with a single hand. She glared at her father defiantly, but said nothing more as she led the horse and cart away.

"Ye see, Kane." Cullen smirked. "A biddable lass."

*Biddable, but not beddable*, Kane thought, despite the lusty look she gave him.

"Marry her off quickly, Cullen," Kane advised. "Else ye will have a daughter with a bastard by her side."

"Aye." Cullen rubbed his chin. "Would ye reconsider taking her fer yerself?"

"Nay." Kane shook his head. "Ye would be sorely disappointed in my ability to husband her properly."

Sighing, Cullen patted Kane on the back. "Come then, me friend, let us prepare for the festival and perhaps discover which female might be willing to let ye satiate yer lust on her this eve."

## Chapter Two

"I want my daughter home, Armond."

"Impossible!" The king of the fae swung about, his translucent, glimmering cloak fanning his royal essence of gold and blue through the air. "She's human."

"She is half-fae." Gwyndolen stood rigid, squarely facing King Armond, a determined look on her perfectly symmetrical, faerie face.

Armond studied her for a moment, taking in her pristine beauty, pleased she was his mate. "Is it my fault you chose to conceive a child with a mortal?"

Tipping her head into a nonchalant tilt, the queen cast her glance upward and askew, as if in pensive thought. A sensual smile creased her mouth. "The mortal caught my eye."

"And caught it well from what I've seen and heard."

"Yes," the queen moaned an amorous sound as she mused over her human lover. "He was quite … stimulating."

Armond crooked a brow. "Indeed."

Not that he was jealous.

Those of the otherworld took many lovers when it pleased them to do so. The resulting offspring was a matter of fact, and nothing more. But the child had been sired by a human and the king would not consider having a mortal living freely amongst his kind, even if she was a half-breed fae.

"Your daughter is a skilled, druid healer," Armond tried to reason with the queen. He moved closer to Gwyndolen, shrinking the gap until there was just a wisp of space between them. Taking advantage of her aroused state he smoothed his hands up the side of her ribcage and then fondled her breasts, admiring their perfect roundness and perfect weight. "The humans need her."

Gwyndolen allowed the king's hands to linger a bit, enjoying his caress, before forcing them off of her with a quick yank. "Fallon has lived in the mortal world for twenty and two years, learning their ways. It is time she is educated in her otherworld breeding. She should refine her magical flairs."

Stepping back, she crossed her arms over her chest. "Aside from that, I miss her."

Armond regarded her comment for a moment before speaking. "You are fae. Your quintessence would never ache with such tenderness."

Gwyndolen winced at the straining in her chest and the king's indifference to her feelings. "It does."

"It will pass, Gwyndolen. Such responses always do with our kind."

Armond's statement was truth, for the beings of the faerie otherworld rarely held strong sentiments overlong. Though emotions could be suddenly impressive at times, flaring with little warning, they in like, dispelled just as swiftly.

Turning her back to the king, Gwyndolen gazed at the swirling, crystalline milieu that was the atmosphere of their world--the veil to the mortal lands beyond. "Well, it hasn't. And crossing the veils twice yearly to catch a glimpse of my daughter is no longer satisfying to me. I want her home!"

She cared not that her outburst sounded more like a childish tantrum than a queen's demand.

"My queen, you must consider your thoughts with rational consultation." Armond took a step, coming to stand at Gwyndolen's side. Clasping his fingers behind his back, he too stared at the glittering mist. "Her fae essence may rejoice at being with our populace, but her human side shall weep. Without a fae lover to keep her by his side, misery would be her keeper. She would not appreciate being held captive for many here to exploit, those of our kind who lust after humans. Your thinking is illogical."

"I think like a mother."

"Mother is mortal and you are neither." Armond took no heed in his comment, aware that he was insulting his queen. But he was becoming annoyed at her improper behavior, and had no need to listen to such maudlin nonsense. He would never accept a free roaming human within their domain.

Gwyndolen's head snapped to the side and she narrowed her eyes at Armond. Her body shook with obvious irritation as she pressed her lips into an angry pucker.

"I can not inoculate what seizes control in here." The queen pounded a fist to her chest. "It is what it is."

Armond sighed. "You are aware of our bylaws, Gwyndolen. No mortal may enter our midst unless invited."

"Then I will bid her to come."

The king's lips twitched with amusement as he swiveled toward Gwyndolen. Cupping her beneath the chin, he tipped her face upward while at the same time bending his head toward her.

His tongue darted out and he ran it across her lips.

"And make her your paramour, Gwyndolen?" he murmured, a mocking edge in his voice. "A mortal is only invited to become a faerie's lover."

"Don't be ridiculous. I'm her mother!" Gwyndolen shoved Armond away, her action drawing a boisterous laugh from him.

Armond's eyes sparkled in anticipation as the queen's aura turned red. She was angry, but still aroused. Now, if only he could provoke her anger further, their love play would be delightful this eve.

Anger always incited the queen's lust and she was quite a

vigorous lover when she was in this state of mind.

"It wouldn't be unheard of amongst our kind," he said. "You might enjoy your daughter as such."

Snarling, the queen lunged toward Armond and pressed her body up against him. She dug her fingers through his silky white hair, intent on ripping it from his skull. But instead, she curled her fingers around the back of his head and drew his mouth toward her, kissing him ravenously.

And then she jerked back her head, lifting suspicious brows. "You purposely rile me for a reason, don't you, Armond?"

Her essence turned to a mix of pale yellow and gold as her emotions began to abandon her. But underlying that, a red glimmer still shone through, a mere wisp that peaked like a struggling flame, flaring and dissipating with her changing mood. "Now why might that be?"

Slipping his arms around her, Armond grasped her bottom and pressed Gwyndolen to him. Intent on fanning the flames he ground against her. He would take advantage of her amorous anger to satiate his carnal appetite.

Gwyndolen's lids drifted shut.

"My king." Throwing her head back, she arched in his arms, reveling in the hardness that was between his thighs.

Armond suckled her throat, and a subtle chiming sound emanated from Gwyndolen's body as the auras of passion radiated around her.

She moaned her delight.

When next she opened her eyes, Gwyndolen saw that they were no longer alone. Someone stood behind her, the image upside down in her line of sight because of the position of her tossed back head.

It was human flesh, she could tell, by the skin exposed through his sandaled feet. And as her gaze stretched along his bare legs she stopped to appreciate his sinewy thighs before realizing that the figure was completely nude. Regardless of this, the queen continued to peer at him, taking in the luscious shape of his lean hips and the deliciously formed masculine gem between his legs.

She knew that gem. She knew that body well.

"Aori?" It was the name given to the seventh born of an Olympian god.

Armond stilled. "He is here?"

"Completely in the flesh." The figure flashed a snide grin. "Well, almost completely."

"Moros!" the king growled as he lifted his face away from Gwyndolen.

"May I join you?" Moros leered. "Looks like you're having immense fun."

In the most lewd of manners, he grasped his shaft and jiggled it.

Armond was peeved at the intrusion coupled with his annoyance for the fae known to wreak havoc wherever he stepped. Aside from that he had no need to see the Greek wiggling his cock. "What are you doing in our midst, fae?"

Moros tipped his head askew his expression turning annoyed. "You still call me fae, Armond. I'm a god."

"In your own mind, Aori. You are no less or more than we." Armond stood upright, bringing Gwendolyn with him. Releasing her he stalked toward Moros. "On second consideration let me rephrase that. You are lower than we."

"If you say." Unbothered by the king's taunt, Moros strolled to one of the chaise sofas and reclined to his side. "Though I'll never agree."

Drawing up a knee, he draped an arm over it, his presentation showing every bit of the arrogance he possessed. "How are you this millennium, Gwyn?"

He made no attempt to further acknowledge the king.

Beaming a smile, Gwyndolen sauntered to the chaise. "What brings you to us this time, lover?"

She lowered herself to the floor in front of Moros and then let her fingers run the length of his flesh from his calf to the crease at his thigh. "So warm, so mortal."

Licking her lips, Gwyndolen turned a lustful eye on his face.

"You always did have a fetish for the human form." Moros grazed his knuckles along her glowing cheek and then frowned when a linen loin suddenly appeared from nowhere and wrapped around his hips. His gaze snapped toward the culprit, Armond of course.

"Should you not be living a mortal life somewhere and causing misery to some poor, unfortunate human soul?" Armond said, now that he had the Greek fae's attention away from Gwyndolen.

"The Olympian Origins have given me temporary reprieve from my chastisement." Moros stretched his arms and yawned before resting them behind his head. "The faerie realm is a good place for a holiday. Don't you agree?"

"No I don't agree, at least not for you." Armond rubbed his chin, wondering why the Origins would consent to such a retreat.

Moros had a penchant for continuously disrupting harmony in the universe, and the Olympian council found it necessary to hand down punishment to Moros by stripping him of his ethereal body and his magic. Though in essence he was still immortal, his life's eternity was confined to that of human flesh, sentenced to be born, live and die as a mortal creature, over and over again in various dimensions, in various times. It was an existence none of their kind wished to endure, for death was a torturous experience for a fae--or a god, so they were called in some domains.

"They took pity on you?" Gwyndolen looked at him with surprise. It was a rare occurrence by the Olympians to allow respite for one put to shame.

Sitting upright, Moros' demeanor became obviously tense. "Even the Origins cringed at my last human death endeavor."

"Tell me," Gwyndolen asked with utmost interest, ignoring Armond's grunt of disapproval behind her.

"I was drawn and quartered."

"A horrible death!" Gwyndolen pressed her finger to her chest bone.

"Likely a deserving death," Armond snorted.

Gwyndolen ignored the king. "What did you do to deserve such a thing?"

"You need to ask, Gwyndolen?" Armond returned. "Obviously it was for treason."

"Damn king. Not much of a sense of humor, that one. His daughter, however...." Pausing, Moros smirked as he scratched his temple. "Ah, never mind. Let's just say it was no great enjoyment watching my own entrails being cut from my body and burned."

"Ghastly!" Gwyndolen sucked in a breath. "Such barbaric, human behavior."

"Ah, well, I can never predict what lot in a particular mortal life will pour down upon me. I do my best."

"I would think by now you might've become wiser in the behaviors that have earned you such a fate, Moros." Armond reclined in a chaise on the opposite side of the room, his demeanor emitting a nonchalant pose. With a wave of his hand, a human appeared at his feet.

"I am who I am, Armond. How can I change that which is innate?" Moros studied the woman who sat submissively near the king. Clad in nothing but a sheer wrap, Moros took note of her lackluster eyes, her pretty face and her perky little breasts.

Humans invited across the veils eventually became mindless beings, though it appeared to be a contented state. Nevertheless, it was a detail all fae ignored when deciding whether to return the mortals home or keep them in the faerie domain.

But Moros believed it was better to live with blissful insanity in the faerie world than to be returned to earth and shunned by your kind as a mental basket case. This woman had obviously chosen to stay or wasn't offered the choice. Nevertheless, her witless destiny was permanently sealed until she would come to meet her last day.

Sometimes it was good, Moros thought, that humans failed to live overlong and that death for them was a forever thing. Thinking about his own predicament, Moros sighed at the lack of permanence with each of the deaths he'd experienced. Always he was judged by the Olympian Origins and sent to live yet another mortal life and suffer yet another mortal death.

It was rather unappealing.

Moros watched as the pretty female smiled blandly and lifted her hand obediently to give Armond a drink she'd poured from the decanter at her side.

Taking the drink from his human lover, Armond focused on the sparkling liquid in the cup before sipping it. He then set it aside, his attention returning to the Greek fae.

"Are you still here?" the king said with annoyance. Gwyndolen was caressing Moros' cheek, and seemed quite engrossed in the deed.

Armond's lip twitched slightly. Maybe he was a tad bit jealous of his queen's fancy with the creature. But it was more likely that he was irritated with Moros' mere presence, for he was sure that the Greek faerie would somehow manage to disrupt the serenity in the faerie.

The king wanted Moros gone. "Here is not the place to seek your reprieve."

With a swirling of his hands, Armond began the chant that would cast Moros away, but Gwyndolen interceded.

"Wait!" she said, standing abruptly. Stretching out her arms, she stepped in front of Moros as to shield him. "I have a thought."

Armond halted his banishing spell and winced. Gwyndolen's thoughts were typically not thoughts at all, but plots--plots that would bring him grief. "Gwyndolen, what scheme is churning in your mind now?"

Looking at Armond, Gwyndolen's lips turned up into a grin and her eyes gleamed with a satisfied sparkle.

The king waited apprehensively for her to complete her *so-called* thought, knowing without a doubt he was going to object to it.

"My daughter, Fallon, she needs to come home." Gwyndolen turned toward Moros.

Groaning, Armond shook his head. Truly, he thought the subject was closed.

"How does that involve me, my favorite queen?" Scratching the back of his neck--damn human flesh, it always seemed to itch somewhere--Moros wondered how Gwyn's idea would include him, for it was acutely apparent by the manner in which she was gazing at him that the queen intended on his participation.

"Armond has made it perfectly clear that Fallon, who is of mixed breed, must catch the eye of a fae to be brought to our realm."

Moros bolted upright. "Surely you don't mean me, fair queen?"

Whether she was half-blooded or not, he lacked the desire for a human lover. After tasting plenty of females in the many mortal lives he'd been ordered to exist in, Moros had grown quite bored with human women. He had come to the midst to enjoy the lusts of the fae.

"Do you listen with only partial hearing, Gwyndolen?" Armond asked. "As I have told you, her human half would suffer amongst our kind."

Gwyndolen smiled. And in a near float, she glided across the palace floor.

Keeping her back to both of them, she stared at the now thinning veils to the human world and said, "Not if Moros keeps her while she trains. My daughter would then be safe from becoming prey to our others. He could forbid all from touching her."

"No," Moros protested. Training a faerie properly could take centuries, if the half-breed lived that long, and he refuse to be shackled to a female for such a lengthy time. It would ruin *all* of his holidays.

A bellowing guffaw burst from Armond's mouth, knowing the Greek would never agree. At his mocking laugh, the queen spun to face him and glowered. After only a short moment, however, her expression softened and again she smiled, her gaze shifting to Moros. "You are handsome and enticing."

"Yes, I am," Moros agreed. "But the answer is still *no*."

Gwyndolen ignored him. "And though it's contrived, being part in the human flesh as you are right, Fallon would be more at ease in accepting your offering."

"No," Moros repeated once again, this time louder.

As if he had said nothing, the queen continued. "I can think of no other who would be more appropriate to bring her home to me."

Snorting, Moros reclined onto the chaise again. He decided on a different approach. "And what makes you think I would concur?"

"Immortality, my handsome, Greek fae," Gwyndolen answered. "The complete return of your ethereal body."

Armond's eyes widened. "No."

If Moros agreed, the king would be doomed to be in his presence for eternity hereafter. Trouble would abound. His life would become miserable.

With limited interest, Moros smirked. He didn't believe Gwyn was capable of superseding a spell cast by a Greek deity. In fact, he knew she wasn't. "And please tell, Gwyndolen. How would you accomplish such feat?"

"Demeter owes me a very large favor."

That caught Moros' full attention. Demeter was the Origin who convinced the Greek Olympians that the horrible spell he'd been despising for centuries was a fitting punishment for his offenses-- not that Moros thought any of his actions could be viewed as misdeeds.

What did it matter that he let loose the dark spirits in the Alderian galaxy which resulted in one of the solar system's sun imploding? The inhabitants on the nearby planet were nothing but disgusting, brainless little cretins anyway. And he was justified with his attempt to overpower an entire world, bringing down the demise of thousands of peoples. The planet belonged to him. It said so in their Book of Edicts.

"You believe that in your name, Demeter might concede?" Moros finally asked, his interest peaking.

"No," Armond answered, standing to his feet.

"I am completely certain." Gwyndolen ignored the king. *Well, she wasn't completely certain, but it was a possibility.* "Let me repeat, she owes me."

"No!" Armond started forward, but there was a pull on one of his legs that stopped him.

"I would have my ethereal body returned?" Moros questioned to verify the queen's previous offering.

"Of course."

"No!" Armond said a bit louder.

"And my magic?" Euphoria arose in Moros at the thought.

"I would plead for all of it," Gwyndolen answered. "In fact, I can grant you limited magic while you're tending to my requested task."

"Will you allow it to remain as long as I'm on reprieve?" This was getting better and better.

Gwyndolen tapped a pensive finger against her lips. "Yes."

"I'll do it!" Moros agreed.

"No, you can't!" Armond looked down at his leg. His human lover was gripping his limb. He attempted to walk forward, but she didn't let go.

Moro's snorted at the king's limping gait as he attempted to drag the clinging female along the floor. Somehow it diminished his typically formidable persona. "I can and I will."

"Off!" Armond flapped a hand at his human slave as he bellowed his command.

The woman vanished.

Beaming with faerie delight, Gwyndolen's aura sparkled around her. "Superb!"

"Gwyndolen, you must reconsider," Armond begged her.

"The deal is done!" With an upward swing of Gwyndolen's arms, Moros began to fade.

He disappeared within a cloud of glimmering dust and all Armond could do was groan with worry. This surely couldn't bring any good.

## Chapter Three

"Aimin' on catchin' a fae's eye, Kane?" Cullen snickered at his friend. He leaned back on his elbows trying to get more comfortable on the grassy hillock where they sat.

Always a man to challenge danger or fate, Kane held the whitethorn in front of him and examined his weave. "Nay."

He returned Cullen's snicker.

"Then why do ye fashion the whitethorn wreath instead of the rowan, which repels the faeries away?"

"'Tis me favorite wood," Kane stated simply. "The flowers are one of the first ta bloom during the growing season, and 'tis said the boiled leaves make a tea that brings peace to a man's soul. 'Tis also the best wood for the fire, burnin' hot and bright."

"Aye," Cullen agreed. "But also attracts the fae who seek mischief during Bealtuinn."

Kane smirked. After witnessing the horrors of battle, no simple faerie could shiver his bones. "I will save it for Samhuinn then, when the faeries are more biddable."

"But ye look through the sprig now. A dangerous thin'."

"'Tis still the light of day, Cullen. The fae will no' seek prey until the eve hours arrive when the fires have been lit."

Stretching out his arms fully, Kane continued to gaze through the wreath's opening, framing the various villagers in the market area below as they scampered about, making ready for the Bealtuinn feast. He smiled at some of the antics going on--woman and men in flirtatious teasing, children playing their pranks. There was even a rhymester reciting his doggerel, entertaining the crowd that gathered round.

Moving the ring to the edge of the village, Kane caught sight of the two pyres being prepared for the season's sacred rituals.

Suddenly his view was obscured.

Kane's lips parted, his heart thumped as he blew out a slow breath. He was unprepared for the vision that stepped into his sight.

A woman, so stunningly beautiful he was nearly blindsided. Her hair was black as midnight, yet glimmered like the dawning sun on serene waters, highlights of lavender strumming through it. Her face looked so smooth and silky that he longed to run his fingertips along it. Her skin was dark, and her body--it was perfection personified. Kane was whelmed by a sudden ache to wrap himself around her, to mold her to him, to feel her essence threading through his soul.

"What do ye see through there?" Cullen asked.

But when Kane said nothing, Cullen studied him for a moment and then noted the mesmerized expression on his friend's face. Following the line of the warrior's gaze, Cullen frowned disapprovingly when he saw who had captured Kane's attention.

"Nay, nay! Ye do no' want that one."

"So lovely. Who might the lass be?" Despite Cullen's protest, Kane could not tear his eyes from the woman.

"'Tis the druid healer, Fallon Moireach, who should catch no man's eyes."

"And why do ye say such a thing?" Kane asked, watching as the lass set down her collected bundle of apple wood branches. She arched her back to stretch, her pleasingly round breasts jutting upward as she turned her face to the sun. Her movement was so simple, yet so enticingly sensual, it had Kane swallowing away the lump in his throat and focusing on the growing lump between his thighs.

"She be the issue of Marlow Moireach and the queen of the fae."

Without taking his eyes from Fallon, Kane crooked a curious brow. "This man, Marlow caught the eye of the royal faerie?"

"Aye, 'twas nearly twenty and three years ago this verra day." Cullen shuttered as he spoke. "Saw it with me own eyes."

Kane's mouth turned up into a half smile. He had heard that the faerie queen was an extraordinary beauty. It would explain the astonishing loveliness of the druid woman who was engaging his full attention right now.

"She came upon the Bealtuinn fires whilst Marlow, who was the druid leader at the time, led the rites." Cullen continued. "And afore we could discern what was happenin', she snatched his sight and took him away."

"And that be the last of him?" Kane asked.

"Ach! Nay," Cullen returned. "Marlow Moreach was returned on Samhuinn, barmy as a the cold is long. And Fallon, she was left at Marlow's hearth the followin' Bealtuinn."

Standing, Kane continued to eye the woman. Despite Cullen's tale, he was reluctant to believe that the druid posed any harm to him. It was then that she briefly glanced his way, and Kane sucked in a breath, causing him to reconsider that thought, for he would swear on the future king's life that she had lavender eyes. But she turned from too quickly for Kane to be sure.

"She *is* quite lovely, is she not?"

A stranger was speaking.

Still looking through the whitethorn wreath, Kane turned to see who it was.

A man sat upon Cullen's thighs.

"Cease to view me through that ring Gael, for I do no' fancy that way."

"Well then, if ye do no' fancy that way, stranger, kindly remove yerself from me lap," Cullen said with utmost irritation in his voice.

The stranger slashed his hand through the air, and in an instant, he was standing.

Kane lowered the sprig slowly. He blinked, for he failed to see the man move.

"Who might ye be?" Kane furled his brows, watching Cullen's eyes widen and his complexion pale to nearly white as he scampered away on his bottom.

"I be The Bryan," the man answered.

Lifting a brow, Kane stared at him. "*The* Bryan?"

What half-wit used the word *the* as a title?

An arrogant one he supposed.

There was something odd about the man, something that Kane could not quite discern. "Whence did ye come, stranger?"

The Bryan lifted a hand upward. "From beyond the veils."

Kane snorted. "Are ye claimin' to be a fae, man?"

The stranger had human flesh, though there was a wraithlike mien about him. But a fae?

"A fae-man," The Bryan laughed, repeating Kane's words. "Aye, 'tis exactly what I be."

"'Tis truth he speaks," Cullen choked out as he jumped to his feet. He continued backing away, putting more distance between himself and The Bryan. "There was nothin' and then he was there in me lap. Came out of thin air I tell ye, and then vanished from me lap to be standin'!"

"And what brings ye to our midst?" Wariness began surfacing and Kane's body stiffened as he kept a watchful eye on the fae. Slipping his arm across his body he curled his fingers around the grip of his *durk*. Kane had a deep, visceral sense that this man or faerie or whatever he was, could not be trusted.

"I be here because 'tis Bealtuinn, friend," The Bryan explained, a condescending tone threading his voice. "I have crossed the veils for a spell."

"'Tis the *eve* of Bealtuinn, friend," Kane returned, his dislike for the man-fae rising. He also did not like the fae-man's use of the word *spell*, pondering that there was twofold meaning in his comment.

"Aye, well, no matter. I be here nonetheless."

Looking beyond The Bryan, Kane watched as Cullen vigorously shook his head from side to side. It was a warning, and Kane knew that he should take heed when engaging a faerie. They were quick to anger and quick to react when irritated by a human being. Kane might find himself missing part of his brain or another part of himself he was rather fond of.

Tightening his fingers around his dagger's grip, Kane pondered what the faerie's intent might be.

From what he understood, the immortals always had a purpose

for descending on man. Whether it be for arduous pleasures, simple mischief or evil intent, there was good reason to be mindful.

"For what reason have ye come?" Kane asked him again and waited for The Bryan to answer him.

With his lip curling up to one side, the fae shifted his gaze to where Kane held the blade, and then his eyes snapped up to lock onto Kane's eyes. The Bryan's pupils dilated.

Kane wavered. The hand holding the *durk* loosened, and his arm dropped to his side. Gritting his teeth, a wave of dizziness came over Kane, and his body suddenly felt as though it were being pricked by an abundance of tiny metal shards.

It was painful.

"Do ye think to pierce me with yer weapon, Gael?" The Bryan laughed mockingly. "With just a pierce of me eyes I have you under me power."

Wariness turned to irritation when Kane realized that the fae was responsible for his present, discomfiting condition. Jerking his head to one side, Kane shook off The Bryan's hex, his rising ire overshadowing any fear he would be wise to have of the fae. He most assuredly disliked the creature and the expression that stretched across Kane's face clearly exposed his feelings.

Immediately it was noticed by Cullen who spoke loudly in warning. "Beware ta anger a faerie, Kane Siosal! 'Twill bring doom upon yer head."

He turned to run.

The Bryan snickered at the comment. Doom and gloom were what he was known for best. Without looking behind him, he lifted his arm and snapped a finger causing Cullen to halt. In mid-step he became statuesque, his body frozen within the space around him.

Stiffening, Kane approached the faerie, grabbing him by the shoulders. "Release him."

And The Bryan laughed. "Such bravery for a mere mortal."

"Release him now or I shall...."

"Ye will what, Gael?" The Bryan voice lowered to a formidable level. "Kill me?"

Pushing roughly at The Bryan's shoulders, Kane grunted and stalked a few paces away. Of course the notion was absurd. A fae could not be killed. Yet Kane, unlike his friend, was not afraid of the being.

"Ye still have not explained yer presence, faerie." Kane spun to face The Bryan, fearlessly looking him directly in the eye.

The Bryan was amused. The one behind him was a coward, but this mortal was a human that could be reckoned with. He would enjoy watching him struggle not to fall.

As before, The Bryan snapped his finger and Cullen, released from the spell, crumpled to the ground.

"I have come for the wench," the faerie said pointing in the direction where the druid woman stood. "Fallon Moireach shall be mine."

Kane looked toward the area The Bryan indicated, and saw that Fallon Moireach was gone, leaving her pile of apple wood behind. Had the fae-man already taken her? Anger ran rampant through Kane's blood. How dare the faerie stake such a claim. It was beside the point that Kane had desire for the lass. He heard legends of what the stealing away of a human by a fae meant. It resulted in the ruining of the mortal spirit and emptying of the mortal mind. For this, most humans feared and despised the fae, and Kane could not stomach such a fate for any human, save the pretty druid, half-fae or not. It was a matter of valiancy and honor that drove a rising need in him to protect her.

"Over me lifeless body ye shall have her, The Bryan," Kane sneered.

"That might be arranged," The Bryan returned. "Do ye challenge me, Kane Siosal?"

There was nothing in the mortal world, or any world, that The Bryan enjoyed more than a challenge.

Stiffening in his stance, Kane glared at the fae. "'Tis a challenge I would easily win!"

"Nay! Kane, ye fool. Do no' provoke him," Cullen warned, a crease of angst forming on his brow. "If he desires the druid, she shall be his."

Both Kane and The Bryan ignored Cullen as they glared at each other with confrontational rapport.

The Bryan nodded, his eyes alit eagerly. "A wager, then?"

"Expain yer meaning," Kane asked.

Holding out the palm of his hand, The Bryan revealed a small sack, tied closed with a thin twine. He tossed it toward Kane and it landed at Kane's feet. Squatting down, Kane picked up the sack and shook it. There was a clanking sound inside.

He looked up questioningly at the fae. "Coinage?"

"Thirty silver pieces ta the victor!" The Bryan smirked.

"What victory dost ye speak of, fae?"

"The one to bed the druid first."

Kane's mouth twisted with disgust. To him it was seamy wager in which he would not engage.

"Ye are able ta match it I am ta assume, Gael?" The Bryan asked before Kane was able to respond further.

Cocking back his shoulders, Kane's irritation pushed further to the surface. "Aye, of course, I be able ta match it."

"Agreed then!" The Bryan interrupted. "The spoils be set."

And with a wave of his arms the faerie vanished.

"Ach, Kane!" With a heavy stride Cullen moved closer to his friend. "Have ye gone mad?"

"I do no' like him," Kane returned sharply.

"'Twas quite apparent that." Cullen rubbed a palm across his chin. "But ta take a wager with a fae, you can no' win."

"I have no intention of protectin' a woman or beddin' her for the prospect of compensation, especially from the likes of a scalawag fae." Kane tossed the sack of silver toward Cullen, who snatched it out of the air. "If ye see The Bryan, return that ta him."

"Oh nay! May he have left without returnin', for all our sakes!"

"Friend, I believe 'tis unlikely." Kane gave Cullen a doubting look as he walked toward him. He patted Cullen on the shoulder. "Now then, show me where I might find the druid, Fallon. I wish ta meet her."

## Chapter Four

"Why did I look upon him?" Fallon Moireach paced across the dirt floor of her home. "Why did he look upon me? And through the whitethorn sprig, no less!"

With an irritated shake of her shoulders Fallon stalked to the fire and picked up the poker, stabbing it several times into the flames. "I can no' believe I was carryin' the apple wood at the time."

One of the nine sacred woods burned in the Bealtuinn fires, apple was the sacred harbinger of love.

"Well, he will no' have any brain left after a tumble with me!" She dropped the poker and it hit the hearth stone with a clank. "Ach! I can no' believe I jest said such a thing."

Fallon Moireach had not a single intention of *tumbling* with any man.

"Oh horrid curse!" Fallon balled her hands into a fist, squeezing tightly.

Never had she looked upon a man, for Fallon had been told by many, the elder women, the Chieftain, Alanna, her friend, that because of her half-fae blood, to do so would set a man's mind upon her. His pursuit would be relentless.

And should he succeed in taking her to his bed, madness would become his only companion until his dying day.

It was the truth they all spoke. Fallon sincerely believed this, attested by her papa's manner after he tangled with an immortal. Marlow Moireach was snatched away after catching the eye of the queen faerie one Bealtuinn eve, many seasons past. Once a respected druid sage amongst the clans, he was returned some thirty and one days later, dullard in mind. The following season, Fallon, nearly a newborn babe, was set on his doorstep. It was said the queen was forbidden by the faerie king to keep her and thus gave her to Marlow to care for.

In all of Fallon's years, she never had a normal conversation with her papa. His only utterances for as long as she could remember were restricted to the recitation of the druid orations.

It was how she learned her trade. That and an innate wisdom that allowed her to comprehend the prayers and chants he had spoken throughout the years.

Fallon spun around to study her father. He stared at her blankly from where he sat on a bench near the hearth. Well, she had no intention of being blamed for a man becoming witless, and because of that she remained aloof from all human males.

And catching the eye of a faerie? That was no option either, for the mortal half of her mind would be consumed.

Aside from that, men, may they be of the human world or the next, were not to be trusted. Many a season she comforted a wailing woman tossed aside by her bored, male lover after the handfasting of a year and a day had passed. It was a ritual that Fallon despised, believing it benefited the men more than it did the women.

*Nay!* Fallon Moireach was destined to always walk alone.

She had no need for a man, fae or mortal, to fill her days, especially with one the likes of … of….

*I wonder what his name be?*

A small smile creased Fallon's lips.

*He was quite pleasing to the eye,* she thought.

"Ach! I do no' care!"

Flattening a palm against her breastbone, she denied the odd leaping in her chest.

*Nay, nay!* said her human heart, but her fae blood was singing.

"Curses!"

Frowning, Fallon strolled over to her father and re-arranged the fur about his shoulders. "Are ye warm enough, Papa?"

He did not answer.

"Will ye ever talk to me, Papa, in the common sense?" Fallon dropped to her knees in front of Marlow Moireach and set her cheek on his knees. His hand came up and he stroked her hair, but he uttered not a single word.

"Give me wisdom, Papa."

A lengthy silence followed while Falion sat at her father's feet. She closed her eyes enjoying his fatherly affection and listening to the soothing sound of the wood sizzling and crackling in the hearth.

"Inta a closed fist nothin' enters." Marlow finally spoke.

"Aye," Fallon said in return. "I be strong of will, Papa, and none shall enter me heart."

There was a knock at the door and Fallon rose to answer it. "Alanna be early."

Fallon's friend was to come by to help her ready for the Bealtuinn blessings.

"The heart is as eternal as the soul," Marlow added.

"Aye, Papa." Fallon yanked the wooden door open and stiffened as her eyes met the stranger's gaze.

"And so be loneliness with nothin' ta fill the heart," Marlow mumbled.

"Curses!" Quickly Fallon snapped her gaze away. How could she have been so careless as to look into his eyes, twofold no less! "What do ye here, stranger?"

Her stomach fluttered as she swallowed a gasp. It was him, the man who held the whitethorn sprig.

"Control yer emotions or they will control ye."

"Hush, Papa!" Closing the door behind her, Fallon stepped outside.

*Aye,* Kane thought. Her eyes were a lovely lavender color, just as he suspected. Bending to get a closer look, Kane attempted to once again meet her gaze.

But she turned her head away, avoiding the visual contact. The action brought a smirk to Kane's face for he knew it was not an act of shyness. She failed to drop her eyes to the ground submissively. It was more a reaction of obduracy, it seemed, as her eyes diverted to the side.

It amused him.

"Ye have failed ta answer me question, stranger."

Kane side-stepped to the direction the druid gazed in. Crouching at the knees he again attempted to get her to look at him. Once more she turned away.

Kane chuckled as he introduced himself. "I be Kane Siosal,"

"Ah, I see." Fallon smiled--a respectable name. "And now that I know yer identity, man, tell me what brings ye ta me threshold?"

Inhaling deeply, Fallon pushed aside the incredible yearning to look at his face. Instead she shifted her attention to his muscular thighs.

It was less than a help.

On an intake of air her eyes wandered upward to his hips--lean and sensual. Her thoughts turned to passion and a physical ache so overwhelming, she had to turn her back to him in an attempt to dissuade her mind, but the feeling stubbornly remained.

Curse her faerie lust!

"I have come ta give ye warnin', lass." Kane moved around to the front of Fallon, intent on looking into her face, but with solid resolution to avoid his gaze, she snapped her head away, closing her eyes this time.

"Warnin' about what, Kane Siosal?" Turning to him, Fallon opened her eyes, purposely keeping them level. She found herself staring at his massive chest.

`Twas a wonderful chest, so masculine and broad.

Her mind wandered to thoughts of how glorious it would appear absent of the garment that draped it. Without so much as a warning, Fallon's nipples peaked and the urge to rub them against his bare skin assailed her. Her cheeks immediately flushed--heated desire, fused with irritation at her lack of command, along with a bit of chagrin over her ruttish thoughts.

"Why will ye no look at me, lass?" Kane leveled his head with hers. *Was she blushin'?*

At the same instant Fallon covered her face with her hands to hide both her eyes and her mazed expression. "'Twould be dangerous ta yer wits."

"How so?" Kane grinned as he straightened his knees. He was finding her ever so delightful a woman.

"I am half-fae, Kane Siosal," Fallon mumbled through her palms. "Ta catch me eye would bring upon ye a mental demise."

"I will take me chances, lass."

Fallon dropped her arms and stared beyond him, deciding it was safer to study the trees in the forests around her than to dare chance a glance at the handsome warrior in front of her. "Ye are a big fool then, Kane Siosal."

Ignoring her comment, Kane bent askew and attempted to meet her face yet again, determination to see her gaze driving him. But as before, she avoided the visual connection by snapping her lids shut.

Kane chuckled at her reaction. She was truly skilled at this avoiding task, and she was truly amusing him, as well. Still, however, he wanted very much to see the color of her eyes. Having stolen a glimpse of them already, he knew it would be entirely enchanting to gaze upon them for longer than a split of a moment. Reaching forward, Kane placed the thumb of one hand just below Fallon's right brow, his other thumb at her lower lashes and attempted to pry her lid open.

"Ach!" Fallon squeezed her eyelids tightly and jerked her head askew. "Ye lookin' ta poke me eye out, warrior?"

"Nay, but 'tis a thought," Kane teased. "If ye be blind I could gaze upon yer beautiful eyes for an eternity."

"Cease, Kane Siosal!" Fallon slapped at his hands. And then she burst out laughing. It was such an absurd thing he was doing! "Have ye no care fer yer well-bein'?"

Relenting, Kane dropped his arms and strolled over to a nearby well wall. He leaned against it, crossing one booted foot over the other. "Have no' a concern, Fallon. I have already caught a fae's eye this day, a true blooded one at that, and me mind has no' been taken."

"Ye have no'!" Fallon denied he did such a risky thing.

"Aye, I have. His name be The Bryan."

A male? Fallon's eyes burst open and she gasped, finding herself staring directly into....

She blew out a relieved breath. It was his horse's eyes. Thank the gods Kane Siosal was off to her right side.

But then Fallon's chest tightened though she denied it was a reaction to what he had just said. She pondered why he would seek the sight of a male fae. Such a pity if Kane Siosal preferred his own gender. A pity for the other women....

Not her....

...of course.

"Well then, perhaps ye should be seekin' yer faerie lover instead of botherin' me," she said to Kane.

*His faerie lover?*

"Ha!" Kane slapped his thigh and stalked toward Fallon stopping a hand's length away. "I assure ye, lass, a male is far from what I desire in me bed. Aside from that 'tis no' me he seeks, but still he will come ta where I rest me feet."

"And why that be?" Folding her arms, Fallon spoke to the empty air in front of her, ignoring how close Kane was to her side and how tantalizing his hot breath felt against her temple when he spoke.

He smelled good, as well--like fresh earth on a dewy spring morn.

Like nature in its breeding hour.

*Ach!*

She was apparently in her breeding hour.

"The Bryan will come ta where I be because I will be nearby ye, and 'tis ye he seeks."

"Me?" Fallon nearly turned to look at Kane, but halted and instead dropped her head downward.

"I heard the words from his verra mouth."

*What*, Fallon wondered, *dost a fae want with me?* "I see. So ye plannin' on bein' me protector, Kane?"

"Aye, that I be committed ta doin'."

Fallon liked the idea of Kane Siosal following her about, but she refused to acknowledge that outwardly ... or inwardly for that matter--denial being a more favorable companion than admitting her attraction to the man. She tried not to think on the fact he had now captured her gaze twice over.

"For what reason would ye partake of such a task? Ye do no' know me, man."

"'Tis true, but I do no' like the man-fae and I do no' like his comin' here ta stake a claim on one of our own."

*On ye, Fallon Moireach*, Kane thought silently.

He desired the pretty druid and bidding himself to be her protector, Kane had to admit, was a reasonable excuse to be near her. Though he would protect her anyway.

"Ah, so 'tis yer honor that persuades ye?" Fallon snorted, for she knew a mortal had nary a chance of defeating a faerie. "And how do ye think ta safeguard me from an immortal?"

That comment was thought provoking to Kane. How *would* he, a mere mortal, defeat a creature possessing mystical powers?

"I do no' know," Kane answered with a barefaced shrug. "'Tis a bridge I will cross when I come ta it."

Fallon laughed loudly. "A man with a solid plan. Ye are interestin' indeed, Kane Siosal."

She had to confess she was amused by him. But it was nothing more than that….

Amusement….

…of course.

Scratching his head, Kane smirked in return. He was not appearing as much of a guardian at the moment.

"Dost ye no' think I may put him off on me own, Kane?" Fallon paced forward, her stride taking her closer to Kane's mighty horse. She admired the beast--a beautiful destrier--clucking her tongue at him and petting his snout. "After all, I also be half-faerie and no' so easily persuaded."

Tipping his head at an angle, Kane smiled. His horse was a mean-tempered beast to most others aside him, nipping and snorting and scraping its hoof when others moved a bit too close. Yet, with Fallon, it bowed its head almost reverently as she administered her affections on him.

Interesting thing that.

"May I ride the beast?" Fallon asked without turning around.

Kane lifted an incredulous brow. "The druid is a brave lass, albeit no' a wise one."

"He senses me oneness with nature and shall no' harm me."

"He shall throw ye, Fallon."

"Nay, he shall no'." With that, Fallon mounted the horse, straddling it, her action causing Kane's heart to drop to his stomach. He darted forward, visions of his horse bucking and tossing and stomping Fallon, playing in his head.

But the horse remained still with Fallon perched upon it. The beast's only movement was the bobbing of his head as she gently stroked his mane.

Kane halted and watched the interplay with amazement. He rubbed his brow with the palm of his hand and released a relieved breath. "It appears I be underestimated yer abilities, lass."

Fallon slashed a hand through the air, and then, lifting her chin, she tilted her head into a smug pose. "Nary a worry, Kane Siosal. 'Tis a common error with mere mortal men."

Kane laughed, knowing she teased him, for he noticed how she pressed her lips tightly together to stifle a smirk. Still, he was not about to chance her becoming hurt by his horse so he climbed into the saddle behind her.

Without warning he was overcome by the press of her body against him, heat spreading through him, his shaft twitching.

Closing his eyes, Kane savored her warmth and the sweet smell of her hair, unable to resist touching her. His hands slipped around her hips, coming to rest on her bare thighs exposed by the hiking of her skirts as she straddled his horse.

Kane bit his tingling lips to tamp the craving to kiss her, for to do so would surely earn him a slap. But he could do nothing about the tightening in his gut or the thumping in his heart that he swore was audible through the awkward silence that now passed between them. His mind held visions of her thighs straddling him instead of the beast.

Fallon's grip tightened on the horse's mane as Kane pressed against her. She shuddered at his nearness, and the obvious male reaction probing at her bottom.

Drawing in a breath, she held it, a sudden urge pushed at her to sink into him, to have him hold her closer--to look at him. Fallon attempted to stifle the demanding sensations, ignore how tantalizing his warm hands felt against her flesh, how his muscular legs wrapped around her like a comfortable bed fur....

*Ach!* Fallon winced. *I can no' believe I just likened him ta a thing I would enjoy in me bed!*

Perhaps looking twofold into his eyes was causing her to lose wit.

She released the air in her lungs and the pace of her breathing quickened. Unable to endure it any longer, Fallon did the only thing she could think of. She swung a leg over the horse's head and leapt from its back, dashing immediately into the house.

The door slammed behind her and Kane stared at it for a lengthy time, feeling a bit astounded. He expected to be awed by the female druid, perhaps even a bit intimidated by the spirit powers she possessed.

But where other men revered the druid, shunned the immortal, mostly out of fear, what Kane found in her was a charming, desirable woman.

To him, Fallon Moireach was more human than fae. And he wanted her in earnest.

Chapter Five

"Dost he continue ta follow behind us?"

Fallon and Alanna ambled along the forest path collecting the remainder of the nine woods Fallon needed to offer up at the celebration.

"Why do ye no' look fer yerself?" Alanna smirked.

Flashing her friend a sidelong glance, Fallon blew out an annoyed breath in response. "Ye know I can no' do that. The druid virtue of honor requires me to always do the right thing. Even if it means self-denial."

"Do ye wish ta be alone all of yer days, Fallon?"

"'Tis me fate."

"A fate ye have chosen yerself."

"And what if I do catch his eye?" Fallon questioned her friend as she walked over to examine the tiny, fragile flowers sprouting from a whitethorn tree. "He'll no' be much of a companion after he is vacant of mind."

"'Tis worth the chance. Do ye no' think?" Alanna fanned her face with her hand and exhaled long and slow through puckered lips, as if to cool herself down. "Kane Siosal is verra pleasin' ta the eye."

"Aye, that he be," Fallon agreed as she fingered the various twigs on the tree. And then she frowned. "Well, as much as I have seen of him is quite fetchin'."

Gently caressing the gnarly branch, Fallon gave homage to the whitethorn murmuring humbly, "I thank ye fer yer gift."

With great care, she broke a few of the older stems away from its branches. Placing them in the basket she carried, Fallon returned to the path where Alanna waited for her.

"I be bettin' that what lies beneath his leine is impressive as well." Alanna bumped Fallon's shoulder with her own. "Do ye think he has a large man part?"

"Oh, Alanna!" Fallon's eyes widened with astonishment at her friend's comment. "Yer mind wanders on a single path."

Heat flooded her cheeks and Fallon's face reddened, for she was thinking the very same thing.

She had *felt* the very same thing.

And it was quite impressive.

"Aye!" Alanna laughed. "But I see by yer face that ye are also considerin' the pleasures that the warrior might give ta yer body."

"Shush, Alanna! He will hear ye."

"Then let him hear. Me thinks he fancies ye anaway, Fallon."

"Nay, he dost no'."

"So ye think. And he trails us, for what reason?"

"I have told ye. He quarrels with a fae who seeks me."

"Ach! I was listenin', Fallon. Kane Siosal made no pretense about wantin' ta protect ye, and ye bein' a total stranger and ev'rythin'. Well surely 'tis because he favors ye."

"Hmph." Fallon disregarded her words. "No man with stable musings would find interest in a woman he knew would drive him mad. Unless he be already mad."

"Well if he be already mad, then ye have no worries."

With a huff, Fallon abandoned Alanna, saying nothing more about it. She continued walking down the path, still a bit annoyed with her friend for hiding behind a bush near her house when Kane Siosal came calling. Alanna had been eavesdropping on the whole of the conversation exchanged between Fallon and the warrior, only to reveal her presence once Kane departed.

"Ye can run, but ye can no' hide from yer feelin's!" Alanna yelled and then quickened her pace. Catching up with Fallon, she snatched her friend by the upper arm and gently yanked.

Annoyed, Fallon stopped in her tracks and turned to Alanna. "What do ye want now?"

"Offer yerself ta him."

"Nay," Fallon returned with a snort. "'Tis better unmarried than ill-married."

Lifting her brows, Alanna placed her hands askew. "Now who be talkin' about marriage?"

"Then what mean ye, Alanna?" Fallon regarded the question, feigning ignorance, though she could tell by the sparkle in Alanna's eyes exactly her word's intent.

A wily smile crested Alanna's lips. "Take Kane Siosal ta the forests this eve, after the offerin's and allow him ta have ye."

"A single night of pleasure?" Fallon wrinkled her brows. "What would be the purpose in a thin' such as that?"

*Aside from the obvious.*

Shrugging, Alanna turned, shifting her gaze down the path from whence they had come, her sight settled on the man who followed them. He too had halted, perched upon his horse--far enough away not to hear--near enough to keep watch.

"What better way ta give guidance ta a bedded woman who seeks yer advice, if you have the experience yerself."

Fallon blinked at Alanna.

*'Twas no' arguin' with that perspective*, she reasoned.

Fallon would fare much better in her counsel to the women if she had an understanding of the lovemaking act. She thought about it momentarily as she studied Alanna's expression, and then snickered when she realized Alanna's purpose. "Ach! Ye care no' about my counselin' duties, Alanna. Yer jest goadin' me inta seekin' me lusts."

"Aye," Alanna agreed with a sly grin and a nod. "And why should I no' encourage ye, Fallon? Ye deserve it, lass."

Leaning her head closer to Fallon's ear she whispered, "Kane Siosal is the kind of man that would have a woman shriekin' with delight."

An intriguing thought that nearly had Fallon turning her head to cast a glance toward where Kane Siosal sat on the path. Stiffening at the last moment, Fallon faced Alanna. "Nay, I do no' want him."

Alanna opened her mouth to respond, but a voice interrupted her.

"If ye do no' want *him*, then perhaps ye will give yer attentions ta me."

Fallon turned to the male voice that seemed to appear from nowhere. "And who might ye be?" Fallon asked.

Accustomed to looking beyond the faces of those who spoke to her, she focused on an area just past his shoulder, but the aura she sensed around the man told her he was not of this world.

To her side, Alanna gasped, so overcome at the sight of the faerie, she fainted dead away, dropping to the ground with a thud.

The sound of hooves pounding the path rushed up behind Fallon, Kane Siosal's voice bellowing through the breeze, commanding the faerie to keep away.

Far be it from a faerie to listen to a mortal, for he took a step toward Fallon who started to back away. "What do ye here, fae?"

"I have come ta claim ye, Fallon Moireach," the faerie responded with a low, chilling snicker that sent an unsettling shudder through her. "Now look me in the eye."

"Oh, I do no' think so." With that, Fallon buried her face in her basket of woods, determined fend off the fae's request.

"Keep yer hands from her, The Bryan!" Kane yelled as he closed in on them.

Snickering, The Bryan waved a hand causing Kane and his horse to come to a sharp halt. Kane's horse bucked and nickered at an unseen barrier that rushed like a wind so mighty and a roar so loud it caused Kane to grind his teeth. Kane's hair whipped around his head and his eyes watered making it difficult for him to see. His horse became skittish, kicking out his hind legs and bucked so ferociously, Kane was thrown from his mount. He hit the ground harshly and rolled a few times before stopping. With a grunt of pain, Kane forced himself to his feet, keenly aware that a rib was cracked, the warm moisture beneath his shirt a sure indication he was bleeding. He pushed aside the thought of a rib likely poking through his skin and ignored the pain. Instead, Kane's eyes darted down the path, and he rushed forward, but was halted once more by the wall that the faerie created. Unable to reach them, Kane watched with outrage as The Bryan grasped Fallon by her arm. She screamed, struggling to pull away.

The Fae looked in Kane's direction, a mocking expression on his face. His hand came up and he snapped his fingers. A loud, booming noise rent the air, and as it did, The Bryan and Fallon vanished.

"Nay!" Kane yelled.

Withdrawing his *durk*, he slashed at the indiscernible wall. There was a crackling sound and Kane fell through. Stumbling forward, he fought and then gained control of his feet.

He listened carefully to his surroundings. If Fallon had looked the fae in the eye, she would be gone to the otherworld.

His stomach churned with the thought.

But if she resisted, Fallon would still be here, hopefully nearby.

A female screech gave him his answer.

*Fallon.*

"Oh," Alanna moaned as she began to recover from her swoon. "Fallon?"

"Remain here," Kane ordered her.

Already he was breaking through the wooded foliage, heading toward the sound of Fallon's voice. Still holding his blade, Kane came upon a clearing. He slowed his pace in an attempt to quiet the sound of his treading feet and stopped just short of bursting through the brush. He saw Fallon struggling against the faerie-man, her eyes tightly shut as she swung her fists at him. The string of curses that spewed from her mouth would have had Kane chuckling if he was not so worried about how he was going to rescue her from the grips of The Bryan. It would have to be accomplished unawares or else the faerie would vanish with Fallon once more.

Crouching low, Kane summoned incredible strength against his temptation to rush upon them.

"Look inta me eyes!" The Bryan commanded.

Fallon bucked and twisted beneath his body, turning her face from side to side to avoid his attempts to kiss her. The Bryan rolled to his side taking Fallon with him. His hand came up and he squeezed her breast. So appalled was Fallon that without a twice over thought, she kneed him in the groin, the impact so painfully accurate The Bryan yelled out, releasing her immediately. He drew himself up to all fours and then lifted his head to glare at Fallon. His anger surged and he lunged, pinning Fallon to the ground.

He clenched her chin in his demanding hand. "Look at me now, wench!"

"Aye, a tantrum will surely gain me favor, faerie!" And with that, Fallon spit in his face.

Swiping at the spittle on his face, The Bryan laughed heartily at her valiant efforts "'Twill be entertainin' makin' ye me whore."

One of his hands shifted and pushed beneath Fallon's skirts.

"Gods damn ye!" Fallon screeched.

"The thought be belated, wench." The Bryan snickered. "I be already damned by the gods."

At the sight of the violation against Fallon, Kane spewed a silent growl from where he watched and was seized by a possessiveness and bloodlust so fierce he was determined to kill the fae.

Lunging forward, Kane flung himself at the faerie's back, grasping him by the shoulders. He jerked The Bryan from Fallon's body and threw him to the ground. The faerie landed on his back. Lifting his blade Kane forcefully drove it downward but met only solid ground as The Bryan's body dispelled before his eyes.

Reality caught in Kane's brain. A faerie, being immortal, could not be killed. It was foolish to even try. And then he realized something else. His attempt was a dangerous thing.

Kane quaked.

Had he thrust the blade at The Bryan's back whilst he was still atop of Fallon, his *durk* would have pierced her chest when the faerie vanished.

But there had to be a way to defeat the fae. Kane would ponder that dilemma at a later time. For now, he turned his attention to Fallon who cursed uproariously as she jumped to her feet and started to flee. Kane chased after her, grasping her about the waist and dragging her backwards. She fought him, her legs and arms flailing, her mouth still spewing outrageous expletives and Kane laughed at her spunk. Losing his footing they both fell and Fallon landed in Kane's lap. She threw a tightly clenched fist at his head and Kane dodged it, jerking his head aside.

"Fallon, cease!" Kane bellowed as he snatched her wrists to stay her swinging fists. His command was followed with a grunt of pain caused from the shifting of his broken rib. "'Tis me, Kane! The fae be gone."

"Kane?" Fallon went still. Her eyes remained closed as her head turned toward him. She shifted where she sat, her bottom grazing his groin. "The faerie?"

Much to Kane's dismay--or delight--he was unsure, his shaft perked to life at her movement.

"Aye, gone," he answered through clenched teeth as Fallon exhaled in relief and then swept her arms around his neck pressing her body to him.

Pain mixed with arousal, and Kane was unable to ignore the stabbing sharpness in his ribs, but also unable to ignore the stimulating feel of Fallon's breasts squashed against his chest.

It was an odd combination.

And it was a simple choice to toss aside the pain in lieu of desire.

Smoothing, his hands along Fallon's sides, Kane allowed them to settle on her hips, but he resisted the urge to grind his shaft against her.

"Open yer eyes, lass," he rasped out.

At the sound of Kane Siosal's sensuous voice and the rousing shift of his hardness beneath her, Fallon felt a stirring in her belly. Nuzzling her face to his shoulder, she held him tightly. She very much wanted to gaze into his eyes, but dared not. Hearing him, *feeling him* would have to suffice.

With her lids still shut, Fallon drew back and touched her lips to his cheek.

*A kiss of gratitude*, she told herself, denying that the thumping of her heart was a reaction to being touched by him.

An impish grin creased Fallon's lips. Who was she trying to fool? Being held by Kane felt rather pleasing.

And her need for soothing from her frightful encounter with the faerie was a good excuse to linger overlong in Kane Siosal's embrace--though Fallon had to admit she was not overmuch distressed by the event. The faerie--*what had Kane called him? Aye, The Bryan*--incited more fury in her than fear.

But with her fury now subsiding, Fallon discovered that deep inside, her carnal cravings were demanding to be freed.

She was helpless to disregard it. Druid oath insisted she forever tell the truth to all, whether it be her gods, or her people, or even to herself. Though this particular truth was not very difficult nor was it a dreadful thing to confess to.

Curling closer to Kane, she sighed.

*Perhaps Alanna is right,* she thought. *If Kane Siosal be willin', why no' seek me pleasures?*

After all, it was the eve of Bealtuinn, when discretion was unbridled. *Why should I be deprived?*

Abandoning her human logic to resist the sexual spoils, Fallon surrendered to her faerie lust. She lifted her face and pressed her lips to Kane's chin.

On an intake of breath, Kane cranked back his head and then tipped it forward to gaze down at Fallon as he exhaled. He half expected to find himself looking into her eyes, but *nay*, they remained shut.

Though he was disappointed at that, Kane could not ignore Fallon's sensual posturing. Her face was tipped up, and her lips ... *aye* ... her lips were full and inviting.

The sight was too enticing for Kane to resist.

Lowering his head, he covered her lips with his mouth, a gentle taking, coaxing them softly. And she responded with an open request, parting her lips so he could slip his tongue inside. And when Fallon's tongue eagerly slid along his, Kane's body quaked and came roaring to life.

Never before had he been so intensely aroused by a woman.

The feel of her nestled in his arms, how easily she accepted his embrace and how tantalizing her lips were to fully taste, had his flesh raging with desire and his mind reeling with thoughts of her naked body pressed beneath him.

Kane's hands skimmed upward, seeking, yearning, and settling on one of her breasts.

*A perfect fit*, he thought as he fondled it, pleased when her nipple pushed through her garments, peaking against the palm of his hand.

She gave no protest when he pushed her *brat* aside. And Kane noticed that the lavender color in the plaid matched one of the three colors in his own *brat*--fate perhaps?

Again, he was reminded of her eyes, and his attention shifted upward, as he tried to imagine the lovely lavender hidden beneath her closed lids.

He longed to see them once more, but Kane would be patient. In time, Fallon might trust him enough to know that gazing into them would not cause him to lose his wits. Of this, Kane was convinced, believing that his mind was stronger than her faerie persuasions.

For now, he concentrated on his fingers, which found the bindings holding her *leine* closed. He deftly untied them, pushed the garment from her shoulders and then further still, to reveal her breasts to his eyes. His mouth watered and his shaft surged as he moved from kissing her throat, seeking the tender flesh of her breast, craving to taste her there as well.

Fallon responded with a soft mew. Tipping her head back, she exhaled slowly as Kane kissed her throat and then skimmed lower until his mouth was on the swell of her breast. She pushed toward his mouth in a beckoning gesture to have the peak of her breasts suckled.

*Ye were more than right, Alanna*, Fallon mused. Kane's seductive skills were setting her ablaze. Never had she been so amorously inflamed by a man.

Not that she tried over much. Not that she *wanted* to try over much. But with Kane--there was something about the man she was unable to defy.

"Do ye want me, Fallon?" Kane asked, his voice revealing his arousal with its raspy tenor. He would proceed no further unless she gave consent.

"Aye," Fallon returned as she pressed her palms to his chest. "'Twould be an interestin' adventure."

Kane chuckled at her choice of words and then lowered his head to take her breast into his mouth.

Moaning with delight, Fallon's palms mapped the contours of his muscular chest through his garment. Soon she would be exploring his flesh.

Such a rousing thought!

Sensations began stirring between her thighs, and Fallon shifted in Kane's lap, yielding to the yearning to rub against his groin. Her hands moved lower, to grasp Kane's side.

But suddenly he stiffened. And on a fierce jolt he yelped.

It was not a sound of pleasure.

Fallon's brows drew together. She felt moisture on her palm and a lump beneath the cloth.

Opening her eyes, she looked down as she pulled away from Kane and turned her hand over.

"Ach, Kane!" Her hand was bloody. "Ye are injured, man."

"'Tis naught," Kane answered, but suddenly all he could taste was pain.

Fallon slid from his lap, her hands fumbling at the ties of his *leine*. Frustrated that she was unable get them loosened quickly enough, Fallon relented and instead ripped the garment open.

She grimaced at the wound.

"Naught, ye say?" Fallon clucked her tongue. 'Tis a bone there, Kane."

"'Twill heal."

"'Twill fester!" With that, Fallon pushed at his shoulder. "Now lie back, man."

Obeying, Kane reclined to the dirt, the pain of his wound dousing his lust. He preferred it the other way around.

Reaching into one of the three pouches tied at her waist, Fallon scooped out a powdery substance and then cupped her hands together, lifting them into the air as she chanted an orison.

"What do ye, Fallon?" Kane lifted his head to watch her.

"I be healin ye." With that, she blew at her palm, sending the dust toward his face.

As the substance blustered in his eyes, Kane squeezed his lids shut and turned his head aside. Unintentionally, he sucked in a breath, inhaling a hefty dose of the powder. Within moments his head felt heavy and it thumped to the ground.

Withdrawing a ground herb from a second sack, Fallon once again lifted her hands in offering to the gods and then patted the substance on Kane's wound. With the sharp edge of her blade, she slashed her palm and pressed it against Kane's broken flesh where the bone broke through. Her healing blood seeped as she pushed the bone back into place, drawing only a slight grunt from Kane, as he was well muddled by her remedies.

Fallon held her hand in place, closing her eyes to feel the energies of curative power that strummed through her veins and course directly into Kane's body. She sensed the bone mending and felt the wound sealing beneath her palm.

Quietly she gave thanks to the heavens that bestowed on her the druid gift of healing, as she dropped her head in humbled praise.

"Ach! So much for the druid oath of devotion ta friendship!"

"Oh." Fallon's gaze snapped up to the edge of the clearing where Alanna stood with her arms akimbo and the most piqued expression on her face. Fallon had been so preoccupied with Kane, she had forgotten that Alanna had swooned on the path.

*How unforgivably self-servin' of me!*

"Here I be layin' in the dirt from me fright whilst ye are cavortin' in the forests.'"

"I am no' cavortin'." Fallon scowled. Was Alanna hiding in the bushes this time as well? "The man be injured and I be healin' him."

"Aye," Alanna nodded. "Far be it from me ta question a druid who heals a man with her breasts."

With her eyes widening, Fallon looked down and grimaced with chagrin at her exposed chest. Quickly, she pulled up her *leine* to cover herself, redoing the ties. She snatched up her *brat* and threw it over her shoulders.

Standing, she walked to where Alanna stood and then cast a glance behind her to look at Kane. He was a tempting man, even in his sleep.

Fallon sighed.

"Ah, ye like him." Alanna grinned at her.

"Nay," Fallon denied.

"Then why were yer breasts flappin' in the breeze?"

Fallon's gaze shifted from Kane to Alanna. "I jest be experimentin' 'tis all. 'Twas a mistake ta dally with him."

"Humbuggery!" Folding her arms Alanna stared smugly at Fallon. "Yer fancy for him is etched all over yer face, no' ta mention the suckling marks on yer breasts."

With an intense glower, Fallon grabbed Alanna's wrist and began tugging on her. "I have ta be gettin' ready for the rituals."

She would inspect her skin later.

"Yer bein' a fool!" Alanna stumbled forward as Fallon dragged her. "He dost no' fear lookin' upon ye, lass."

There was merit in Alanna's words, Fallon accepted. No male for as long as she was aware of them had ever dared to give a single glance to her. All men feared her--feared succumbing to lunacy--so she was told and she believed.

"I will no' discuss this further, Alanna." Again Fallon tugged on her friend's arm, but Alanna dug in her heels.

"Are ye jest gonna be leavin' him there?" Alanna looked empathetically at the slumbering Kane Siosal.

Blowing out an exasperated breath of air, Fallon released her hold on Alanna. "He shall awaken healed and hearty, I assure ye."

"And layin' in the dirt, alone and forgotten."

Fallon pursed her lips in irritation at Alanna's goading. Spinning on her heels she headed toward the path. "I be walkin' away now, Alanna!"

"Tsk, tsk." Alanna placed a palm to the center of her chest as she called to Fallon's back. And then she started to follow her. "What manner of concern ye have fer yer friends. 'Tis shameful!"

"I am no' listenin' ta ye, Alanna!" Fallon returned without looking back.

## Chapter Six

Kane awoke in the dirt, free of pain, his hand immediately seeking the wound he suffered, but it was gone. He could feel nothing where the bone was prior, except the slight hardened ridge of a scar.

He also sought out Fallon. But in like with his wound, she too had disappeared, though the taste of her still remained impressed in his memory.

For a moment Kane worried that The Bryan had returned and seized her, so he whistled for his horse and then frantically searched the forest and the paths for Fallon or Alanna, or signs that there might have been a struggle.

Much to his relief, Kane found the two women back at the village, and he followed closely by them as they went about their preparations for the feast and rituals forthcoming.

He and Fallon did not speak. In fact, she refused to acknowledge him despite his efforts to engage her. Alanna, on the other hand, was relentlessly garrulous towards Kane, bending his ear until near dusk, poking and prodding him for information. *Where were ye sired … how many kin do ye have … how did ye earn the honor of a thrice wrapped brat … and the colors, did ye notice one of them matches Fallon's eyes?*

It was almost like the scrutiny he had undergone at his request to take arms for the future king.

Kane politely answered most of Alanna's questions as best he could, all whilst wishing silently that she would make herself scarce so that he might speak with Fallon. But she stuck to them like thistles in molasses.

"Do ye have any bastards?"

Reacting to the bold question, Fallon stopped pounding the oats in front of her and glared across the table where Alanna was working.

But Alanna paid Fallon no heed, and instead, focused on shaping her *bannochs*.

"Pleasant good day." A woman approached, carrying a platter of steaming shellfish.

Looking up, Alanna swiped the sweat from her brow. "And a pleasant day ta ye, as well, Lila."

Alanna's eyes dropped to the platter and a wily grin began spreading across her lips. "I shall be takin' that."

Lila handed over the platter, and Alanna turned to Fallon. She held the platter at arms length, reaching across the table and sticking it beneath Fallon's nose. "Care for a bite?"

Fallon scooped her pounded oats into a bowl. With a resounding thud, she dropped the bowl in front of Alanna and scowled at her.

Shellfish was a commonly used and very potent aphrodisiac--strawberries were another. There was no misunderstanding Alanna's aim.

Shrugging off Fallon's obvious irritation, Alanna placed the platter to the side and reached for a nearby bowl. This too she shoved beneath Fallon's nose. "Strawberry?"

Lila's eyes widened. "Ye are a brave woman ta taunt a druid fae."

"Ye have no idea, Lila," Fallon responded through gritted teeth. "A wart would look mighty fine in the center of yer nose, Alanna."

"Ach! I'll have no part in this," Lila exclaimed as she turned about and walked away.

Alanna snorted. "Temper, druid, temper."

She shook her finger at Fallon.

Fallon drew a few irritated breaths through her flared nostrils, silently chanting. *Thou shalt no' lose thy temper in the face of being provoked ... thou shalt no' lose thy temper in the face of being provoked ... thou ... shalt no' ... turn thy friend inta a toad, though shalt no' turn thy friend inta a toad ... though I would be sorely pleased ta do so....*

Kane watched the byplay between Fallon and Alanna as he finished pouring a bucket of water into a large pot that would be used to boil the *haggis*. Dropping the bucket to the ground, he leaned against the table and picked up his ale. Scratching his whiskered chin, he pensively studied the two women. It was difficult to recognize their friendship by the manner in which Fallon was glowering and Alanna was smirking.

*Hmph.* Taking a sip of his ale, Kane began to swallow.

"So how many women have ye bedded?" Alanna returned her attention to Kane.

Kane spit his drink upon the ground and started coughing.

"What?!" he choked out. Alanna was quite the brazen woman.

After regaining command of his convulsing lungs, Kane blinked, dumbfounded by Alanna's query. To Kane, what she asked was a private thing, one not for the telling. And then, he could not believe it, but heat flushed his cheeks.

He was blushing!

Kane's eyes swung to Fallon, who pounded her oats with a force so tremendous he thought the wooden table would splinter.

"Are ye experienced with women?" Alanna continued to look at Kane, a nonchalant expression on her face, waiting, as if she expected him to answer such a thing.

Kane's mouth fell agape. His tongue seemed to stick in his mouth.

In a goading manner, Alanna picked up the platter and held it out toward Kane. "Shellfish?"

She winked at Kane whilst at the same time tipping her head to indicate Fallon.

Kane's brow lifted though he said nothing. His mouth snapped shut.

But Fallon--oh Fallon--she was beginning to seethe! Halting in her task, she lifted her head and bore a glare at Alanna so icy it could have frozen a raging forest fire in a midsummer's heat.

"'Tis time fer me ta meditate fer the rites," Fallon hissed through her teeth.

With that, she turned about and began stalking away, but unforeseen, a boy child of no more than four, rushed by and tripped over Fallon's extended foot. Stumbling, the young bairn crashed head first into the table. Rebounding, he fell backwards landing flat on his back. Air expelled from his lungs and began thrashing about, blood dripping from a gash in his forehead.

"Oh gods!" Dropping to her knees, Fallon swiped at the boy's forehead, whilst Kane and Alanna rushed around to the other side of the table to see what happened.

The boy had gone still, his complexion turning an unhealthy shade of blue.

A crowd began to gather as Fallon reached for her pouches. She withdrew the herbs from one of them. Tipping her eyes skyward and lifting her hands, she quickly recited a chant before sprinkling her medicament over the oozing wound. Fallon then slipped her blade from its sheath and slashed it across the palm of her hand, drawing blood. She pressed her hand to the boy's gash, her head dropping down to his face, her hair draping all around the boy's head like a protective cocoon, and she willed her breath into him.

The healing energies surged through Fallon, and she droned her magical chant, her mind, her soul reaching out, connecting with the boy's quintessence whilst she channeled her restorative blood and her life-giving breath. Within her meditative trance, Fallon gave praise to the spirits beseeching them and thanking them for sanctioning her body to be the vessel for their curative powers.

And as Fallon murmured her intonations, Kane watched, his hand seeking the area where his rib had been broken. Never had he seen a druid healing. Mostly, with the druids he ever encountered, he witnessed them only in prayer. What Kane saw before him now awed him. An aura seemed to bend around Fallon, first emanating yellow--the color of discipline and wisdom, and then shifting to a green that was deep at first, but then grew vigorously bright.

It was the healing color and the color of the growing season as well.

Admiration--*nay,* 'twas more--a longing for Fallon besieged Kane.

He yearned to have her in his arms.

She was perfect. Everything a man could want in a woman--gentle and giving, yet strong of will and determined. Kane wanted Fallon with a ferocity that went beyond his lust, beyond the enchantment of looking into her faerie eyes, something his heart could not describe.

Kneeling beside Fallon, Kane reached for her, and touched her shoulder. He felt a sudden bonding with her--pure and mighty.

It blew through him like a hasty wind.

And amidst admiring her druid bestowments, his desire for her was fortified. He felt her essence, caped in the enchantments she spoke aloud, and in the silence of the words she did not speak. His core cried out for her--a blending of human souls--a mingling of spiritual with an incredible human yearning, and Kane wondered if it was just his imagination or if Fallon was aware of it too.

He did not have to wait long to know the answer. Her head turned up to him. And though she avoided looking him in the eyes, Fallon must have understood, for she gasped. And on her intake of breath, Kane was drawn in, grasping at her, seeking to snare her heart and make it his own.

Fallon rose to her feet, and Kane stood with her, but rather than acknowledging what passed between them, she turned her back to Kane. Looking down at the child, Fallon was pleased to see him sitting upright. He blinked his confusion, but was otherwise well and healed. The mother came to her child, scooping him into her arms whilst bowing reverently toward Fallon and thanking her for her gifts. And she walked off with the boy, leaving the appreciative crowd behind along with Alanna who praised Fallon's druid abilities aloud with thankful prayers.

But Kane did neither of those things. He merely stared in amazement and a great longing for the human woman who stood in the dirt before him.

"Do no' come closer ta me," Fallon said tersely as Kane stepped toward her.

Turning about, Fallon lifted her palm, flattening it on Kane's chest to stay him. Through the gap of his *leine*, where she had torn it apart prior, Fallon made contact with his bare flesh. The heat from his skin radiated and seemed to permeate through her, and though she attempted to ignore its presence, ignore the urge to curl her fingers through his masculine hair, the sensation, nevertheless, stemmed the length of her arm and flooded into her.

Her insides quivered.

Fallon's breath caught, but she refused to swallow the lump in her throat, refused to acknowledge the fierce, aching need for the warrior, Kane Siosal.

Relieved that Kane halted, obliging her request, Fallon finally inhaled. But Kane's hands moved and he held her healing hand between his own. Turning it over, his eyes fell to her palm where blood continued to ooze from the self-inflicted slash.

Kane skimmed his thumb across the wound, and watched it slowly fade before vanishing, leaving not even a suggestion that it ever was. His gaze lifted to Fallon's face finding that her eyes were fixed askew and away from him. At the same time she attempted to yank her hand free, but with quickened reflexes, Kane tightened his grip and held her fast. Lowering his head, he pressed his lips to her now mended palm.

"I want ye, Fallon," he proclaimed in a lowered voice though it was louder than a whisper. The crowd around murmured at his proclamation.

He paused, stunned by his own blatantly indiscreet admission.

But though the feeling took him unawares, Kane was unable to deny it was intrinsically natural to say such a thing to Fallon, as if the words, the feelings, had been stowed within his being, tucked safely away to be used at this very moment.

Fallon did not move.

Whether it was from shock at his declaration--or perhaps it was fear--no man had ever expressed desire for her before. Not in public, nor in private, until Kane.

She was clueless as to how to react.

Particularly with so many eyes upon them.

It was something the teachings in druid ethics failed to address. It was an issue a father should address--or a mother.

She had neither.

For the first time in her life, Fallon was confused. And from that confusion, her attention snapped toward Alanna, silently seeking answers, only to find her friend smiling broadly at her.

It was obvious Alanna approved.

Beside her, Cullen slapped a hand to his forehead. It was an obvious, opposite reaction to Alanna's.

"Shoo, shoo!" Alanna flapped her hands at the villagers. "Off with all of ye. 'Tis well inta dusk and we have much ta do."

As the crowd began to disperse, Alanna turned to Fallon and Kane. "Will we be witnessin' the two of ye, leapin' the flames this eve?"

Kane paled.

*A marriage vow?*

It escaped him to consider something so extreme.

At the same moment he was pondering exactly what it was he wanted from Fallon, she jerked her hand free. With not another word spoken between them, she spun away from Kane and stalked from the village.

Starting forward to chase after her, Kane felt a hand upon his upper arm. Turning, he expected to see Cullen, but *nay*, it was Alanna who stopped him. With his brows drawing together, he gave her a questioning look.

"She goes ta meditate," Alanna answered to his unspoken inquiry. "This she must do alone."

Nodding with understanding, Kane watched as Fallon reached the brim of the village and then disappeared over the knoll. For several moments Kane was silent, whilst Alanna and Cullen stood quietly beside him.

"What 'tis it ye are thinkin'?" Cullen asked as he studied Kane's pensive expression.

Kane inhaled, held the breath briefly and then released it slowly.

"Did ye see the colors that shone about her?"

"Colors?" Alanna repeated with a sparkle in her eyes. "Ye have seen inta her soul, Kane Siosal."

"Ach," Cullen groaned. "'Tis jest the beginnin'. Ye will be witless afore long."

Listening to Cullen's surmising about his forthcoming condition of mind, Kane's eyes remained fixed to where Fallon had retreated from his sight.

He pushed Cullen's warning aside.

If having a woman as lovely as Fallon Moireach made him a barmy man, then so be it.

## Chapter Seven

The wolves howled, the sounds of their cries echoing ominously from the forests beyond--stalking, like other unseen creatures--spirits or fae--immortal beings waiting to seize their prey.

Beneath the luminous, rounded moon, the clans marched, singing their hymns by the beat of a single drummer and the chimes of the cruit strummer, beckoning the gods for the sun's healthful warmth and the rains that would nourish the dirt.

Led by Fallon, the procession moved along the paths. From homestead to homestead they went, hanging rowan wreaths upon every door to dissuade any faeries from raising mischief.

Fires were extinguished in each dwelling's hearth and would be rekindled later by flames taken from the Bealtuinn pyres.

To do so would bring blessings abundant.

Kane walked by Fallon's side.

Wrapped from head to toe in a green, hooded cloak, Fallon's ritual garment concealed every aspect of her face and form. And aware from prior celebrations, that Bealtuinn was a time of deepening spiritual revelation for the druids--a time when their souls bonded with the earth as they beseeched the gods for fertility and a plentiful harvest, Kane honored Fallon's meditative state, saying not a word to her.

Behind him, Nevin and Glenna walked, and just behind them, Alanna, her father, Cullen, and his wife, whom Kane had yet to meet.

The remainder of the clans followed, one hundred and two in

number, and a bevy of offspring, their feet moving in rhythmic accord to murmurs of their chanting.

They ended the procession at the top of the knoll just beyond the village. There, two pyres, foregathered with the nine sacred woods, waited to be ignited.

At the base of the hill, the deep bellows of the cattle could be heard. Amidst them, the farmers held their sedge torches to purify the air. And they stood heedful, intent on protecting the livestock from the hungry wolves whose cries echoed through the air once more.

Fallon set herself in between the two pyres, as the remainder of the clans gathered in a circle around. She lifted her arms and waited patiently until all in gathering fell silent.

"Let the fires be kindled." Fallon pushed the cloak from her body, and the garment crumpled to the ground, revealing her body in its most natural state--unclad.

Stretching her arms skyward Fallon gave praise, offering homage to the fertility spirits. With a reverberating boom, smoke went up, a crackling, a spark, and the kindling burst into flames proclaiming victory of the light season over dark.

The villagers rejoiced loudly with hearkened rapture and Kane stood amongst them, though he was very still.

Despite the merriment around him, all sound was null to his ears as his gaze became fixated on Fallon.

He was seized to the core.

Kane saw not the druid giving adulation and beseeching the gods. He saw not the healer who was revered by the peoples in the clans. What he saw was Fallon, beautiful and womanly in her naked presence and he worshipped her body with his thoughts and his eyes.

It was sinful, such musings, when all around were thinking only of the blessings they sought. But Kane cared not, his lust surging, his desire for Fallon crying out.

And then it occurred to him.

What man, mortal or other, could refuse to look upon such a breathtaking woman without being racked with a libidinous thirst?

His thoughts were confirmed, for as Kane scanned the area about him, he found that most men present attended to Fallon with lustful grins and leering eyes.

A growl formed low in his throat, more intimidating than the wolves that howled from the forests beyond. He glared at each and every man until they caught his angry gaze and lowered their eyes away from Fallon.

"Nine woods we give ye," Fallon shouted and reached for the basket at her feet, picking it up. "Ta the god, we give oak. Bring the wholesome rains down upon the grounds and nourish our seed. Birch for the goddess, bless us with bright days and bring growth aplenty."

Removing several token twigs from the basket, Fallon began tossing them into each of the two Bealtuinn fires.

"We give fir for healthy births," she continued, tossing more branches. "Willow ta celebrate death, rowan ta dissuade the evil magic and apple…."

Fallon hesitated and then gulped an ever so discreet swallow that Kane did not miss. Something happened in his chest--an ache--as she faltered over her words.

"…apple for love." Fallon's gaze darted to where Kane stood, but she failed to meet his eyes.

"Aye!" several of the villagers answered at once.

"Better short and sweet, than long and lax!" someone called out, drawing hoots of laughter from the crowd.

Fallon ignored their jesting and instead persisted with her invocations. "We give ye grapevine ta bring joy, hazel for wisdom, and whitethorn ta celebrate the purity of the season."

"May the flames bring us ripe harvest and fruits aplenty! May the fires bring streams of fish, forests of hardy woods."

"Clean water!" one of the villagers yelled.

"Ornaments of silver and gold!" another added.

"Oh gods!" a male cried loudly. "We do no' ask ye ta give us wealth, but show us where 'tis!"

"Aye," another said. "And even the deaf man will hear the clink of coinage!"

Several of the villagers laughed and then nodded their agreement along with cohesive murmurs.

Stepping from the center of the two pyres, Fallon moved to the side.

"*Eadar theine Bhealltuinn.*" Amidst the Bealtuinn fires, she said and summoned the livestock.

The farmers hooted, thwacking the animals' hindquarters, driving them forth. The cattle were rushed up the hill bellowing their protests and urged between the sacred flames.

It was the ritual of blessing to drive scourge from the beasts and ensure their fertility for the mating season.

The incense were lit and then Fallon began dancing around the flames as the fragrance of jasmine and sandalwood, rose petal and frankincense filled the air, permeating and blending with the smokes from the fires.

And all inhaled the pleasant aromas.

"Free us from invasion!" Fallon prayed. "Bring ease ta ev'ry home."

Round and round the flames she stepped, her hair fluttering to and fro as she twirled and weaved about the Bealtuinn fires, weaved about the onlookers.

All watched her, and Kane relented, seeing it was hopeless that the men could restrain their interest in her. Fallon danced the steps of the season that would bring blessings to all, and all desired to witness this great event.

Pushing aside his covetousness of Fallon, Kane explored the activity around him. He smiled as he caught Nevin fondling and kissing his wife.

So much for the neighbor's woman.

Suddenly feeling lonely, Kane cast a glance beyond the gathering, staring into the darkness beyond. It was then that he spied the figure sitting upon a rock a short distance outside of the circle.

Shielding his eyes from the glare of the blaze, Kane narrowed his gaze as he attempted to get a cleaner glimpse.

The Bryan. There was no mistake about it.

As if sensing the attention upon him, the faerie-man turned his head toward him, and Kane went rigid at the sight of The Bryan's faerie eyes.

They glowed--ethereal--like two round moons, reflecting the fires of the ritual and lighting the arrogant smile on his faerie lips.

And then, The Bryan turned his eyes back to Fallon, uncaring of the warning rage in Kane's façade.

"Gods of the flame we beseech ye," Fallon cried out.

Kane started.

The Bryan rose and was moving. His pace was slow, purposeful, as he stalked in an arc around the perimeter of the gathering.

"Guide our bondin' with nature," Fallon chanted as she twirled around, unaware of the male aggression befalling outside of the throng. "Bring forth the nurturin' spirits of fertility and future."

Kane's eyes riveted to the fae whose interest fell directly on Fallon. Every nerve in Kane's flesh rippled with anger and worry as he treaded swiftly toward the immortal. The Bryan paid no heed to Kane, disregarding his advance as if he were just a mere nuisance to be dealt with later.

The drum beat louder, voices rose higher as the clans sang out their singing praises. All seemed ignorant of the faerie in their midst, save Kane.

"Give unta us the blessin' of the blossoms and the gift of creatures here in these lands ta bear offspring," Fallon beseeched.

The Bryan picked up his pace, changing direction and moving directly toward Fallon.

Kane began to run.

"Bestow on us wisdom ta honor your ascendancy over all things. In the lightin' of these Bealtuinn fires may we find fulfillment of passions in the flames. May the power of winter be broken!" Fallon cried out. She halted and spread her arms wide. "'Tis done!"

"Let us eat and be merry!" someone shouted.

Crossing paths with the fae, Kane halted and drew his weapon, knowing full well the faerie had the magic to pass directly through him, disregard the blade, yet Kane did not know what else to do.

But The Bryan halted in front of Kane, and looking directly into Kane's eyes, he crooked a mocking smile. Before Kane could blink, the faerie was gone.

Twisting to look over his shoulder, Kane's eyes snapped to Fallon. She had retrieved her robe to cover herself and was sitting on the ground, amongst the clans. In a possessive suggestion, sensing The Bryan was still nearby, Kane stalked back to the gathering and positioned himself at Fallon's side, his hip touching hers.

Fallon's only acknowledgement of Kane's presence was to shift her bottom away from him, but as she did, Kane shifted with her. Fallon continued to shift and Kane continued to follow until there was no more room for Fallon to go, her opposite hip abutting up against Alanna, who sat to her other side.

Fallon suddenly found herself squashed between her friend and Kane.

As Alanna felt the increased pressure from Fallon's body, she turned to look at her and saw Kane too, pressed up against Fallon.

Alanna snorted.

"Well now, this be cozy," she said and shoved a trencher of food at Fallon.

Jerking the platter from Alanna's hands, Fallon scowled, passing the food to Kane whilst keeping her irritated gaze on Alanna.

Fallon leaned in and whispered, "He will no' go away."

Alanna cranked her head back and with an utmost serious expression she raised her brows. "Do ye wish him ta go?"

"I...." Fallon opened her mouth to speak, but her jaw just hung there with no more words coming out. To say she wanted Kane to leave would be a blatant lie. And druids never lied.

Fabricated a bit occasionally, but did not lie.

Crooking a finger under Fallon's chin, Alanna closed Fallon's lax mouth. "'Tis what I thought."

There was smug edge in Alanna's voice that had Fallon sighing in defeat. "What shall I do, Alanna?"

"Enjoy his company." Alanna bit into her *bannoch*. She noticed that Kane devoured his fare like a man desperate to fill some insatiable need which seemed to have nothing to do with the food he was ingesting.

And he was, though food was no great substitute for the sensations that failed to subside. Sitting so close to Fallon was causing Kane's manly hungers to rise.

It was nearly more than he could withstand.

Never could Kane recall desiring a woman with such ferocity as he did Fallon.

Heaving a sigh, Kane scooped a bit of *haggis* to eat, and then stuffed his mouth with fruited bread. He washed it down with his wine, wishing the drink were more potent.

"Swallow it up and do no' let it come back," Alanna said. Reaching around Fallon, she refilled Kane's mug from the flagon she held.

Kane chuckled, accepting the drink.

As the celebration progressed, dish after dish was passed, drink after drink was swigged. What food remained after the feast would be buried as an offering to the earth. To save the leavings to be consumed the following day was considered ill-luck.

But for now, the villagers took their fill.

Except for Fallon.

She did not eat--could not eat, not with the churning in her belly that was something other than hunger.

It was nerves.

And rarely did Fallon feel uneasy, but with Kane so near to her the feeling refused to settle.

Swallowing hard, Fallon watched as lovers leapt the now low-burning flames, announcing their aim to marry. They would handfast for a year and a day. At the next Bealtuinn, the couples could choose to stay together or part ways dissolving any further obligation between.

Whatever the decision, any children resulting from such *greenwood* joinings were considered offspring of the spirits, and the care of them would be shared by each of the clans.

Four children resulted from last season's pairings and Fallon could almost predict which of the pairs would separate, founded on their behavior during the past season and the behavior she was witnessing at the moment. Clyde Stukly, who handfasted with Cordelia Mckie last season, had his hand beneath Tara Lobdale's skirts, unconcerned that Cordelia took to the forests with Rhys Gairden. And Dallas Athol and Dermot Egan who paired last Bealtuinn were nowhere to be seen, though Fallon knew they were not off together, having observed each of them creeping off with different partners.

Others, as well, were beginning to succumb to salacious intoxications, though Fallon had less concern for their doings. Those mates who were committed one to the other for a number of seasons, it was expected they would sample variety in the flesh this eve.

Fallon inhaled the still fragrant air, and observing the cheery sights and the sounds of merriment amongst the clans.

And then the frenzy began.

All were becoming intoxicated--on the drink, on the excitement of the growing season, on the fire-struck enchantments of the Bealtuinn eve.

Those not otherwise occupied ushered the children off to bed to hide their innocent eyes from the fertility rites that followed the feast.

Fallon sat quietly, and to her pleasure, Kane remained at her side. She half expected he would seek his lusts, since it was an eve of open freedom to do so, but he did not.

Women began stripping their clothes and the men followed. Wedding vows were tossed to the wind, and married or not, many villagers paired off, some rutting in full view of the gathering, whilst others scattered to the forests beyond.

Some were merely at ease to dance and sing around the pyres, Alanna amongst them. Naked and wild, she pulled her plait free, and romped about the flames.

Kane watched her and the other women for a bit, admiring their nude, female bodies, as did the other men who had yet to meet with a lover.

Fallon also watched the lionizing clans. During prior Bealtuinn celebrations she never paid them much heed. After offering her obligatory blessings, she usually retired early to sup with her father. She could not have cared less as to what proceeded with the clans after she departed, though Fallon was well aware of their doings, mostly from overhearing the tittle-tattle that ensued the following day.

But this eve she remained, observing the dancing and singing and the rutting--especially the rutting--with intense curiosity.

*Aye*, tonight she stayed, and was loath to admit why.

It was Kane.

Despite the worry over what could befall him, Fallon found it difficult to break away from him. Was it because twice he had caught her faerie eyes, or was it her human side that beckoned her to be near the warrior?

She thought about her father and the madness he succumbed to after his romp with the queen faerie. Though others had told her he was once the wisest of druids, Fallon only knew him as a witless man.

If she took Kane to her bed could she resist snatching Kane's gaze, risking that he too, would become the same?

*Nay.* She could not.

Rising to her feet, Fallon snatched a torch newly lit by the sacred fires and started to walk away, but halted when she felt a hand wrap around her ankle.

"Do no' leave, Fallon," Kane requested.

Fallon closed her eyes and summoned every power of will within her.

"I must attend ta me papa. Please…." She begged he would adhere. "Release me."

Much to her relief, Kane let go. Without a glance backwards, Fallon left the knoll and the festivities, heading off into the darkness.

## Chapter Eight

He followed her, of course.

Snatching a torch of his own to light his way, Kane trailed just a short distance behind Fallon as she made her way down the path. Though he was close enough for her to be aware of his presence, not once did she speak or turn around.

But Kane had to be sure she was protected. The Bryan was lurking about. Of that, Kane was certain. And as long as the veils between this and the otherworld were thinned, Fallon's existence on earth would be threatened.

On the morrow's daylight breaking, the faerie-man would no longer be free to roam in this his realm, as the shrouds would be congealed. Fallon would be safe, at least until the Samhuinn celebrations following the harvest season, when once again the wall separating their worlds would wither.

By then however, Kane would be long-departed from the village, thinking of the druid woman no more.

Such foolishness!

Kane winced.

He was deceiving himself if he believed that Fallon Moireach would ever leave his head….

Or his heart.

It was then Kane became fully conscious of his own intent and his emotions. His desire for Fallon went beyond the lust that failed to fade.

He was falling in love with her.

How was it possible? They had just met this very day. Pondering that for a moment, Kane wondered if it was her faerie blood that charmed him. Twice over he gazed into her eyes, after all.

*Nay.*

Kane was certain there was a definitive between enchanted possession and true human emotion. He knew his own heart, and what it revealed to him now was comfortable and sincere. It felt virtuous and just--untainted.

Of this, his mind was decisively clear.

What he would do about it was decisively unclear.

Turning down the path that led to Fallon's home Kane appraised his surroundings, searching for The Bryan. He heard a door creak shut as Fallon went inside. But he refused to depart even though any faerie was forbidden to enter a house uninvited.

Particularly with the rowan wreath hung upon the entry.

Kane would sleep upon the ground this night, just to ensure The Bryan did not show his face and attempt to lure Fallon to him.

Amidst making this decision, Kane heard the creaking of the dwelling's door once more and Fallon stepped outside. She no longer carried the torch and Kane noticed a glow coming from within the dwelling, likely from the hearth, newly stoked with the

Bealtuinn flame Fallon carried inside.

Fallon released a heavy sigh when she spied that Kane was still present. Brushing by him, she shook her head as Kane followed behind her. Still saying nothing to him, Fallon departed from the path and moved into the woods. Deeper and deeper she treaded, the sounds of twigs snapping and foliage crunching beneath her feet, until it became so tall and thick it was impossible to stray any further.

"Do ye wish fer me ta set the forest afire?" Kane asked, referring to the torch he carried.

Glancing around, Fallon determined she had no choice but to return the way she came. "I did no' ask ye ta pursue me, warrior."

With that, Fallon brushed by Kane once more.

"Fallon?"

"Aye?" She halted her steps.

"I shall be trailin' after ye." Kane spoke to her back.

"I prefer you do no'."

"I must."

"Why?"

"I be lost."

"Ah." Fallon chuckled. "Well I can no' leave ye ta rot in the forests."

"'Twould be much appreciated."

"This be the way." Fallon started forward, leading Kane through the brush until they were once again on the path.

"Now then, I shall go this way." Fallon pointed down the path, and then circling her arm around, she indicated the opposite direction. "And ye shall go that way."

"Nay," Kane said, cuffing his hand around her wrist. "Look inta me eyes, Fallon."

Ignoring his request, Fallon closed her lids and took a quick breath. "Why do ye insist on protectin' me, Kane Siosal?"

What could he say? *Because I am drawn ta ye, Fallon, because I want ta bed ye, because I want ta kiss yer beautiful lips until the stars fade away?*

"The Bryan--"

"Is no' a concern," Fallon interrupted.

Dropping her head to the ground she smiled. It was admirable that Kane wished to guard her from the faerie when most would have run off with fear.

But Fallon was needless of Kane's protection.

She, in like, was needless of his hand upon her as such. His touch was confusing her senses, stirring unprompted feelings deep within her that were both unwanted and wanted at the same time.

Regardless, she failed to pull away.

"The faerie-man was forcin' his way with ye, when last the two of ye met."

"True," Fallon agreed. "He took liberty beneath me skirts, but 'twould have been dire punishment for him by ruling fae had he persisted."

She paused. "Unless, of course, I invited him. Rest with assurance, Kane, 'twill no' happen."

Lifting her head, Fallon looked over her left shoulder, giving him her profile. His hand slid from her wrist and Kane held Fallon's hand as he stepped a bit closer to her. He was pleased she did not protest the contact. It was the truth she spoke, that a fae seeking her was of no worry if she refused him. Still, he was opposed to leaving Fallon's side.

"'Tis dark in the forests and I thought ye might not be able ta see yer way," Kane offered, lifting the torch slightly. It was a fair reason to accompany her.

"I be able ta negotiate these woodlands with me eyes closed, which they are most of the time." Fallon chuckled. "Me vision is verra acute in the darkness."

*Ah,* Kane thought. He wondered how she managed the forest so easily with it being so black. He should think on another reason to stay by her side.

"The wolves, they howl this eve and I thought ye might be afraid of becomin' their prey." Unconsciously, Kane skimmed his thumb in circular motions over the top of Fallon's hand as he spoke.

"I have told ye afore, warrior. I be one with nature." Fallon drew her brows together aware of Kane's subtle caress, even more aware of the subtle tremor that purged from her body. Again she closed her eyes, attempting to shake away the sensation, but occluding her vision had the contrary effect. She could hear his breathing, almost feel the heat of his body that seemed to diffuse and girdle the air all around her. Even his scent tickled her more profoundly. Without her sight available, Fallon was more keenly alert to Kane's presence, and his closeness to her. His touch was even more profound.

"The wolf will no' harm me." Her voice emerged in a breathy whisper. *Ye, on the other hand, Kane Siosal, are a grave risk ta me wellbeing.* Whenever Kane was around, Fallon seemed to have difficulty thinking clearly.

A howl rose up from the beyond the trees, and as if on cue a lone wolf appeared from the darkness, growling and bearing its teeth. With his eyes widening, Kane released Fallon and stepped in front of her. He pointed the torch in the wolf's direction as his other hand sought his *durk*.

But putting proof to her words, Fallon moved around Kane's body. He grabbed her shoulder to pull her back, but Fallon shook herself free and stepped forward. Staring directly into the wolf's eyes, she waved a shooing hand at the beast. The wolf yapped once and then scampered back whence it came.

*Now*, Fallon wondered. *What shall I do about the wolf lurkin' behind me?*

She could not deny that Kane intimidated her--well, if she were to admit more truthfully--her *reaction* to Kane intimidated her.

More than any wolf or faerie creature could possibly.

On that thought Fallon gulped when she felt Kane pressing his body against her backside. Extending an arm, he held the torch out to his side, whilst his other hand slipped around Fallon's waist, pulling her to him.

Kane began nuzzling her cheek.

"Ye are an amazin' woman," he whispered low, though the effect of his sumptuously deep voice rocked her like thunder.

*I be an amazin'ly warm woman right now*, Fallon mused silently.

Her nostrils flared, and she sucked in a short breath, whilst stiffening at the same time. It was not because she disliked the feeling of pleasure Kane was giving her, but because she was overly enjoying it--in great abundance.

And she did not wish to enjoy it.

At least she did not *think* she wished to enjoy it.

Cupping his hand beneath her chin, Kane tipped Fallon's head back. Her lids reflexively closed.

*Oh gods! She wished so very, very much to enjoy it!*

"Look inta me eyes, Fallon," he beckoned and touched his lips to hers.

Kane's breath feathered across Fallon's mouth and she nearly melted as she waited for yet another kiss from him, but thoughts of her father and his madness seeped into her brain and Fallon summoned her strength. On a shudder and an exhale, she reluctantly broke free, stepping forward and away from Kane's embrace.

On a sigh at Fallon's reluctance, Kane wedged the torch between two nearby boulders. His attention moved to a small grove of whitethorn trees and he walked over to examine them. After murmuring a few words of praise and gratitude, he fingered the sprouting white flowers gently. "I have a question for ye, Fallon."

"Speak yer piece." Fallon watched Kane's actions with curiosity. His homage to the tree seemed an almost intimate thing.

"The scar." Kane felt the area where Fallon healed him. "I was jest wonderin'. On me, on the child, after ye healed us, scars lingered, yet where ye cut yerself, there is no' a trace."

"'Tis my will."

Careful to avoid its sharply-pointed thorns Kane snapped a tiny blossom from the whitethorn, and held it beneath his nose. He inhaled the rich, heady scent. "Then ye are able ta heal a wound with no' a sign of it followin'?"

He swiveled to face Fallon.

Immediately, she angled her face to the side. "Aye, that I can do."

"Then why do ye no' do so?"

"If no token of the affliction persists, then no forethought ta riskin' life and limb would be considered the next time danger reared."

Stepping closer until he was just a span in distance from Fallon, Kane touched her, his palm coming to rest on her cheek.

"'Tis verra wise thinkin'." He nodded in agreement, admiring this unique woman.

"A druid must use all bestowed gifts prudently." Fallon attempted to ignore Kane's touch upon her face, but to no avail. The heat from his flesh seemed to ensnare her, flowing impressively within her, spreading from her cheek and through the extent of her body in one demanding sweep.

And though she refused to look at him, through the corner of her eyes she knew his gaze was locked on her face.

Kane lifted the flower to his nose and inhaled its scent once more.

Fallon's attention snapped toward him whilst at the same time his gaze fell to her mouth. With leisurely purpose, he brushed the petals across her lips.

A tingling sensation caused by the soft petals being stroked across them caused Fallon's mouth to slacken. She closed her eyes, taking the sensual fragrance deeply into her nostrils, finding it impossible to dissuade the intruding desires and pleasures that began racking all of her at once. It was bad enough Kane alone exhumed these feelings in her, but now, with the addition of the highly erotic whitethorn aroma, her senses became implausibly heightened.

She yearned to be held by Kane, to be kissed and caressed and taken away to the depths of euphoric ecstasy.

"Do ye have harmony with the whitethorn tree, Kane?" Fallon whispered.

Was she swaying?

"Why do ye ask?" Kane whispered in return, his voice a low, sensual pitch.

"Ye stroked the sacred branches, appeased the tree before snapping off the bud, more so than the common man would."

"The tree is meaningful ta me, aye." Kane traced Fallon's cheek with the blossom and then continued along her jaw line. Moving inward, he skimmed the petals along the edge of her lower lip, his gaze tracking its path as he appreciated the exquisite contrast of the white flower against her dark skin.

In a seductive motion, Kane lightly dragged the bud downward, following the line of Fallon's throat until he reached the swelling of her breasts.

Fallon's head dropped back, and she inhaled a long, languishing breath.

Kane's gaze flicked upward resting on her face.

"I was born beneath the whitethorn moon," he told her.

*By gods she is beautiful.*

Fallon's lids fluttered open as her head tipped toward Kane. She nearly caught his gaze, but averted the path of her vision at the last moment. "Then ye know of its legends."

It was an honor to be born under the whitethorn sign for the offspring of such a tree were honest and loving and wise.

"Aye." Kane smiled warmly at Fallon, noticing she watched his lips as he did so. It was not the same as her looking into his eyes, but he felt affection in her action just the same. "I know that when worn or carried the sprig brings happiness."

He tucked the bloom behind Fallon's left ear and then smoothed admiring fingertips along the length of her long, silky hair, arranging it over her shoulders. "And a child of the whitethorn is ready ta meet any challenge."

"The whitethorn is the protector of faeries," Fallon returned, gulping at Kane's tender regard. Her heartbeat strummed a pounding tune. It felt as though it was about to burst.

Kane's smile grew wider. "Then 'tis good I have come ta safeguard ye from The Bryan."

"Perhaps 'tis The Bryan who will need the protectin' from me."

Chuckling at her remark, Kane slipped his arms around Fallon, gathering her to him.

Bending his head, Kane's mouth met hers. A slight whimper left Fallon's mouth and Kane felt her lashes flicker against his cheek. He pulled back, but *nay*, her eyes remained shut. He lowered his mouth to hers once more.

Yielding to his touch, his taste, Fallon relaxed in his arms, no longer able to deny the impact of Kane Siosal on her being. She was falling in love with him and there was no turning away from it.

Fallon could not resist.

Nor could she protest when Kane's fingers undid the fastener holding her cloak closed and he pushed it from her shoulders, revealing her naked body as the garment dropped to the ground.

Unabashed at her bareness, Fallon allowed Kane's hands to roam her flesh, his palms smoothing along her back and over her bottom. He held her to him, shifting his hips against her, the ardor of his hardness increasing her need, inflaming the ache between her thighs with yearning to have him inside of her body.

A purely male murmur rumbled from Kane's throat, the desire smoldering as his mouth took Fallon's in a frenzied claiming, their tongues sweeping one over the other with a heated urgency clearly definable as passion unleashing.

Kane lowered Fallon to the ground, resting her atop of her cloak.

And beneath the gleam of the copious moon, to the wispy sounds of a subtle breeze blowing through the brush, and the distant howls of creatures, mortal and mystic, Kane began making love to his faerie woman.

Chapter Nine

His hands sought her breasts, caressing them, his thumb skimming over the nipples as they peaked beneath his touch. His lips explored her, kissing her jaw, her neck, the top of her shoulder and then trailing back to her mouth. Her parting lips drew on him, taking his breath and he gave it to her.

Kane moved to her throat and lower, nuzzling between her breasts, before dragging his tongue across a nipple, and then sucking it into his mouth. He was deeply emboldened by Fallon's quiet moans and the arching of her back telling him she was begging for more.

Lower he moved, worshipping her flesh, adoring her navel as his tongue swirled around it. And he kissed her lower still, nipping at her belly and then brushing his mouth along her female mound.

On a whimper and a request, Fallon's legs parted, and Kane groaned his reply.

He tasted her there. Grazing his tongue and suckling the budding of her female flesh. Her scent as intoxicating as the whitethorn flower, he took in her flaming passion, drank of the feast known only to him as Fallon Moireach, the woman he desired.

She bucked and rubbed against his mouth, and Kane could take no more.

Rising over Fallon, his knees placed to each side of her hips, Kane unlatched the belt that held his blade and sheath, tossing it aside. He pulled the *leine* over the top of his head, and then looked down at her.

She focused on his shaft.

Her hands came up, one cupping his sack, the other surrounding his jutting erection.

With earnest she studied it, ran her fingers along its length, felt the smoothness of the skin and its alluring warmth.

"Have ye ever seen one before, lass?" Kane shuddered, resisting the urge to plunge into her. He wanted the moment to last.

Fallon's eyes lifted and roamed about Kane's face. She looked at his chin, his nose, his hair, coming perilously close to capturing his eyes, but she successfully failed. "I have seen more than I can number."

"Ye are no' untouched?" Kane's heart fell.

He was so hoping to be her first lover.

Releasing a short laugh, Fallon pushed at Kane's chest urging him back to his haunches and she followed him to a sit. Without hesitation she leaned forward, pressing her lips to the tip of Kane's shaft drawing a hiss of pleasure from him.

"Ye are forgettin', warrior, I am a druid healer," she returned. "I have seen many men in various states of undress."

"Aye," Kane groaned at her lustful kisses upon his member and the way her voice vibrated on its tip when she answered him.

"'Tis their eyes on which I have never set me glance. And *nay*, I have never given over me body."

Reaching for her, Kane dug his fingers through her hair and they both rose up to their knees, their naked bodies coming together into an intimate press for the very first time.

"Look inta me eyes, Fallon." Kane stroked his shaft against her as he whispered in her ear. He nipped her lobe gently. "Invite me in, faerie beauty."

"The madness…." Fallon's head tipped back.

Her breathing quickened.

"'Tis too late." He kissed the side of her neck. "Twofold I have seen inta yer eyes, and the madness already beseeches me."

"*Nay.*" Fallon frowned, denying that her new lover would go insane.

"'Tis in me heart, Fallon." Kane set his lips upon her worried brow and then took hold of her hand, flattening her palm to the center of his chest. "'Tis here the madness calls out for ye, lass."

Releasing a gasp that was part relief, part delight, Fallon swept her arms around Kane's neck and pulled his lips to her mouth. She leaned back against his embracing arms, her weight bringing Kane forward, and they reclined to the ground, Kane coming down atop of her, their lips remained locked in a searing kiss and Fallon's thighs fell apart, taking Kane's hips between them.

"Invite me in, beauty." Kane propped to his forearms and swept his thumbs across her closed lids. His heart thumped a hardened beat, and he stroked his shaft along her folds, savoring in the feel of her naked flesh pressed beneath him.

She opened her eyes.

Her gaze pierced him and Kane was awestruck.

Sucking in a breath Kane held it.

Though he requested it, desired it, craved it, her gaze took him unaware.

Shook him to the core.

Kane was captured--snared by an enchanting pool of lavender, her eyes ensnared him and refused to let go. Snagged in euphoria, entwined for eternity, he bent his head to kiss her, their eyes remaining locked.

Hopelessly lost in her splendor, he cradled it, cherished it, breathed it into his soul.

He could claim her now.

Lifting his hips, Kane found the path to her opening and he slipped inside of her. She was warm and wet and welcoming, moaning her reception to his taking.

Gently Kane pushed against the soft, but firm barrier within her.

Refusing to close his eyes to relish her moist heat, Kane muttered, his voice raspy and uncontrolled, his breathing harsh. He felt her squeeze tightly around him, beckoning him into her.

He groaned.

And Fallon waited--for pleasure, for pain, she did not know which, for by legend it was said the female faerie found ecstasy with the breeching, her body surging to an exquisite, forceful peak.

But her human side might feel tremendous pain and she would bleed.

Fallon felt both.

Kane plunged, ripping through her--a burning sensation igniting as she tore.

Fallon screamed, clinging tightly to him, relieved when it quickly receded, replaced by a burgeoning fire of pleasure that spread through her and rippled along her flesh in a powerful bursting that pushed the human agony of being shredded into an incredible surging of erotic, faerie bliss.

It flowed through her and ruptured through the breadth of her flesh.

"Kane!" Fallon's voice echoed throughout the forests.

*"Mi gabh bhuat neo-chiontach, mi chi sibh a breagha bioreannach,"* Kane whispered to her. I take yer innocence and I leave a beautiful woman.

On a rising cry, Fallon began peaking, her hips moving in a frenzied rhythm with Kane's increasing thrusts and heavy breathing--her body quaking to a shattering rush, her climax broke through as Kane frantically pumped into her. And not once did she avert her gaze, staring directly into Kane's eyes, watching with excitement as rapture flooded through him.

And with a forceful plunge and a heavy growl Kane released his climax inside of her, accepting that it was he who was claimed but welcoming being lost in her forever.

Kane collapsed, his head dropping, his lips planting kisses on Fallon's cheek and then paying homage to her mouth. Finally, they both closed their eyes, breaking the intimate gaze that fed their passion, and Kane rolled to his side, dragging Fallon against him. He held her tightly, wrapped his body around her, his hand finding her breast and plying it tenderly, and they listened to the sounds of their passion's breathing slowly subside into quiet, satiated silence.

"Kane?" Fallon twisted in his arms looking into his eyes with a gaze that refused to let go of his soul.

And Kane received it, welcomed it.

"Aye?" He smiled.

"'Twas good?" Fallon asked simply.

Kane's smile widened--a warm presentation at her innocent appraisal of their love-making act. "'Twas verra good, Fallon."

Fallon returned Kane's smile and snuggling closer to him, she relaxed in his arms.

"Well, isn't this special?"

Jolted by the sound of The Bryan's voice, Kane snatched his *durk* and jumped to his feet pointing the blade toward the faerie, whilst Fallon scampered backwards and away.

"I should thank you, Gael, for breaking in the druid for me." The Bryan glared at Kane, a patronizing gleam in his eyes. "It's such a messy business, debauching a woman, don't you think?"

"Be gone, faerie!" Fallon rose to her feet, her line of sight passing beyond where The Bryan stood. "Ye have no dealings here."

The Bryan's mouth turned up on one side. He took liberty in perusing up and down Fallon's form. And Kane saw his own red aura as his blood began boiling to an angry height. With his eyes still riveted to The Bryan, he bent to snatch up Fallon's cloak and tossed it to her.

She swept the garment around her body and then clutched it tightly closed, concealing her nakedness from the faerie's leering eyes.

"Your lusty cries were ear-shattering, druid." The Bryan wriggled a finger in his ear as he snickered. "And the vigorous way your body moved ... tell me, did it feel good?"

Disgust and outrage racked Kane--at the faerie-man's invasion, at his abhorrent taunts, at the strange way he used his words and the crudeness in them.

That he intrusively watched Kane and Fallon sharing their passion.

Raising his blade further, Kane prepared to strike, but with a jerk of The Bryan's head, the weapon was whisked away from Kane's clutch. It flew through the air impaling a nearby whitethorn trunk, and Kane could swear he heard the spirits shriek.

The cut was an insult to the sacred tree, an assault to its glory. The spirits that lived within it would be sorely irate for the disrespect. Ill fortune would be brought down upon all of their heads.

"For what purpose do ye come here, fae?" Kane demanded. He would never surrender Fallon.

With a casual strut, The Bryan strolled to the whitethorn. Yanking the blade from it, he examined the weapon, blew a breath on the blade and polished it with his sleeve. "Why to hand over your swag."

Kane eyed the faerie-man suspiciously. "What swag do ye speak of?"

"Your silver." The Bryan tucked the *durk* into his belt, looked toward Kane and snickered. "You win. I lose."

"What dost he mean?" Fallon questioned.

"Oh," The Bryan clucked his tongue. "Perhaps I should've kept silent. Of course she wouldn't know."

"Know of what, Kane?" Fallon frowned.

"Why the wager as to which one of us would bed you first," The Bryan answered flippantly whilst eyeing Fallon at the same time. His attention shifted back toward Kane. "Did I say too much?"

"Nay!" Kane growled. "The fae lies!"

The Bryan responded with a shrug. Turning up his palm, he slashed it through the air in front of him.

Cullen appeared lying face down in the dirt, and he was completely unclad. Somewhere in the distance and beyond the trees a woman screamed that her lover had been stolen by a faerie.

Looking up from his prone position, Cullen's face showed his puzzlement as he glanced first at Fallon and then to Kane. He lifted a brow at Kane's nudity and was about to speak when he spied the faerie.

Standing abruptly, Cullen realized his own naked state. And thinking about what he had just been taken from, his confusion turned to discomfiture as he covered his still swollen shaft with one of his hands.

"The silver, mortal," The Bryan demanded, and something materialized in Cullen's other hand--the sack containing the faerie's coinage.

Fallon looked on with confusion and dread as The Bryan stalked toward Cullen and snatched the sack of coins from his grasp. Turning, he tossed it through the air, and the sack landed at Kane's feet, the coinage clinking inside.

Kane did not pick it up.

"Nay, Kane," Fallon gasped with dismay. "Say 'tis no' true."

With anger in his voice, Kane gainsaid The Bryan's accusation.

"I did no' wager with ye faerie!"

"'Tis a bet I would easily win." The Bryan's face went expressionless, his eyes a chilly glare. "Aren't those your words, Gael?"

"Did ye say such a thing, Kane?" Fallon's body quivered with unease. She held her breath as she waited for Kane to answer.

Doom rent the air.

It was not a good sign.

Thinking carefully on his meeting with The Bryan earlier, Kane sifted through the conversation he exchanged with the faerie. He could have chopped off his own tongue with his teeth, his words coming back to haunt him. Kane *had* said those words, but not in the circumstance that The Bryan was attempting to convey at the moment.

"Kane?" Fallon gave him a troubled look.

Turning to her, Kane's chest wrenched at the worry on her face. "Those be my words Fallon, but…."

"And did you not say you could match the wager?" The Bryan stepped forward interrupting Kane before he could say more.

Kane's body shook with fury as he realized what the faerie-man was attempting to do. He was going to kill the immortal with his bare hands.

"Ach." Cullen spit into the ground. "I warned ye 'twas foolish ta bargain with a faerie."

The words hit Fallon's ears, her eyes snapping to and fro as she thought about all that was being said.

"'Tis true?" Fallon asked. "Ye wagered me body for a sack of silver?"

Fallon shook her head at Kane and her lovely lavender eyes seemed to drain of their luster. Her expression twisted with horror and disbelief.

Hurt--abominable hurt--spread across her face.

"Ye must listen, Fallon," Kane pleaded. She was misconstruing what occurred.

"I think…." Fallon released a low, anguished cry. "…I be hearin' enough."

The Bryan stepped closer to Fallon, holding out his hand. "Come to me, druid, your mother awaits."

*Me mother?* Fallon's eyes dropped away from Kane, the faerie catching her ear. All of her life she wanted to know her mother-- the enchanted mother who stole her father's mind away.

"*Nay!*" Kane rushed forward, but The Bryan waved a hand and

Kane's movements became progressively sluggish until he could go no further. Kane likened it to being trammeled in a thickened pit of mud from which there was no escape.

"Ye will take me ta me mother?" Fallon asked The Bryan whilst ignoring Kane.

"Look into my eyes and it will be done." Reaching out, The Bryan took Fallon's hand into his own.

Her head lifted.

"Fallon, Nay!" Kane shouted. He was desperate to tell her the truth. "I did no'...."

His voice faded.

His mouth moved but no words could be heard, and Kane knew in an instant that The Bryan's magic was the culprit.

"Why would me mother send ye in her place?" Fallon queried.

Mist began swirling around them, and Fallon seemed oblivious to Kane's distressed shouts, though she was well aware of the shattering that ravaged her heart.

Still holding her hand, The Bryan explained, "The fae cross the veils seeking mortal lovers, druid. Your mother couldn't come for this reason...."

"She is me mother." Fallon finished his sentence. It was quite easy to understand. Her mother could not bring Fallon to the faerie realm unless she made Fallon her paramour.

What mother would do such a thing?

Nodding, The Bryan softened his gaze, feigning concern and tenderness for Fallon.

"Give me your eyes, Fallon." His voice whispered a gentle beckoning.

Fallon's gaze moved toward the faerie.

Her heart wept.

Kane had betrayed her.

He had taken her maidenhead on a wager, stolen her love in a bargain and for nothing more than a sack of silver. She wanted no part of mortal life or mortal men anymore.

*Nay! Nay! Nay!* Kane mouthed silently as he pushed and pushed at the invisible sludge, frantic to break free.

And then it was too late. He watched in horror and tremendous grief as Fallon's eyes met the fae's. The mist around them condensed, shrouding Fallon and The Bryan from his sight.

Within moments, the mist cleared, and when it did, Fallon--his love, and The Bryan had vanished.

All that remained was Kane's *durk*, lying in the dirt, the

whitethorn he presented to Fallon atop of it.

## Chapter Ten

"What's wrong with her?" Gwyndolen took in Fallon's disheveled appearance as she looked to where Fallon slumped motionless on the floor.

Moros moved to a chaise and reclined on it. "Beats the hell out of me."

"I highly doubt the hell will ever get beaten out of you." Armond entered the palace's grand hall, his stroll an easy glide. His eyes dropped to Fallon and he frowned at the tangled mass of hair that fell over her bowed face. "I see you've gotten your way, my queen."

"I'm wondering at what price." Gwyndolen knelt in front of Fallon. "She's a mess."

"A simple mood swing," Moros said, addressing the faerie queen. "You of all should know that faeries are prone to erratic fits, since you've had many."

"This is no mood swing!" Gwydolen placed her hand beneath Fallon's chin. "And I'll ignore that last comment."

Tipping Fallon's face upward the queen examined it. She pressed her lips together, concern wrinkling her brow. "Ach! She has emotional suffering. I can see it in her eyes."

"Mother?" Fallon mumbled. Her heart should have felt elation, but it only felt pain.

"She'll mend," Moros answered in an indifferent manor as he casually inspected his fingernails.

Gwyndolen pulled Fallon's green cloak open. She drew back upon seeing the virginal blood gracing her daughter's inner thighs. "What have you done? Did you ravish her?"

"I've done no such thing!" Moros bolted upright from the couch. "I haven't a need to force my way with women. They freely come to me."

Armond snorted. "Freely as long as you've enchanted them."

"I take offense to that, Armond." Moros glowered at the king as he resettled himself atop the sofa.

"I take offense at your presence, fae."

"Enough of this squabbling!" Gwyndolen stood, her expression turning sharp with warning. "Who was the man that took my daughter's virginity?"

Moros shrugged a shoulder. "Just some half-wit Gael. No one of import."

"Hmm," Gwyndolen scoffed. "I think he was of significant import to my daughter by the looks of her. How did you lure her away?"

"Gwyndolen," Armond beseeched her. "You have your daughter. Just leave it alone."

Shaking her head, the faerie queen reached for Fallon grasping her by the upper arms, urging her to a stand. A single tear trickled down her daughter's cheek and Gwyndolen's annoyed demeanor immediately softened.

Fallon lifted her lids.

Their eyes met and Fallon saw lavender. Their eyes were the same.

"I want to know how you swayed my daughter's gaze, when it's so obvious she pines for another." With a protective embrace around Fallon's shoulders, Gwyndolen led her to an empty chaise and sat with her.

Moros grinned. "She was unable to resist me."

"My daughter is strong of will, Moros! If she loved another she wouldn't be so easily swayed."

*Moros?* Fallon looked The Bryan's way. She knew that legendary name. Moros was an immortal of the underworld who favored bringing fate in the form of misery and doom. He was punished for it.

"I demand you tell me," Gwyndolen persisted. "Or else I will deny the favor I offered you to bring her here."

*Favor?* Fallon wondered. She could not stomach being a pawn in yet another game. *What favor?*

Moros grunted his annoyance at the queen's insistence of an explanation. At the same time he snared Fallon's gaze and eyed her with carnal intent.

Fallon shrank back. And it took tremendous strength--faerie strength, to pull her sight away from him, but she managed to look away.

A full-blooded human would be at his mercy.

"Very well, if you must know," Moros began. It should be enough that he brought the queen her daughter, but it wasn't. "I won her in a wager."

Fallon grimaced, and she choked out a small cry, the painful sound drawing Gwyndolen's attention to her.

The queen stroked Fallon's hair. "Details, Moros."

"A sack of silver to the one who bedded her."

"What?" Gwydolen narrowed outraged eyes at Moros.

Armond lifted curious brows toward the Greek fae. He wasn't the least bit surprised that Moros accomplished the queen's request in a deviant way. Taking a seat on an overstuffed chair, he rested his hands in his lap and waited to hear the rest of the tale.

"He won," Moros continued. "So I appeared to them to give him the silver."

The queen gave him a confused look. "Why would you enter such a wager?"

"He was pursuing the druid, and was intent on having her." Moros stared at Fallon as he spoke. "Believe me, Gwyn, there was no other way."

"The warrior agreed to this?" Gwyndolen's mouth twisted with disgust. She would cross the veils and kill the man outright for bringing such grave hurt to her daughter.

"Well, not exactly," Moros snickered.

Fallon went still. *No' exactly?* Her heart thumped with hope.

"This is getting quite interesting," Armond commented. "Please continue, I for one, want to hear more."

"Fallon," Moros beckoned her and Fallon's head snapped around, her eyes immediately locking to his.

That he could so easily summon her left Fallon feeling dismayed. She was not in the least bit enamored by The Bryan, yet he was still able to snatch her gaze.

"Come to me," The Bryan said to her.

Ill of her resolve Fallon stood and her feet moved. It irritated her tremendously, yet she was unable to defy him.

"Sit Fallon," Gwyndolen ordered.

"Come to me, Fallon."

Standing, Moros didn't wait for her to obey. Swaggering to Fallon, he took her hand, and led her back to his chaise. He sat back down and indicated to the floor. "Sit at my feet."

Fallon glared daggers at Moros. "Should I be supposin' ye will be requestin' fer me ta kiss them next?"

"I might."

Shaking indignantly, Fallon sat on the couch, demonstrating her defiance toward him.

Moros laughed loudly at her insolence, knowing full-well that her faerie blood would fight him. "I'm going to enjoy mastering you, druid."

"You will only master her until she's learned the faerie ways, Moros." Gwyndolen scowled. "And then you will release her."

"Maybe I will, and maybe I won't," Moros answered. He relished the seething reaction the queen expressed at his words. This was so much more entertaining than having his guts cut out before his eyes.

"Finish the story!" Armond bellowed his impatience. "How did you acquire the queen's daughter?"

Never one reluctant to talk about himself, Moros relaxed into the sofa's cushions. He summoned a drink. From the air, a human captive appeared and brought one to him immediately. After taking a sip of the scintillating fluid it contained, he set the cup aside and ordered the human away.

He vanished.

Moros smiled pensively. He was immensely enjoying having his magic returned, even if it was only in part. Inhaling, he began his sordid story.

"The Gael took interest in her and it annoyed me."

"I'm sure it did," Gwyndolen said.

"The humans, ah well, you know how they fear the fae. But this Gael." Moros shook his head with resentment. "He didn't fear me. Nor would he concede when I told him I wanted Fallon."

Moros continued to convey his tale--relaying his attempt to draw Kane Siosal into a wager and how the Gael protected Fallon and captured her interest. With an arrogant beaming, Moros told them how he lured Fallon and the scheme he used that caused her to reject the Gael's heart.

"...and when the man, Cullen, confirmed it by reprimanding the warrior for entering any bargain with a faerie." Moros snickered. "I nearly busted a gut with laughter the timing was so perfect."

"I see," Gwyndolen ascertained. "So you revealed this pretentious plot in Fallon's presence, to make her turn to you, to make my daughter believe her lover had betrayed her, when he most certainly did not?"

"It worked quite well," Moros said, waving a hand to indicate Fallon. "As you can see."

Staring at the glittering mist beyond the palace columns, Fallon carefully took in all that she heard, but saying nothing. Joy melted through her. Kane had not deceived her.

*Oh!* She had allowed the faerie to capture her gaze and take her away....

…from Kane.

He must hate her for mistrusting him. Fallon released a small, pained cry. *What have I done?*

"Release me," Fallon insisted fervidly from her sitting position next to The Bryan.

"What?" He looked at her. "I gave you no permission to speak."

Fallon met his eyes, and with the most obdurate of glares. With relative ease she dispelled his enchantment of her. "I say ta ye, send me back ta him!"

"No," he answered, a bit miffed that he was unable to hold her with his spell.

Fallon drew back. *Nay?*

The queen studied Moros with annoyance, disliking his deceitful methods and very disturbed at the disrespectful way he was treating her daughter. "You don't own her, Moros."

With a grin on his face Moros propped his arms on the back of the chaise and stretched out his legs. He crossed one ankle over the other. "Oh but I do."

"A fae is forbidden to own another fae!" Gwyndolen protested. "It's written in our decrees."

"True. But she's only half-fae. It's her human half I own, and a fae can own a human." Moros paused, angling his head at a cocksure tilt, his expression smug. "By decree."

Gwyndolen shot to her feet. "This is absurd! When I requested you beckon my daughter, it was to keep her by your side as a mate, not as a slave!"

Moros shrugged. "I suppose you should have thought this through better then."

"Deceitful!" Armond burst out laughing, slapping a hand to his knee. "I warned you, my queen."

"Shut up, Armond!" The queen turned a furious eye to her mate.

"You need to calm down, Gwyndolen." Armond stood. With his hands clasped behind his back he glided across the floor until his back was to the three of them. "As much as it loathes me to say this, Moros is correct. He claimed her, and he now owns her … er … well, at least he owns half of her."

Fallon shook with irritation. "I am no' an object ta be halved and divvied up."

Reaching behind her head, Moros grabbed a tuft of Fallon's hair and jerked her head back. "You will only speak when spoken to, druid."

"'Tis the faerie side of me that now speaks." Fallon glared at him rebelliously, finding enormous strength from within. "That blood ye will never conquer."

"Let her go!" Gwyndolen scowled. "How dare you treat my daughter as such. She is royalty."

"I will treat her in whatever manner I feel." With that, Moros squeezed Fallon's face between his hands and kissed her roughly.

Almost immediately, a harsh yowl ripped from Moros' mouth. It was so loud that Armond spun around to see what was happening. He hooted with laughter at the sight of Fallon's teeth clenching down on Moros' bottom lip.

Moros clamped a hand at Fallon's throat and squeezed. She released him immediately and started coughing.

"She bit me!" Moros jerked away and glared into Fallon's angry eyes.

Gwyndolen's mouth turned up into a satisfied smile. "So she did."

Moros' nostrils flared as he rubbed his swelling lip. "A faerie is bound to never hurt one of their kind. You'd better learn that quickly, druid, or you will suffer gravely."

"'Twas no' the faerie blood that bit you," Fallon snarled at him. "'Twas the human side."

Crossing one arm over his body, Moros lifted his hand to strike her.

But Armond intervened, conjuring a spell that threw the faerie to the floor. "There will be none of that, Moros."

Fallon jumped to her feet and scurried to her mother's side, for protection and to put distance between her and The Bryan.

"Come back here!" Moros said as he rose to his feet and shook off the effects of being thrown.

"Ye shall never possess me, fae," Fallon returned. "I shall fight ye till me last breath."

"Speaking of last breaths," Armond said to Moros. "Shouldn't your reprieve from punishment be just about near its end?"

"How quickly we forget." Moros strolled across the hall moving closer to Gwyndolen and Fallon. With his eyes on Fallon, he halted in front of the two women and watched as the druid averted her gaze away from him. "The queen is to seek audience with Demeter if I brought her daughter and I expect her to do so as promised."

*So this be the favor of which they spoke of earlier.* Feeling like a pawn in a meaningless game, Fallon looked at her mother's face. "Did ye agree ta such a thin'?"

"I'm afraid it's true, my daughter," Gwyndolen said regretfully.

"'Twas selfish, Mother." Fallon pressed her lips into a frown, but her face suddenly expressed monumental pain when Kane returned to her thoughts. Tears welled within her, but she choked them back. "Ye did no' consider me own wishes. I do no' desire to be here."

Gwyndolen never considered that. She assumed her daughter would welcome the faerie realm with open arms. What faerie, or even half-blooded faerie would not? Where the human world was riddled with war--oppressed and bleak, this domain was such a wonderful and perfect existence.

At least it was in Gwyndolen's opinion.

Something happened inside of her chest at the sight of her daughter's afflicted expression. It was a feeling she'd never felt before.

She felt Fallon's deep sorrow.

Plotting to have her daughter by her side was an enormous mistake--a difficult thing for Gwyndolen to admit to her perfect self. But despite what Armond said, she was Fallon's mother and she most certainly bore maternal emotions for her. How could she have let her faerie selfishness get in the way of her daughter's own wishes, her own happiness?

Gwyndolen gazed at Fallon's face and then stroked loving fingers along her cheek. And Fallon couldn't help herself, she walked into her longed for mother's embrace.

At the tender exchange between mother and daughter, Moros snorted, drawing Gwyndolen's attention to him.

Moros' expression then turned stern as his eyes shifted toward Fallon. "Look at me."

His voice was commanding, and the pull of it was strong on her. Fallon felt her head turn though she did not will it to do so. The Bryan speared her gaze with his eyes, the pull of it even stronger than before as he held her sight to him.

Fallon's head spun.

Something was happening to her senses.

Sorting through the odd sensations Fallon could barely rationalize it was faerie enchantment that was consuming her, forcing her eyes to linger on The Bryan, pushing her desire to move toward him. Fallon's free will was abandoning her. And if she failed to fight it, her rational mind would vanish as well.

The fae queen recognized the glaze that spread through Fallon's eyes. Moros was gaining command of her daughter and

Gwyndolen was powerless to break the binding spell he held over her. The enchantment was a part of the faerie's essence--an innate gift.

There was no interfering with it.

"Release her," Gwyndolen demanded.

Ignoring the queen, Moros pulled Fallon away from the fae queen and swept his arms around her. He forcefully yanked her body up against his. "Tell me you love me, Fallon."

Closing in on Fallon, Moros bent over her, his lips coming to within a hairsbreadth from her mouth.

Fallon struggled to break the spell that held her entranced, but she knew very well the gaze of a fae was overwhelmingly captivating. No human would have a chance.

But Fallon was only half human.

"Tell me you love me," Moros demanded of her once again.

"I love…." Fallon's heart was sinking. She was about to say the words. Searching her head and her heart, Fallon sought her genuine feelings, reached for them, snatched and took hold of them, fed them to her soul. She wanted her Gaelic warrior, not this repugnant creature named Moros.

Her mouth opened against her will. "I … I…."

Fighting it with all of her faerie might, Fallon yelled loudly. "I love … Kane!"

Her voice came out in an echoing shriek that nearly had the palace quaking and Fallon broke away from both his grasp and his gaze. Holding up her hands she pushed at his chest and then backed away giving him a vehement warning. "Stay away from me, faerie! I do no' want ye. I shall nev'r want ye!"

Gwyndolen stepped between Fallon and Moros, relieved that her daughter had the strength to break from him, irritated at herself for accepting Moros into the faerie domain when Armond wanted to banish him. She should've listened to the king. "If I beseech Demeter will you let her go?"

"Hmm." Moros tucked one arm over the other and strummed his fingers against his arm as if considering it. He was silent for a moment, and then he said, "No."

"And why not?" Gwyndolen asked.

"Because I like her." *And because I like annoying you … and the king … and everyone else for that matter.*

"Release her or I will not beseech Demeter on your behalf!"

"Either way, I'm afraid you must, my queen." Armond spoke up, though his voice revealed he was less than enthusiastic about what he was saying. "A promise is a promise, by our decree, and I will see that it's not broken."

"Damn decrees!" The faerie queen shook with irritation.

"I warned you." Armond shrugged. "Moros thrives on misery and doom, Gwyndolen. And there is nothing that I'm willing to do about this particular venture he's chosen to engage in."

"*Willing* to do?" Gwyndolen repeated his words. She knew precisely what he meant by the word and she scowled at him for the purpose in it.

Truth be told, Armond, as fae king had the power to command Moros to release Fallon, but if the queen was able to persuade Demeter to denounce Moros' punishment, Armond would rather have the Greek fae pawing a half-breed druid, than drooling over Gwyndolen from now until eternity. It was a selfish maneuver by the king.

"This is not turning out the way I planned." Gwyndolen sulked in defeat. She wanted her daughter with her, but not if it meant misery for her. "Well, if you won't do anything about this Armond, I will!"

With that, Gwyndolen spun about, her glittering cloak fluttering and spreading sparkling faerie dust throughout the air as she stalked from the palace hall.

## Chapter Eleven

Kane stood in front of Fallon's dwelling, pondering what he would say to Fallon's father as he lifted his knuckles to rap on the door.

Though on the Bealtuinn eve it was customary for all human visitors who appeared at one's threshold to be welcomed inside, Kane was not calling to sup with Marlow Moireach. He was not calling to celebrate the season.

He carried with him grave news. That Fallon Moireach-- Marlow's daughter had been snatched by a faerie.

There was also another motive for paying a visit. Kane wanted Fallon returned, not only to the earth, but to him, as well. His heart ached for her, the pain more dreadful than any wound he had ever suffered. The hollowness inside of him caused by her departure felt like death, vacant and abandoned, and the anguish of never holding Fallon again left Kane feeling cold.

"Fallon," he whispered her name most grievously. She thought he deceived her, though her belief was false. It was The Bryan who was the betraying one. If Kane ever saw Fallon again--*when* Kane saw her again, somehow he would find a way make her see the truth.

Kane knocked upon the door and then waited. No answer came. He knocked again and then put his ear to the wood and listened. Not a sound could be heard inside. Finally, he opened the door and stepped over the threshold, his eyes immediately falling to the man sitting by the fire lit hearth.

"Marlow Moireach?" Kane addressed the man.

How angry would Fallon's father be that Kane failed to protect his daughter? Did he even have enough wit in his brain to understand what had happened to Fallon or to aid Kane in retrieving her?

He had little choice in the matter. Not one other in the village had knowledge enough to advise Kane on what to do.

Grabbing a small bench, Kane set it in front of Fallon's father and sat down. He began explaining the eve's happenings, save the love-making he and Fallon shared, telling him the false wager was for Fallon's heart instead of her body. Some things were better left unsaid, particularly to one's sire.

Marlow Moireach sat quietly, unblinking, unmoving, and Kane was hesitant to believe the man even heard a single word he expressed.

But Kane remained. Though the glaze in Marlow's eyes revealed a witless state, there seemed to be underlying wisdom within. Still, the man failed to speak or respond with any emotion to Kane's tale, his expression remaining blank.

Hope abandoned Kane and he began rising to leave. "Ye be nothing but a witless fool."

"*S minig a thainig comhairle ghlic a ceann amadain.*"

Kane halted. In mid-stance he stared into Marlow Moireach's eyes and Marlow stared back. Often has wise counsel come from a fool's head, was what the man said.

Slowly lowering himself to the chair, Kane curiously waited for Marlow to say more, but he only stared at Kane. After a bit, there was still nothing but silence from the man's mouth.

Pressing his lips together in disappointment, Kane rose once more. "Jest foolish blabberin', I can only suppose."

"*An rud a líonas an tsúil líonann sé an croí.*" 'Tis the mark of a wise man that he can listen to fools and learn from them.

Lifting a brow, Kane pondered those words.

And then he understood.

With a nod, he sat down again. Marlow Moireach was speaking in maxims and it was likely that the man expected Kane to interpret.

"Aye, ole man. Ye have me ear."

Marlow Moireach's entranced gaze seemed to change. Life filled it.

"*An áit a bhfuil do chroí is ann a thabharfas do chosa thú*," he said. What fills the eye fills the heart.

Again Kane nodded. "I caught yer daughter's eye and me heart is indeed filled."

"*E cruaidh sgarachdainn, cha robh dithis gun dealachadh*," Marlow answered. Though separation be hard, two nev'r met but had ta part.

"Nay." Kane shook his head. "I can no' think on it. Nev'r will I accept it. I love yer daughter and I would give me life to have her back."

"What is meant for ye will no' pass ye by," Marlow said.

Taking a deep breath Kane thought about that. "But if Fallon be meant fer me by what means do I find her?"

"Yer feet and yer eyes will bring ye ta where yer heart be."

"Me feet … me eyes?" Kane furled his brow. "I know no' what yer meaning be."

"The moon be wanin'." Marlow's drone voice changed, becoming almost eerie in tone. Lifting a single finger he pointed upward, his entire arm quivering as he did so. "'Tis no' a good sign."

Glancing toward the shuttered window, Kane understood exactly what Fallon's father meant by that comment. The dawning would arrive soon, and when it did, the veils to the otherworld would close. Not a soul would be able to pass through them.

At least not until the passing of the growing season, when the harvest would come.

It would be Samhuinn.

For this eve, Kane would soon lose the darkness of the night. He would lose his chance to retrieve Fallon.

Shaking his head, Kane pushed away the thoughts of what might happen to her until the harvest came. Worse over, he was terribly troubled about what might be happening to her at this very moment.

Whatever course he was to take, it must be accomplished before the break of day. "Ye must tell me what ta do, ole man."

Marlow drew back his shaky finger, pressing it to his lips. His eyes darted about the room and Kane searched with him, seeing nothing odd.

"A faerie comes ta speak," Marlow returned with a low, animated whisper.

"What faerie?" Kane stood with alarm.

Spinning about, he hunted for the creature but he saw none. "Talk ta me, ole man.

Of what faerie do ye refer?"

*The Bryan? Perhaps Fallon found a way to return? Who … could it be?*

Silence followed Kane's question and he turned back to Marlow.

The man's head dropped and he appeared to be asleep.

No matter. Kane knew exactly what it was he needed to do. Heading for the door, Kane halted and looked over his shoulder. "I be grateful to ye fer yer help, Marlow Moireach."

He left the dwelling with full understanding of what he had to do. Kane was also keenly aware that the undertaking was a risk to both his life and his mind.

But Kane cared not.

Without Fallon neither held value to him. He had to find her.

Through half-closed lids, Marlow Moireach waited until he was sure the warrior, Kane Siosal would not return. He lifted his head and his gaze shifted to the beautiful lavender eyes that fixed upon him.

A smile crested his face, as he warmly looked into them. "Why did ye abandon me?"

"I couldn't stand it any more--watching you slip from wisdom to a state of mindless nothingness. It was too painful."

"'Twas bliss for me." Marlow's expression turned moony.

"It's the same reason I left Fallon in your care. Armond was loath to have an unclaimed human blood in our midst … such prejudice." The queen fae knelt in front of Marlow. "For me it was more than that. I was afraid her human mind would be taken by a faerie's eye and I would be unable to protect her."

Marlow lifted a hand to cup her cheek. "Tis been so long, Gwyndolen."

"There's a purpose for my presence here." Gwyndolen nuzzled her cheek against Marlow's hand.

"Our daughter." Marlow's expression went somber. "How she be?"

"Sorrowful … in despair."

"Aye. So be that warrior."

"They were betrayed, and it's my fault." The queen set her cheek upon Marlow's lap. "I have come to seek him."

Marlow's face wrenched with angst. "Then ye have no' come ta take me back?"

Tipping her head, Gwyndolen looked upon Marlow with sadness. "It can never be. I returned you home with at least some of your mind intact and I will not steal the rest."

Marlow smiled at her. "'Twas a small price ta pay ta be with ye."

Gwynolen stood. "I must leave you for now Marlow. There's a dark faerie who must meet his fate."

## Chapter Twelve

Kane set himself beneath the whitethorn tree near the path where he and Fallon first found passion. After speaking with her father and leaving the dwelling, Kane wandered through the forests, and just as Marlow foretold, it was where his feet carried him.

Giving praise to the new season and the spirits, he fell into deep prayer beseeching assistance for the grave task he was about to undertake.

Before long he felt the presence of the ancient one and his heart was gladdened. And though Kane was unable to see her, the ancient one's essence stemmed through his head as well as his thoughts.

*I have not abandoned you, warrior.*

"Truly I be grateful ye have come."

*Your fate is my eyes and I will tell you that the outcome is not good.*

"I beg of ye, tell me what ta do."

Kane inhaled as the goddess swept through his body and mind, explaining what was about to befall him and how he could change the course of his future. When she was through, the goddess withdrew her spirit from within Kane, but continued to remain in the air around him, waiting for his reply.

Searching the dark forests, Kane collected his thoughts and considered what the ancient one revealed to him. His future did indeed look bleak.

Finally he spoke. "I loathe deception, goddess."

*In this case the end will justify the means.*

"Aye, though I do no' favor this act of trickery ye suggest."

*You are a principled man, and I respect you for that. But sometimes, warrior, it becomes necessary to fight fire with fire.*

"I do have understandin' of this, goddess. But I shall first attempt ta face this task in a more honorable way, if ye grant me."

*The choice is yours, if you wish.*

"I bid ye me humble thanks."

*Your gratitude is always appreciated. And now I will depart. Farewell for now, warrior. I will see you soon.*

Kane felt the ancient one's essence diffuse away until he was alone. But he was not abandoned. She gave her blessing for him to do the thing he considered. And now it was time to act upon it.

Always his practice, Kane gave praise to the sacred whitethorn tree before breaking off a few branches. He began weaving, fashioning a new wreath and thinking about Marlow's words.

*What fills the eye fills the heart.*

And now he would use his eyes to find Fallon.

A fae was in his midst and Kane wished to be lured away.

He hoped it was not The Bryan returning, though Kane was riled with the need to seek revenge on the detestable creature. And he doubted it was Fallon. He also hoped whoever the faerie might be was female, rather than a male with no interest in him, or worse yet, one who might be. Either way, Kane was unsure of what fate held for his body or his mind, should he catch the eyes of a faerie. But he would worry about it at a later time, for he intended to do all in his power to be taken to the otherworld.

It was the only way he could find his heart--find Fallon.

Kane examined his work and then held the wreath to his face. Peering through the rounded opening he framed the glimmering moon, which had moved lower in the sky.

Eve time was fading. The morn would come soon.

Closing his eyes, Kane summoned the inner depths of his mind commanding it to unwind. His head became heavy like honey, and the ruminative power poured through him.

"Faerie of the season, appear ta me," he beckoned. "I wish ta pass from this mortal world and find pleasure across the shrouds."

Silence followed. A wolf howled as Kane repeated his summon.

Again, there was more silence.

Kane waited, and before long the sound of chimes came to his ears.

"Speak," a voice said.

Kane opened his eyes.

A fog filled the whitethorn ring that failed to spread beyond its boundaries. Kane held his breath and his heartbeat quickened as a figure--*no*, two figures came through the haze--a white horse, with a woman perched atop it.

A glimmering aura surrounded her. Brilliant and wraithlike, it was almost painful to the sight. Her moonlit hair glimmered with a lavender sheen blending and weaving amid raven tresses that swept around her glorious face. She was intensely, inhumanly beautiful, Kane's eyes froze upon her. He could not tear his gaze away. All he saw within the depths of the whitethorn wreath--within his thinking--was Fallon Moireach and his heart was filled with joy. "Fallon, ye have returned."

"No, I'm not her," she answered in reply, the sound of her voice so euphoniously enchanting that Kane's mind whirled with longing to hear more it.

"Why do ye no' look at me?" Kane frowned that Fallon's eyes were averted away. Worry seeped in. *Is she still distrustin' of me?*

"I won't capture your gaze until you tell me why you've summoned me, warrior." Gwyndolen refused to bring him to her mists unless she was convinced his emotions for Fallon were true.

"Ye are me love." Kane stood and began approaching her.

"Halt!" she yelled.

Kane stopped immediately and closed his eyes in grief. Fallon was still angry with him. She continued to believe he betrayed her.

"If I steal your gaze, warrior, you might forget your woman."

"I will never forget ye, Fallon."

Gwyndolen smiled at his mistaking her identity.

It meant his heart was likely true, for when mortals spy the faerie, memories of all others are swept from their minds, with the exception of an honest love.

But this man thought she *was* his love, an understandable mistake. She and Fallon were identical in appearance, though Gwyndolen was pure fae and thus emanated a more ethereal presence. And one more alluring at that.

"See me for who I am, Kane Siosal. I am not the one you desire."

Kane felt a rush within his skull that caused his head to feel light.

It dispersed almost immediately and awareness took hold.

No longer could he see Fallon's features, for a bluish glow surrounded and consumed her, revealing only an indistinct form. It was as if he viewed her through an orb filled with wavering, sparkling water. This could not possibly be Fallon. The woman before him had to be pure fae to have such a brilliant color wrapping around her. Kane lowered the whitethorn wreath and looked at her directly, though she still refused to gaze upon him. "Who ye be, faerie?"

And how would he convince her to snatch him away.

"A fae of no import," Gwyndolen answered. "I'm just seeking to amuse myself this eve."

Kane shook with wariness, swallowing hard. The faerie had yet to covet his sight, yet for a moment she snared his mind, forcing him to believe he was seeing Fallon. Her power to consume his human mind with such ease was disturbing. And he also worried that if she was to the otherworld, would she do so again--deceive him into believing he was with Fallon?

"Do ye know Fallon Moireach?" Kane asked. She had to, otherwise how would she know what form to appear to him in?

"I am quite familiar with her," Gwyndolen said.

"Then I bid ye ta take me."

"You seek the druid, not me. Should I be insulted by this, warrior?"

Gwyndolen wondered if he would lie in order to catch her favor and if he did, she would be none too pleased at his attempt at deception. A faerie never takes lightly being told she is admired when indeed she is not. Especially for the purpose of obtaining a favor.

Kane pondered whether to answer her with the truth. She might refuse his request if she thought he desired someone other than her.

"Aye," he finally answered.

Better to be denied his petition than to anger a faerie. Even so, she still might lop off his head. Fooling with an immortal was a dangerous thing.

Gwyndolen admired his integrity. Her daughter had done well in choosing a mate. "If I take you to the otherworld, you may never escape."

"As long as Fallon be with me, 'twill no' matter."

"If I refuse to release you from my enchanted gaze you will forever be mine." Gwyndolen offered him the consequences of acquiring the interest of a fae. "Your body will be shared. You will lose your wit. You will die there."

"Without Fallon, I will die here." Kane pointed to his chest. "She be in yer place and 'tis where I wish ta be.""

Gwyndolen had heard enough. The warrior would sacrifice his mortal existence in this world--sacrifice his life, his mind, just to be near her daughter. "I then choose to honor your request, warrior."

Slowly her gaze began drifting toward him, but Kane immediately looked away.

"Will ye force me ta believe ye are her in your place of dwelling?" he asked. It would be pointless to allow the fae to seize him if he knew not the difference.

*A wise man,* Gwyndolen mused. "I assure you on my honor that you will not envision me any other way than in my true body and face, warrior."

Allowing the glowing drape to fall, the queen revealed her identity. "Regardless, you may desire me over her anyway."

Before Kane could sort what was happening, the faerie's head snapped toward him. He saw Fallon's face, Fallon's eyes.

*The faerie lied!*

She seized his gaze.

Kane fought it.

But he was unable to refuse the fae. Her hold on him was strong. She reached for him, and taking her outstretched hand Kane mounted the horse behind her, as she twisted to side sit on the horse's back, her eyes never leaving his.

And Gwyndolen smiled, seeing how handsome Kane Siosal was. She then sighed. If he wasn't so favored by her daughter, she would keep him for herself.

"Fear not, warrior," she said to him. "This journey won't be long,"

The mist swirled all around them, growing thicker. With a slight buck, the queen's horse sprinted forward and began to trot, though no sound of hooves was heard beneath them.

As for Kane, he was oblivious to the air that blew warmly against them, oblivious to the sights of the celestial air that grew around them, and of the fog that transformed to a glittering mist as they traversed the veils. He was in awe, a blissful sensation streaming through him, his coherence abating as more and more he became mesmerized by the beautiful fae.

Within moments, they reached the aperture of the palace, and

Kane slid from the horse, pulling the faerie down and into his
arms. He wanted to kiss her and bent his head to do so, but she
commanded him to stop.

Kane obeyed.

"Not now, lover." Gwyndolen sighed, wishing she knew of
Kane Siosal before he and Fallon crossed paths. The man was, by
far, too sensual for the mortal realm, even when ceding to the
faerie trance--*especially* when ceding to the faerie trance. It would
be so easy to make Kane her love slave, for in this condition of
mind no resistance would be offered, and his body would
surrender all.

Sliding to her feet, Gwyndolen strolled through the palace doors,
Kane following behind her as she knew he would. She bid Kane
to wait outside and then entered the great hall just in time to hear a
crash and a grunt as Fallon smashed a crystalline platter over
Moros' head. A trickle of blood streamed along his temple.

Moros turned on Fallon, ignoring the blood and the blow, and
lunged toward her, but Armond stayed him with a wave of his
hand, keeping Fallon safe.

"You're pissing me off, you old faggot, I mean fairy," Moros
growled at Armond. He picked a sliver of broken crystal from his
hair and flicked it through the air.

"Very naughty, Aori," Armond returned. "I told you that I refuse
to let harm come to her."

"What goes on here?" Gwyndolen asked. The great hall was a
chaotic mess--broken crystal, a splintered chair, pillows scattered
everywhere.

A few faerie gazed through the roof top with great amusement.

"Fallon has completely broken his allure on her," Armond
answered.

"'Twas quite simple, as well," Fallon added.

Moros scowled at her.

"And I have discovered somethin' in yer absence, Mother."
Fallon ignored his sour expression. "The Bryan feels pain."

Armond bellowed a roaring laugh. "Your daughter is a delight!
She wounds him, and he mends, and then she wounds him again!
This has been great entertainment, Gwyndolen, great fun!"

"Where have you been, Gwynnie?" Moros leaned against a
nearby pillar.

"Oh, just round and about seeking a gift for my daughter," The
queen fae answered. "And I told you to stop calling me
Gwynnie!"

"A gift?" Fallon looked at her mother. "Where be it?"

Gwyndolen smiled warmly at her daughter, but then turned her attention to Moros, her expression turning cold. "Will you release your claim on my daughter?"

Moros swiped at the gash on his brow. Within an instant it vanished. "I don't think so."

"It seems she's giving you nothing but trouble."

"If Armond would cease interfering." Moros leered at the king fae. "I would have her obedience and her body."

To that, Fallon snorted.

"Her full obedience is something that will evade you, Moros." Gwyndolen stepped further into the palace. "Nevertheless, I still want you to release her. You don't deserve my daughter."

"Whether or not I deserve her is beside the point. I claimed her and now I have her."

"Be that as it may, my Greek fae, there is another who does deserve her and has much, much more of a claim on her than you do."

Moros looked upon the queen with a wary gaze. "What do you mean?"

Gwyndolen raised her arm in a summoning motion and Kane, abiding her, stepped into the hall.

"Kane!" Fallon's heart skipped and she flew toward him, wrapping her arms around his chest.

He stood motionless, unresponsive to her embrace.

Tipping her head back, Fallon saw that his sight was set upon Gwyndolen. And there was a haze in his eyes that filled her with worry. "What have ye done, Mother?"

"Under his own request, I brought him here. He is enamored by my gaze."

"Nay! Kane look upon me. 'Tis Fallon."

*Fallon.* Kane's heart battled with his wayward mind.

"Release him, Mother!" Fallon lent pleading eyes to Gwyndolen.

"Of course I'll release him," Gwyndolen responded. "I never had intended to keep your warrior."

But before she withdrew her faerie allure, she studied Kane's face. He was fighting her enchantment.

Armond saw it too. "The warrior is strong of will. A superb human specimen."

"Come to me, Fallon," Moros ordered, and to Kane he said, "She will never be fully yours, Gael."

"Ye can no' covet what ye never owned aforehand, fae." Kane glared at him, his eyes revealing intense control of his mind.

Moros drew back momentarily. The Gael's mind was freed.

And Gwyndolen beamed her delight, for he broke the spell of his own accord.

Kane's attention shifted from The Bryan to Fallon and then to the female faerie who delivered him. His eyes swept back and forth between the two females a few times and then he understood. It was Fallon's mother whose sight he caught, and she was indeed nearly identical in appearance to Fallon with one exception, she was pure fae and emanated an ethereal, faerie appeal.

But it was Fallon who appealed to his heart.

"Fallon," Kane called to her.

She looked directly at him and smiled.

Spreading his arms with invitation, Kane beckoned Fallon, and she moved toward him, stepping into his embrace. Kane wrapped his arms around her possessively. He rested his chin atop her head and speared The Bryan with an angry gaze. "I have come ta retrieve ye, love. Ta take ye home with me."

"You can't have her!" Moros boomed.

"It appears, fae, that I already do," Kane answered, finding his arrogance. His arms tightened around Fallon as he looked to the faerie queen. "I bid ye, send us home."

"I'm afraid she can't do that, mortal," Armond answered.

Kane shifted his attention to the faerie who spoke. "And who, faerie, might ye be?"

"Armond," he returned. "The fae king."

*The king?* Kane was a bit surprised at his sinewy form and his youthful appearance, save the long white hair that stretched nearly to his thighs. He assumed that the ruler of faeries, who likely was long in age, would be of the more stately kind, plump and spoiled. Then again he was immortal and immortals failed to grow old.

"I beg ye then ta tell me for what reason we can no' return," Kane asked him.

"Fallon accepted Moros' invitation and only he can absolve her."

Kane studied Fallon's face. The angst he saw there told him it was the truth. But he would never abandon her. If it meant remaining in the faerie realm then Kane was determined to stay.

Brushing his knuckles along her cheek, Kane spoke softly to Fallon. "I will no' leave ye."

"There is another way." Armond spoke.

"No!" Gwyndolen yelled, for she knew exactly what the king was about to say. "The mortal can't possibly win."

"What be the way?" Kane's interest was caught by the king's statement, particularly if it meant taking Fallon home.

Gwyndolen shook her head. "Armond, no!"

"Yes, Armond." Moros smirked. "Do tell us what the faerie decrees say."

"A challenge!" Armond's voice boomed. "Battle each other for her."

It echoed so loudly through the faerie realm, the sound of it aroused the interest of the other fae in the mist. A few of them materialized within the great hall, curious to see what events were unfolding.

"A challenge for Fallon?" Moros' smile widened. It was a contest he was most willing to accept. There was no way on earth or faerie realm the mortal could win such a bet.

After all, the Gael was a mere human, but Moros was a god!

"If this be the only way, then this be what I shall do." Kane nodded.

Moros laughed. "Then say the words and I'll accept!"

"I challenge ye fae, for Fallon's hand!" There was no mistake this time that Kane was entering into a bargain with the man-fae.

"And I'll meet that challenge!" *Stupid mortal,* Moros thought.

"Nay, Kane!" Fallon looked upon him, her voice pleading, her face expressing worry. "Ye must reconsider."

"'Tis done." Kane cupped her cheek and bent to kiss her lips. "Have faith in me."

In all honesty, Kane was clueless as to what he was doing. Having attempted to down The Bryan before, he knew it would be a difficult undertaking.

Kane stared at Fallon. For her sake, he had to try. There must be a way to accomplish the task, other than what the goddess instructed him to do.

Fallon turned away from him, the worry changing to fear. And looking around, she was amazed to see that from floor to ceiling the hall now rallied with a multitude of fae, eager to witness the battle. Fallon searched their faces for help--for sympathy, but found none.

Her eyes fell on her mother.

Gwyndolen furled her brows at her daughter's hopeless expression "How will we determine a winner?"

Her question was directed to Armond.

"Simple," Moros answered before Armond could. He tapped a finger to his lips. *Now where in one of my mortal lives had a confrontation of this sort occurred before?* He smiled in remembrance recalling the challenge's terms.

Holding out his arms, Moros spun around the hall, presenting himself most arrogantly to the faerie congregation. "The one who dies first, loses."

## Chapter Thirteen

Fury mixed with Fallon's fear. She was angry that the fae, the king, The Bryan, her mother ... *Kane ... oh Kane....*

He could never win this.

"Ye can no' kill what can no' die!" Fallon yelled her protest. "Forbid this competition!"

Shrugging at Fallon, Armond turned to the warrior and then to Moros. "Choose and agree on your weapons."

"Magic!" Moros proposed. He beamed a smile as the faeries present chortled at his ridiculous suggestion.

"That would hardly make the match even, Moros, since the human has none."

"Then, pistols at twenty paces!"

Armond shook his head. "That is not a consideration either."

"And what's wrong with a show down?" Moros held out upturned palms. "Any of us here could produce a couple of guns."

Fallon and Kane exchanged befuddled glances. Neither of them knew what The Bryan was speaking about.

"First and foremost, Aori." Armond tipped his head in disapproval. "The mortal has never seen one, since they do not exist in his century. Secondly, if I recall hearing, during your human stint in the military you trained to be a crack shot."

"There's nothing to it," Moros proposed. "You just stick your finger through the little hole, take aim and pull the trigger ... boom! The deed is done."

"Swords," Kane spoke up. Enough was enough. It was a weapon he knew well.

The fae assembly around them began to murmur amongst themselves, excited to see a sword fight, but all became silent when Armond lifted his hands.

"Will both opponents settle for the blade?"

"Aye," Kane said.

"Sure," Moros agreed with a shrug and a cocky tilt of his head. "Why not?"

"Death! Death! Death!" A few faeries began chanting loudly and the remainder followed.

Kane's attention swept around the hall. There were fae everywhere--atop the pillars, standing on the floors, some peeking through the translucent ceiling above.

"Bloodthirsty barbarians," he mumbled beneath his breath.

"Death! Death! Death…."

Fallon touched his arm. "There is no' understanding ta the meanin' of life when one can no' expire from it."

Kane flinched. Fallon was half-fae and of course would feel some offense at his comment.

He bent to speak in her ear. "I be sorry, Fallon. I did no' mean…."

"'Tis fine," Fallon touched her hand to his lips stopping him from saying more. Stretching up onto her toes she kissed him, and then realized it might be for the last time. Fallon closed her eyes and beseeched the sacred spirits to spare him.

Her heart bled tears at the thought of losing Kane.

"I should no' have doubted you." Lifting her lids, Fallon looked upon him with regret. "I know you did no' betray me."

Kane gently stroked his fingertips along her hair, looking at her tenderly and sighing heavily at the same time. "I would nev'r betray ye, Fallon."

"This cannot be a fight to the death, Armond!" The sound of Gwyndolen yelling above the noisy incantations had both Kane and Fallon looking up. "Moros is on reprieve. He will not die!"

The king pondered that for a moment. There was never a time when mortal human fought immortal faerie to the death, and the human won. Least not a time he could recall. In fact, he could only assume it would be impossible.

Of course his thoughts made sense. An immortal cannot die.

Armond supposed it was unjust to have the warrior engage in a futile contest. What would be the fun in that if they all knew the outcome?

"Silence!" Armond roared, and with the exception of a few faerie giggles that resonated in the air, the hall quieted. "The one to disarm will be deemed the victor."

"I have no doubt I can take off both of the Gael's arms." Moros snickered.

Again the faeries tittered and mumbled.

Armond lifted an irritated brow. "Don't misconstrue my meaning, Greek."

Walking to the great hall's center, Armond motioned for Moros and Kane to come forth. They approached, standing face to face, both with snarling mouths and narrowed, hate filled eyes fixed upon one another.

With his palms turned downward, Armond curled them both into fists and touched them together briefly before spreading his arms outward and away from each other. He opened his hands with a jerk, and a clanking sound was heard. Kane and Moros looked downward. Two golden and brilliantly polished, jeweled swords lay athwart at their feet.

Armond backed away until he was amongst the crowd.

"Begin."

Kane bent, and with speed so remarkable the faeries gasped, the blade was in his hand.

He slashed it upward.

Moros mirrored the movement a fraction of a moment later, and he too slashed his blade upward.

They both jumped back, groans of pain spewing from both of their mouths.

The faerie congress murmured. Fallon shrieked and curled into her mother's embrace, squeezing her eyes closed.

"Oh see there," Moros laughed. "The mortal bleeds."

Kane looked down at his shredded *leine* and the blood seeping through it from the slice in his chest. Lifting a brow he eyed The Bryan, pushing the burn of the wound from his mind. "And so dost the fae."

Looking down, Moros saw that he too was cut in almost the same manner.

"Aye," he said. "But there be a difference between ye and me, Gael."

Purposely, Moros spoke Kane's dialect, a mocking pretense in his words.

"And what might that be?" Kane lifted his blade taking an offensive stance as he began circling around The Bryan.

"This," Moros said and skimmed his fingertips along the bleeding slit. His skin was instantly renewed. "Now I no longer bleed, though you still do."

Incensed, Kane lunged and thrust his sword, but was met by nothing but air. He spun around, his blade swinging, and then spun back. *Where be the bastard?*

Moros had disappeared.

"He is up there!" A female faerie pointed to the palace dome.

All in the palace great hall tipped their heads upward. Moros was perched on the acanthus carving high above the floor. A female faerie reached through an open bay and offered Moros a glittering, blue rose. He took it from her, held it to his nose sniffing it, and then tossed it to the crowd below. Several female fae and a few males, at that, scampered to retrieve it whilst at the same time shrieking their delight.

"Ye do no' fight fair." Kane shook his sword at The Bryan from where he stood on the floor below.

"I never fight fair, Gael," Moros called down. "What would be the fun in that?"

"Forbid The Bryan to use his magic!" Fallon glared at Armond.

But before Armond could issue his order, Moros was gone.

Suddenly, Kane stiffened and arched. His face wrenched as pain scorched the flesh of his back. Reacting in the manner that any well-trained warrior would, Kane spun and slashed his sword at the same time, taking the faerie unaware. The tip of the blade caught the flesh on Moros' shoulder and ripped it thus.

Blood dripped, but then there was none, not even a single sign that Moros had been wounded.

It worried Kane tremendously that the fae was permitted to heal himself.

Lunging at The Bryan, Kane swung his sword and their blades collided, a reverberating clank pealing the air as metal struck metal.

Mortal met immortal, their hatred for each other ablaze and furious. They parried and thrust and parried again, circling round each other, drawing back and then their blades battled once more.

A slash to Kane's thigh and another wound bled. Four in all he received. Few in number, considering the twelve that Kane inflicted, though none could now be seen on the faerie, as all were mended without haste. Even the broken bone to The Bryan's upper arm, caused by the flat of Kane's sword, was gone as well.

Despite his own injuries that could not heal, Kane refused to fall. Drawing on strength from within, Kane continued the clash with every bit of his might.

Over and over they swung their blades, moving to and fro across the hall. And Kane growled his frustration each time he was about to disarm Moros, only to see him disappear and then reappear elsewhere. Even more so, when he knocked the hilt from the faerie's grasp, Kane deemed himself triumphant, but saw that it was not to be, for The Bryan reclaimed it, calling it back and snatching it from the air before it hit the ground.

Kane roared his ire at The Bryan's use of magic to accomplish the task, sure he was a better swordsman and able to defeat the faerie if it were not so. Yet much to his dismay the king failed to stop it, despite the queen and Fallon shrieking their disapproval.

"Ye can no' defeat me mortal," Moros said.

They faced each other, blades raised, and Kane glared at him, his breathing harsh and heavy. Where Moros continued to heal the mass of wounds he sustained, Kane was unable.

Well at least the faerie heaved his weary breath too.

It was a small victory.

At least Kane had that much to be proud of, for there would be no more.

With the loss of blood and no reprieve from combat, Kane had grown immensely weary. Reluctantly, Kane was forced to accept that he was unable to go on any longer.

Still grasping the sword, he fell to his knees.

Fallon darted forward, but Gwyndolen halted her, grabbing her by the upper arm. "It's not over yet. Your warrior still clings to his blade."

"He barely clings to life, Mother!" Fallon broke free, but before moving further, she was restrained by two fae her mother summoned. Though she struggled against them, they were too strong, and they held her firmly. Fallon relented. Escape from them was impossible. All she was able to do was look on in horror.

"Get up, coward." Moros stood over Kane.

And before Moros knew what speared him, Kane's blade was embedded into the fae's groin.

At the sight of such a horrendous blow, the faerie who witnessed groaned in accord. Many shuddered and grimaced at the sight. Some covered their crotches with both hands, as if the pain was their own.

"You son of a bitch!" Gritting his teeth as he healed the incredibly painful wound, Moros pressed the tip of his sword to the underside of Kane's chin. "I should kill you for that."

Lowering his sword, Moros allowed Kane to struggle to his feet.

The least he could do was offer the Gael his dignity as he finished him off. Besides, the act would deem him compassionate, gaining the favor of the female faeries who watched, thus making his bed a rutting place this night, and he would insist Fallon join them.

Kane swayed as he faced the fae. Though he showed little emotion in his expression, defeat riddled his heart. His head throbbed from a blow he received and his stomach felt queasy. Kane could feel the loss of the battle. It was an imminent thing.

He could not win.

"I am but a mere human," he said, despair setting in.

*Fight fire with fire, warrior.*

Kane searched the crowd, finding Fallon amongst and he looked upon her sorrowfully. "If I can no' live with the woman I love, then I have no' wish ta live at all."

Kane dropped his sword.

The faeries all shouted their disbelief.

"Nay!" Fallon screamed as she struggled against the fae who held her.

*Save him!* A voice inside of her head that was not her own commanded Fallon. It was an ancient who spoke.

But Fallon needed no one to bid her to save Kane. Fighting with every bit of her might, Fallon broke free from the fae who held her. She ran toward him.

Closing his eyes, Kane spread his arms out from his sides, an open invitation for The Bryan to take his life.

*I am with you warrior.* The goddess entered his mind.

Silently he waited for the blade to pierce his heart, soothed by the ancient one's presence. Kane would accept whatever fate had in store for him.

"Your wish is my command." Moros shrugged nonchalantly, disregarding the human life in front of him. He grinned victoriously--evilly.

*Hurry!* The ancient one told Fallon.

"Nay, nay!" Fallon threw her body at Kane as The Bryan drove the weapon forward.

The blade pierced Fallon's flesh and then impaled her heart from back to front. It continued onward through her body and straight into Kane's chest, the sound of tearing flesh permeating the palace great hall. And they both released a painful cry.

Moros yanked the bloody blade back and held onto it.

The faerie assembly froze. Armond's eyes widened and Gwyndolen screamed in outrage, her aura turning a mix of red and black.

Kane wrapped his arms around Fallon and gurgled a breath. "What have ye done, woman?"

He tumbled backwards, holding Fallon tightly and bringing her down and atop of him.

Fallon's blood oozed and mixed with Kane's.

"*Tá mo chroí istigh ionat,*" Fallon gasped. My heart is within ye, always. Her head dropped to Kane's chest.

"Literally." Moros frowned.

"*Tha gaol agam ort-fhèin*, Fallon." I love ye, Fallon, Kane said. "Into eternity."

Fallon tipped her head up to Kane's face, their eyes met and locked, as life began draining from each of them.

"All will be well," Fallon whispered. "As ye sacrificed yer life fer me sake, I now sacrifice me life for yers."

## Chapter Fourteen

"Well isn't that a bitch," Moros said. "I was so anticipating the druid naked and in my bed this evening. I guess it's not going to happen now."

He understood the agony of dying, having done it in the mortal state many times before. And just for a moment he felt guilt, but pushed it aside, his sentiment turning cold--uncaring.

It was simply the way of the human existence and nothing more. The mortals all died eventually. Some sooner than others. It was what made them, well, mortal.

"You've killed them!" Gwyndolen screamed. She rushed forward, dropping to her knees besides the bodies of her daughter, Fallon, and the warrior, Kane.

Moros shrugged a shoulder. "It was an accident."

Gwyndolen shook in outrage ready to lash out, but then she gasped at the mist that began swirling in the center of the great hall around her and the fallen bodies. Immediately she rose to her feet, backing away quickly and cowering in a corner.

A figure materialized and was immediately shouting, "Have you all gone mad!"

Faerie shrieks chimed throughout the hall and most of them scattered. A few dropped to the floor, bowing at the Greek

Olympian who had just appeared before their faerie eyes. Some shook with such great fear they could do neither, whilst others stood paralyzed--unmoving.

"Taking vulnerable human lives, mortal creatures, and exploiting them for your own immortal amusements, for your own entertainment!" Demeter spun, her robe spinning in the air as she did so. "I'm appalled! No, I'm beyond appalled! I'm flabbergasted that you all let this go on!"

Her eyes fell to Fallon and Kane briefly before circling her gaze around the great hall, glaring one by one at the fae who remained. "You all disgust me!"

"Hello, Demeter." Moros dropped his sword to the floor and it hit with a resounding clank. He then strolled to an overstuffed chair and plopped into it, crossing his ankle over the opposite knee.

"And of course you had nothing to do with this, Moros." Demeter swung around to face him.

"I didn't start a thing."

"No, but apparently you've finished it."

"I was merely doing the queen fae's bidding."

With an immense frown on her face, Gwyndolen shrank further into the corner she was hiding in as Demeter shifted and then glared at her.

"Ashamed of yourself, Gwyn? Why do you hide? I'm sure the sentiment will pass quickly, and you'll be back to doing whatever it is you do soon, thinking on it no more."

Gwyndolen swallowed hard and closed her eyes. It was more than shame that befell her. It was grief--tremendous, horrible, *unbearable* grief. Her daughter was dead, and it was completely her fault.

"What's the matter, dear?" Demeter said. "You look rather pale for a faerie."

"This was a grave error, goddess." Regaining her composure, the fae queen stepped forward to defend herself. "My only desire was to bring my daughter home to me."

"Grave." Demeter snorted, though humor was far from what she felt. Kneeling down beside Fallon and Kane, she eyed their bodies from top to bottom and then back up again "Well, I guess you have her."

She picked up Fallon's hand from where it rested on Kane's chest, and then releasing her grasp on it, Fallon's arm thumped to the ground, splashing in the blood that pooled around them.

"She's not in very good condition, is she?"

Her attention turned to Kane, and Demeter stroked his hair. "Such a pointless waste of beautiful human flesh."

Demeter looked up, her expression saddened as her gaze again swept the room. "Did none of you here consider that these lives had a right to be spared?"

A single tear fell from the corner of her eye.

Unlike the fae, the Greek immortals were prone to immense emotions that tended to linger overlong. And this occurrence affected Demeter so deeply it would likely stay with her for a very, very lengthy amount of time.

Forgiveness would be a difficult thing to find.

Standing, Demeter faced the king. She inhaled a deep breath before speaking. "I'm none too pleased with you at the moment either, Armond. How could you let this go on?"

"I...." Armond held out upturned palms and stiffened his shoulders, but then they slumped. "I have no answer for you, goddess. Everything just got out of hand. I merely thought...."

Fire raced through Demeter and her fury burst through once more. "You merely thought to feed your pleasures!"

Her voice then rose to a booming, ear shattering pitch that was so loud, the faeries cowered and the entire palace shook. "You merely thought that the druid woman would keep Moros from the fae queen and out of your hair!"

Pausing, Demeter's eyes froze on the fae king and she went still.

"Yes," she finally said, her persona demonstrating her goddess power. "I was not far from your thoughts, any of your thoughts."

She began to pace the floor, shaking her head, but then stopped again. Pointing an angry finger at the king, Demeter bellowed, "You, Armond, are nothing but a mere fool!"

Moros snickered behind Demeter's back. She heard him and spun around. "And I'm far from finished with you, Aori."

"Careful, Demeter, there's steam coming from your ears and nose." Moros answered. His brows twitched, but otherwise his face was expressionless. "I would hate to see you explode."

*He would love to see her explode.*

"What is done can't be undone," he added.

"For them," Demeter snarled as her eyes fell to Kane and Fallon. "But not for you."

"What are you saying?" Moros shot to his feet.

"I'm saying your reprieve is over."

"Now wait just one minute, Demeter...." Moros stopped

speaking.

He and Demeter just stared at each other.

Finally he furled his brows at her silence. "What?"

"I'm waiting one minute to see what nonsense you're about to speak."

"The fae queen has promised to seek audience with you on my behalf."

"I am well aware of the bargain you made with Gwyndolen, Moros." Demeter shot him a stern look. "I'm also aware of the deceitful ruse you rendered on the druid and the warrior. As I told you I always stand with a watchful eye, particularly when it comes to you."

Demeter knelt down by Kane and Fallon once more. Dipping her fingers in the pool of blood, she lifted it to her nose and inhaled.

"A son of the whitethorn," she murmured as her eyes drifted shut.

The scent was unbelievably incredible. It was ecstasy in its utmost glory.

Moros cleared his throat as he looked at Gwyndolen. "Well?"

Gwyndolen shook her head. Aori was truly insane if he thought she would beseech Demeter on his behalf after all that had just happened.

"A promise is a promise, my queen," Armond interceded. "You must make your bid."

Looking between Armond and Demeter, Gwyndolen hesitantly stepped forward.

"Very well, Gwyndolen." Standing, Demeter lifted her chin, emanating her pristine presence and her supremacy over the faerie. "You may have your audience. Go ahead now and speak."

"Yes, well, goddess." Gwyndolen approached and awkwardly bent to one knee, bowing her head in reverence. Humbleness was an enormously difficult thing for a faerie, but Demeter would chastise her if she didn't show respect. As much as Gwyndolen, and all fae for that matter, hated to admit it, the Greek Olympians were much, much more powerful than the faerie creatures were. "I … you…."

"Spit it out, Gwyndolen!" Demeter's voice rose. "I haven't got all century to wait."

Gwyndolen took a deep breath and then blew it out harshly. The desire to do this bidding completely escaped her. In fact, it demoralized her.

"The favor you owe me…." Gwyndolen began. Her gaze fell to her dead daughter's body and she lowered her head in despair, guilt, shame. "I ask that you offer Moros--"

"No," Demeter interrupted before the queen could complete her request.

Gwyndolen tipped her head in confusion. "But, the favor you owe me."

"I know what it is you seek," Demeter returned. "But the answer is *no*."

Gwyndolen rose to her feet and nodded. She was gladdened the asking was denied.

"And why is the request denied?" Moros snarled as he stomped toward Demeter.

"There will be no secession of your punishment, Moros. Especially after what I've witnessed here this day."

"But the favor you owe Gwyndolen." Moros looked at Demeter with an irate gaze. "You dishonor yourself, goddess."

"I do owe her a favor, but this request is one I won't grant."

"For what reason? I did nothing wrong this time. I only did the fae queen's bidding, and there was nothing wrong in what she asked."

Demeter blew out a breath. "Will you never learn?"

Moros crossed one arm over the other. "And what lesson am I to learn this time?"

"He who plots to hurt others often hurts himself."

"Who did I hurt?"

Demeter dropped her head. Moros was surely daft in the brain-- poor descendent traits or something of that nature. It had to be for him to be unable to see the error of his ways. "You disrespected a sacred tree."

Her eyes dropped to Kane and drew her brows together. "To destroy a whitethorn is to incur great peril on oneself."

"It's a damn tree!" Moros objected.

"But the warrior was not." Again Demeter bent and dipped her fingers into the blended blood of Fallon and Kane. Holding her fingertips together she stretched her arm out toward Moros. "You have destroyed the son of a sacred tree and his mate. The spirits weep."

"Oh for the love of…." Moros threw his head back. "You've got to be kidding."

"I'm afraid not." Demeter opened her hand and a crystal pyramid appeared and began rotating above her palm. Rays of variegated colors streamed from it. "You ruled by deceit and your actions were at the expense of two lives."

"This whole thing was a mistake." Moros frowned at the spectrum porthole she held, knowing it was meant for him.

"A very large mistake, I would say. However, it is one that you instigated."

"I didn't instigate it." Moros pointed at Gwyndolen and she frowned at him. "She did!"

The queen fae sneered at Moros. How dare he blame her for this entire event.

"I would say there are many to blame in this," Demeter returned. "But your sword didn't thrust itself into their flesh of its own accord. It was your choice to end it this way."

To that Moros said nothing.

A buzz hummed in his ear and he rubbed it vigorously. He was aware of what it meant. Another human womb awaited him. He would be born again, conceived by miserable human flesh, to live and die another miserable human existence.

Demeter directed the beam of colors to expand, and then waved her hand through it. She set the large cone-shaped spectrum upon the floor. "May your next death be more gruesome than the last one."

Not that Demeter was a vindictive woman by any means, wishing torture on Moros. She only hoped that some day he would come to understand that human suffering was not something for one's exploitation and amusement. All life, whether it be immortal or mortal was worth savoring.

"What a terrible thing to say, Demeter," Moros said as he placed a foot in the beam of colors.

"Oh, and Moros, before you go...."

"What now?" Moros asked, his head dropping to an irritated tilt as he looked at her.

"Release your claim on the druid."

Furling his brows, Moros looked at Fallon's dead body. "What difference does it make at this point?"

"I won't allow you to own a smidgen of her, not even her spirit."

"But I won...."

"You were victorious with nothing! All you managed to do was deceive!" Demeter's anger was flaring at his arguing. "Now do as I say."

"Why should I?" Moros snickered as he pushed further into the porthole that would deliver him to his next human life.

Demeter narrowed furious eyes on him. "Because if you refuse, I will see to it that in your soon to be mortal existence that your appearance is so repulsive that no woman could be forced to turn an amorous eye to you."

Moros pondered that for a moment. No, he wouldn't like that at all. "Very well, I release my claim on the druid Fallon."

Truthfully, Moros didn't really want her anyway. He was just amusing himself.

"Now be gone," Demeter ordered him with a deprecating twist of her mouth. Moros stepped into the beam of light and disappeared.

Demeter summoned the pyramid crystal and it descended and melded with the flesh of her palm. Looking about the palace's great hall, she addressed the faerie crowd that remained there. "What happened here today is a crime within all realms."

Waving her hand over Fallon and Kane, their bodies faded and then vanished. "I expect that this will never happen again, or you will all suffer considerably for it."

She strolled to where Gwyndolen stood and grasped her by the shoulders. Bending, Demeter whispered in her ear. "Save the favor I owe you for another time. This one I could not possibly grant."

Stepping back, she smiled at the faerie queen. "Just be joyous that your daughter is immortal."

Gwyndolen looked at Demeter with surprise.

A half-blooded faerie could be born mortal, immortal or somewhere in between, meaning the offspring could live for centuries or millennia before expiring. But one never knew until they died--or did not die.

In like, they might age or remain youthful forever and that too would only be revealed through the passing of time.

"How do you…?" Gwyndolen opened her mouth to question the goddess, but before she could finish her sentence, Demeter was gone.

Only a moment had passed when Gwyndolen suddenly felt Demeter's presence. But this time she spoke from beyond, sending her thoughts to the queen fae's mind. *She's already died once, Gwyndolen, though she doesn't know it. But there was no one around to tell her that she wasn't just asleep.*

## Epilogue

Fallon caressed the whitethorn tree rendering her most sincere praise. Samhuinn was upon them and the harvest had provided food aplenty. For that, Fallon was immensely thankful. The clans could now claim large stores, which would carry them through most of the next season. Soon all foliage would be asleep, and rare it would be to find a green thing, not alone something to pick and eat. The air would turn cold, bright skies would be few, and the ground would be frozen beneath their feet.

The world around them would become bleak, boredom setting into daily life as all around grew dismal. Hardship was sure to follow.

Rubbing her blossoming belly, Fallon was also humbly thankful for the child she conceived--a *greenwood* babe, though it was not created from a night of rutting, but an intense and unforgettable love. She carried the child of the whitethorn, conceived beneath and by the son of a sacred tree.

Without question she was blessed.

Resting her cheek against the tree trunk, Fallon deepened the thoughts of her lover. It was here in this very place they discovered their love and their passion.

And it was here they were also betrayed.

But Fallon discovered something important that Bealtuinn eve. She could look upon her love with sincere eyes, without fear that he would lose his mind or that her heart might be broken.

She also discovered her immortality.

For that reason Fallon would be eternally thankful to Demeter, or else she might have more to be troubled about this Samhuinn than spending it alone. Once again the veils were thinning and the immortals were free to cross over. Had Demeter failed to force The Bryan's hand in releasing Fallon, the loathsome faerie if otherwise unoccupied in a mortal life elsewhere, might come to seek her. And if he did, this time Fallon would not have her warrior's protection from him.

Pushing the ritual cloak from her shoulders and allowing it to drape down the length of her back, Fallon stroked her fingers between her breasts and caressed the scar that remained there, never to fade.

After taking the brunt of Moros' thrusting sword through her body, the last thing she remembered before going cold, was giving her heart to Kane.

And he gave his in return.

Fallon sighed and closed her eyes. He sacrificed his life for her, fought to the bitter end, all for the sake of loving her.

*Oh,* she missed him so.

Turning her face upward and toward the sunny sky, Fallon savored the warmth on her flesh, appreciating that the sun's heat that would soon be gone. She inhaled what remained of the forest fragrances, letting them seep into her memories.

The scents reminded her of Kane.

Fallon longed for brighter days and warmer suns and of times gone by when happiness was more of a friend to her than it was at this moment.

How would she survive the coming season without him?

And though Fallon was loath to celebrate the harvest rituals alone whilst others found merriment together, she had little choice as druid of the village. The clans needed her to perform the rites this eve.

*Nay.* Fallon must push her aching for Kane aside, and ignore the loneliness within her. It was her duty, not only as a human, but as a faerie as well that she should preside over the *dark time* rituals, lead the clans in preparing for the forthcoming winter's strife.

If only she could find comfort in her father's eyes and warm embrace, but he was no more. Marlow Moireach was nowhere to be found, having disappeared sometime between the Bealtuinn day and Bealtuinn eve last season. No one knew for sure exactly why or when it happened.

But Fallon, however, truly believed he was with her mother.

Sighing, Fallon thought it might be pleasant if the queen crossed the veils this eve, just to spend a short visit. But it was something she refused to count on. Though Fallon forgave her, Gwyndolen was ashamed of the devious scheme that nearly killed both Fallon and Kane. Before they were returned to the earth, the faerie queen promised to stay away, never to meddle in Fallon's life again. Regardless, Fallon would still attempt to summon her mother.

Again Fallon's palms fell to her belly and she caressed it gently.

"I have ye, little one," she whispered. "And because of ye I keep goin'."

And at least she had Alanna's friendship, as well.

Fallon released a small chuckle, thinking about her friend and the days prior when Alanna swept Fallon's hair aside whilst she emptied the contents of her stomach.

Over and over and over and over again.

Alanna kept laughing, irritating Fallon to an extreme degree for refusing to retrieve the herbs that would rid her of the culprit that was making her ill.

*I do no' think 'twould be a culprit ye wish ta be rid of,* Alanna told her.

Fallon completely lost her temper, accusing Alanna of taking vengeance for leaving her swooning on the path the day The Bryan had shown his face to them. She told Alanna that if she was really a true friend, she would practice forgiveness and take pity on Fallon for feeling like a rodent the dog dragged in.

And then Fallon emptied the contents of her stomach once more.

With a hardy laugh Alanna confessed she suspected Fallon carried a bairn in her belly. She further teased Fallon for her lack of insight when for many a seasons it was the very kind of *illness* that women sought the druid's cures for.

Fallon laughed, at first disbelieving of Alanna's claim. But the soreness in her breasts and the fact that, despite her upset stomach, she was hungry, convinced her that she was indeed carrying a bairn.

*No' to mention the manner by which yer moods keep changin',* Alanna commented.

Fallon's delight immediately changed to irritation as she scowled and denied it. *There be nothin' flawed with me moods!*

And she scowled at her friend.

Ignoring Fallon's temper, Alanna brought her bread and broth, which Fallon ate and drank and then promptly vomited. That caused Fallon to weep miserable tears, though she was unsure of what prompted her crying.

It was Kane. She so wished to tell him of the babe they conceived, but he was not there to tell.

"Yer papa would be immensely pleased," Fallon spoke to her belly. "I jest wish he knew of ye."

Fallon closed her eyes. "Well, he be knowin' about ye soon enough."

A horse neighed behind her and Fallon's heart leapt. Had *soon enough* come? Spinning around to see who it was, she blinked, unsure if her eyes deceived her, but they did not.

A broad smile beamed across her face. "Ye have come home!"

Kane waved to Fallon, matching her wide, happy smile with one of his own. "Did ye trust I would have no', woman?"

After nearly half a season's absence, he was returning home

from war.

The horse moved closer and Kane's eyes fell upon his wife. Her ritual cloak was tossed over her shoulders, exposing her naked body to his eyes.

By the gods he was overjoyed to see her. She was just as beautiful as he had remembered.

*Nay.* She was more beautiful than he remembered, and Kane suspected she always would be, to his eyes at least.

Pulling off his leather breastplate, Kane tossed it aside and flashed Fallon a lusty grin. He then unlatched the belt that sheathed his blade. That too, he tossed away.

Fallon laughed, her eyes seeking his, beckoning him toward her as she watched him undress. There was no mistaking his intentions.

Hers were the same.

Just before he reached her, he pulled off his *leine*, and Kane too was naked to her sight, save the fur boots wrapped around his feet and calves, held in place with crisscrossing twines.

Blowing out an amorous breath, Fallon smoothed her hands along her own body as she watched him approach, her gaze gliding all over his muscular form. She ached to graze her fingers through the hair on his chest, trace her tongue along the line that trailed the center of his firm stomach and ran straight downward to the luscious shaft between his thighs. Fallon moaned, watching the manner in which his hips rocked forward and back in a gentle cadence as the horse he sat naked upon ambled. It conjured images of his hips rocking between her thighs as he slid his shaft in and out of her, much in the same rhythm she was seeing now.

Fallon licked her lips. He was a glorious sight to see. Particularly with the center of his desire now thickening and lengthening like a mighty weapon. She was flooded with the yearning to be penetrated by it.

Finding her breasts, Fallon skimmed her thumbs across her nipples causing them to peak. Her passion for Kane surged, fanning her flaming need, and Fallon opened her arms to Kane as he drew nearer, waiting, seeking, craving his embrace, his body.

Kane dismounted from the horse and treaded directly to her. Gathering Fallon into his arms, he sighed at the warmth of her heated, naked body pressed against his longing, aching flesh.

"Ye are home," Fallon whispered as she set her cheek upon his bare chest, and Kane inhaled heavily, the emptiness that pursued him all the days he was away from her and on the battlefield now being relieved by the feel of her in his arms. He was tremendously jubilant to be back in the homelands, and to be with Fallon again.

Cupping her face between his palms, Kane tipped her head back, gazing steadfastly into her eyes. "Aye, love. As by me request, Mor mac Eirc released me from me duties and expressed his gratefulness ta me fer the extended service I gave to him."

Comforted by those words, relief filled Fallon. Kane would depart no more.

It was a terrible hardship on her heart when he left. Fallon and Kane were together only a short time following Bealtuinn when the future king sent word that Kane was needed and must come immediately. Kane hesitated to go, but it was his duty. And Fallon, though she was terrified to see him depart, worrying that he would fall in battle, accepted his loyalty to the would-be king and instead offered her blessings and prayers for his safe return, letting fate take its course.

Whatever was meant to be would be.

Still, she remained hopeful, unable to accept that anything other than Kane coming home was inevitable. He had the shield of Demeter's protection about his head, a shield that saved him that Bealtuinn eve when Moros' sword brought him down. That, and Fallon taking the brunt of Moros thrusting blade.

*Aye.*

Her healing blood spared Kane from impending death, flowing through him in great abundance, seeking his fatal wounds, refusing to allow Kane to meet his doom.

Fallon pressed her lips to the mark that remained on Kane's chest where the sword cut through it. In like with hers, the scars were a reminder to always trust, to always have faith in those you love.

"What be this?" Kane asked as he stepped back to take a look at her. His eyes fixed to her rounded belly.

Tipping her head back, Fallon smiled brightly. "Are ye pleased to be a papa?"

It was more blessing than Kane could possibly hope for and he was mightily pleased, the expression on his face telling it all. "And may we be hallowed with a house of bairns aplenty, or at the verra least, die tryin'."

Fallon chuckled softly, but her amusement turned to heated passion when Kane insinuated his leg between her thighs and their hips melded.

Lifting his hand, Kane strummed his fingers along the scar

between Fallon's breasts, there to remind him how she sacrificed her life for him that day.

Though the goddess guided him on how to defeat the faerie, ensuring him it was the only way for him to remain alive, Demeter never revealed that Fallon would react in such a way. Had Kane known she would put her life in front of his, he with certainty would not have invited The Bryan's blade at all.

He was profoundly relieved Fallon was immortal.

Tightening his embrace around Fallon, Kane lowered his head, taking her mouth, kissing her lips and then dipping his tongue inside. Fallon moaned her pleasure, relaxing into his arms, melting, her heart thumping and her body begging. His hands came up cupping and caressing both of her breasts, intensifying her need for him. And then Kane's mouth sought, ascended, suckling her throat and her breasts, his tongue licking, his lips sucking one and then the other, before returning to her mouth.

Kissing her deeply, Kane's hands skimmed the flesh along Fallon's sides, continuing further to her arms and urging them above her head where her hands found the overhead branches of the whitethorn. She grasped them tightly, and as she did, Kane pressed his naked body against her, forcing her to lean back on the trunk of the sacred tree. In one sweep he wrapped her legs around his hips and plunged his hardened shaft into her.

Fallon released a lustful groan with his deep penetration, moaning out a sharp breath when he grasped her bottom, withdrew his shaft and plunged deep within her again. Over and over his hips moved, in, out, faster and then slower and faster again. Fallon clung tightly to the branches above her for support as Kane's mouth suckled her flesh, licked her throat and breasts, meandering all over her upper body, her passion soaring closer to ecstasy with every thrust Kane gave her. And she panted, her breathy gasps increasing, shifting to sensuous moans that emerged and escalated, threading with the sounds of nature and the whirring of the harvest wind that blew through the branches of the forest trees around them.

Kane thrummed, driving into Fallon, his wife. He was still awestruck by the alluring effect she held over him, but readily accepted and savored it. She was his mate, his heart, his love. And Kane would never surrender her to another, else he would die.

Pumping harder, Kane's heartbeat quickened at the sound of Fallon's passionate wails and the tightness of her squeezing around him as she peaked. His own need surged, igniting and rising higher and higher until Kane felt his own savage fire from within bursting through. And on one last, hard thrust his seed spilled in a riotous rupture, so overwhelming, so gratifying, so depleting that Kane could no longer stand. His knees gave way, and Kane lowered both himself and Fallon to the ground.

"Wife," he murmured, cradling her within his embrace, and he cherished the sound of the word.

On the Bealtuinn past, once Kane came to realize how near to death he was, his life was forever changed. He forecast to the future and saw his own fate, understanding he would not carry on until eternity. Where he tromped the battlegrounds prior, giving little regard to his own life much and tremendous loyalty to the Gaelic cause, Kane's own mortality now became a real thing.

He made love to Fallon the Bealtuinn day they returned from the fae domain. And then they washed in the dew before full dawn, seeking health and happiness.

With one final rite in mind, the two of them revisited the knoll, to the now smoldering sacred pyres. Though there were no witnesses, as all were asleep, Kane took Fallon's hand and they leapt the embers, sealing their marriage for a year and a day. But Kane knew it would be for much, much longer.

He was thankful he rode into the village that day, looking to slake his lusts during the fertility celebrations, he instead found not only passion, but love in the enchanting flames.

\* \* \* \*

Oh, do not tell the Priest our plight,
Or he would call it a sin;
But we have been out in the woods all night,
A-conjuring Summer in!

~Kipling~

*Slan go foill*!
Bye for now!

Printed in the United States
43961LVS00004B/181-234

9 781586 087395